THE GUILTY PARTY

LAURA LYNDHURST

Imprint: Independently published

Cover design by Laura Lyndhurst using Cover design by Laura Lyndhurst using images celebration-7657418_1280.jpg and carnival-3075912_1280.jpg from Pixabay

ISBN: 9798266337299

AUTHOR'S NOTE

This is a work of fiction. The events portrayed are set in the United Kingdom in the late twenty-first century.

The language used is UK English.

CONTENTS

PROLOGUE

I come to with a start, then relax against the pillow. I know where I am. I'm home, in bed, all's well. Except that it isn't. I check the clock; 3 a.m., or a few minutes thereafter, I think.

I turn onto my left side. I can see the window from here, looking over to the East, where the sun will rise, unseen by me, given the dull and cloudy weather we've been having. No sign of any light yet, at all events.

I close my eyes, willing sleep to return, but it's not happening. I reach for my phone, check my e-mail. Nothing important, the usual marketing spam, which I delete. I glance over a crossword puzzle, several answers coming to me without my even thinking. It's a mistake; my brain is awake now, and I know I won't sleep again tonight, unless I doze off again at 6 a.m. or thereabouts. It sometimes happens, and of course I won't want to get up when the time comes. Thank goodness I don't have to go out; not today, anyway.

I think of many things, my life, my daytime occupations, and you. I look across to the right-hand side of the bed; your side, or it would be, were you here. Where are you? Why are you wherever you are, and not here, where you ought to be?

Why are you not dead, as you ought to be?

1: MATT

'Sorry!'

The stout woman wasn't looking where she was going, and collided with him, splashing some of her overfilled glass onto him in the process.

'No harm done.'

He dabbed at the wet patches on his jacket. White wine, or something clear at any rate; gin and tonic, he decided, as he caught the scent of that unmistakeable perfume. At least it wouldn't stain.

Matt asked himself again, as he'd done many times since he'd arrived, what on earth he was doing here. He cursed the need to be polite and carry out duties which he'd rather not. The place was full of people at least twenty years or more older than he, and although there were some of his own age group, they were thin on the ground. His parents' contemporaries, a reunion of a sort, husbands, wives, fathers, mothers, some with their children in tow. Grown children now, including him.

It was many years since they'd been on the Forces circuit, UK and overseas bases, which was what this get-together was all about. His father's oldest and best friend and colleague, long-retired now, as were most of them, looking back, seeking out and inviting many who'd served with him, to this, his seventy-fifth birthday celebration.

Some Matt recognised, others he didn't, but all were

known to Graham. They'd kept in Christmas-card touch, round-robin letters detailing their lives and the achievements of their children. All had a special relationship with Uncle Graham, and Aunt Philippa too. Matt would ask about them later, when Graham wasn't so busy greeting people he hadn't seen for years and getting involved in multiple conversations.

The doctor, for that had been Matt's profession since he'd graduated twenty-something years ago, wondered yet again why he was here. He'd hardly ever been present in whichever married quarter passed for home when his father was serving, and when he himself was old enough to register and remember people. He'd been at boarding school from the age of eight onwards, alongside his younger brother Simon for most of the time, only returning to his parents for the school holidays. So why did he need to be here now? Because Aunt Pippa and Uncle Graham are our oldest friends, his father had said, since he and I were in training together. We were best man to each other when we married, and they're as good as an aunt and uncle to you and Simon. Plus Aunt Pippa's your godmother, and wants to see her godson. That settled it, because Dr Matt, as she called him, with great affection, was too well-versed in good manners and duty to do other than be here.

'Penny for your thoughts. Here's Joe come to see you.'

He'd been thinking about Pippa and here she was, ushering her eldest son Joseph into his presence. She and Graham had four children, two sons and two daughters, and there'd been hopes on the part of the mothers that Matt and Simon might one day marry the girls. All concerned knew real life wasn't like that, although nobody could've foreseen what would happen in actuality. Judith had married a boy she'd met at university, the couple now running a successful business together while raising three children. Bethany hadn't married, going through a series of relationships which never lasted, being a career-woman and serious rock-climber in her spare time.

Pippa left them to it, having other guests to attend to, and Joe, who'd gone into law, joined with Matt in updating each other on recent developments in their lives, personal and professional. Jude and Beth would be here later, Joe added, but Dan was at present painting his way around one of the quieter Greek islands. Interesting, Matt reflected, that in both families the elder brother had gone into a solid, respectable profession, as well as marrying and having children, whilst the younger had embraced an occupation less dependable and somewhat precarious. His own brother Simon wasn't here either, it being high summer and the time of year when, living an itinerant and international lifestyle, Simon worked on yacht cruises in the Mediterranean, having thereby the perfect excuse for non-attendance today.

Their mother Penny was missing too. Although she'd been friends with Pippa and Graham since Graham had been best man to her bridegroom, Frank, she'd divorced the husband who'd returned the favour for Graham and preferred to not be in his company if she could help it. Instead she'd visited her old friends a couple of weeks ago, celebrating the milestone birthday with them through a meal at the local pub and a wealth of catching-up; without the awkward presence of her ex-husband, who was even now seated on a sofa across the room from his son, his second wife by his side.

My stepmother, I suppose, Matt thought, as he looked at the pair; but why had his father married her? He must be lonely, given that visits to see his grandchildren didn't fill all a man's needs, but why this particular woman? She had a sort of long-faded prettiness, for which she appeared to compensate by being groomed to within an inch of her life. Her hair, a suspicious shade of blonde, was streaked with a colour which Matt's wife Jennifer had informed him was known as caramel, and was styled into a neat and immaculate bob which framed the perfect make-up on her face. There wasn't a line or wrinkle in sight, and her forehead was smooth, which made Matt suspect the presence of Botox. Her clothing was neat, classic in style and in colours picked with care to set off what Jen had called her fair, fat and fifty-ish complexion.

An uncharacteristic catty comment, coming from Jen. It'd surprised Matt because she was so polite, as a rule, even to those she didn't like. It was inaccurate too, as Madge was way past her fifties. She admitted to fifty-five, although sixty-five would be closer to the mark, Matt felt, and she wasn't fat, although not slim either. Her figure, which could've been described as matronly when she first got together with his father, had thickened in the years they'd been together, although not by much. She was fair—Jen had been correct about that—but the two hadn't hit it off when they first met, although Jen had been careful not to let her animosity show. Later, however, when she and Matt were alone, she'd made it clear that she felt her father-in-law deserved much better.

"I could've understood it better if she'd had a good mind, a few worthwhile opinions, something to say and the ability to make intelligent conversation. But she speaks in clichés, fashionable key phrases, soundbites. Nothing original ever comes out of her mouth."

Matt smiled at the memory. Jen had a soft spot for his father, meaning her usual good sense took a holiday whenever anything was said to his detriment. Good for Jen, he mused. I'm glad she cares for the old man; he needs all the love he can get since Mum left. If Madge made Frank happy then it made Matt equally so to accept her as a stepmother, even if he'd never connected with her to any great extent.

While he respected his father's choice, Matt wondered

why his own mother had divorced him. She was about the same age as her ex-husband, so older than the new wife—who pretended to be much younger—but still just as fair, although her own blonde hair was greying and she'd never had recourse to a bottle. She was a natural type of person, always had been, and even now in better shape than the woman who'd stepped into the position which Penny had vacated when—having devoted herself to raising her children before they departed for boarding school, and seen them off to university and their own adult lives afterwards—she'd said goodbye to their father and the house he'd bought for their retirement from the Forces, going to live with another man. Another officer, of similar age yet of a higher rank than her husband of almost forty years, and it'd transpired that she'd been having an affair with him. If discovered the matter would've been a scandal, had they still been living in the small society of a military camp somewhere overseas, but as by that time they'd been in the UK, close to a city with a major army base nearby, the family was living out in the wider community and impervious to the raised eyebrows and negative comments of Frank's peers.

Matt's attention returned to Joe who, talking of himself and his own exploits, was unaware that his friend's mind had wandered. As Matt asked a question, to cover his inattention, the eyes of both were drawn to a flurry of activity over by the door caused by a new arrival, a woman. She came through the door like a breath of fresh air, and when Matt saw her he understood why he was here.

She had to be in the older age-bracket, but younger than the upper-sixty and seventy-somethings who formed the major part of Graham's peer-group. She seemed familiar to Matthew, although he couldn't place her. He was intrigued.

'Who's that woman?'

Joe couldn't remember, if he'd ever known.

'An old friend of my parents, but I don't know anything more about her. She used to visit us when I was a kid, but since I left home—.'

He shrugged.

'Best ask my mother'.

Pippa was already there, laughing and making all the right noises of greeting the new arrival. Matt narrowed his eyes to inspect her. Perhaps she was of an age with his parents, but if so she'd lasted better than the rest. He couldn't tell, but it didn't matter. He watched as she laughed with Pippa and Graham, who'd joined his wife to welcome her. A small group soon formed around her, from which she stood out. What made her so different?

It was her lack of artifice, Matt decided. The other women, like stepmother Madge, were groomed with care, to make the best of their fading looks. Hair was dyed in subtle fashion, cut and styled, most often short and sometimes chic in tasteful yet mature styles. Faces were made-up with care, nothing garish, muted colours which blended with the tasteful, well-made clothing; summer dresses in forgiving styles, for the most part. This woman didn't seem to bother with such tricks or make many, if any, concessions. Her hair, a dark reddish-brown turned silvery-grey around the hairline, was worn long and curling. It reached to her waist at the back, and ran riot on its way there. Two combs held it back on either side of her head, which made the grey more obvious.

Another woman, Matthew decided, would have arranged the hair in such a way as to conceal it. Come to that, another woman would have dyed it long ago, most like, and had it cut short at the same time, like the others here. This one did as she wished even if doing so defied accepted convention. Take me as I am or leave me, it's all the same to me, she seemed to announce. Matt admired such an attitude.

Her face bore out his conjecture, lined as it was, although

not as much as might be expected. Those wrinkles present must have been caused by smiles and laughter, for to his expert eye there were no signs of cosmetic surgery, as on some of the other female faces present, including that of Madge. The bearers would have denied any such thing, if asked, but nevertheless, Matt could tell that more than one forehead had been smoothed by Botox, that there was at least one lifted face and various little nips and tucks to chins and upper arms; and that didn't include the changes not on show, lipo-suctioned stomachs and thighs and suchlike.

You didn't have to be a surgeon—although in point of fact that happened to be his profession—to spot the tell-tale signs. He'd spent time with Jeff, his old friend from medical school, who'd followed the big money and gone into the plastic-surgery side of things. He'd given Matt an illustrated talk through some of the most often-desired procedures, hoping to recruit his old friend into practice with him, although accepting defeat with good-natured humour when the latter had decided to stay with the needs of the many inside the confines of the NHS. Matt could tell therefore that this woman hadn't been under the knife, not the visible parts, at least, although he suspected this to be an indication that the invisible parts were likewise untouched; unless she'd attended to the most important areas, those for exclusive access by a husband, or a lover. But that wouldn't make sense, he reasoned, because first you had to attract your lover; so if you were going down the cosmetic surgery route it would make sense to start with the bits on show.

What am I doing? He brought his wandering thoughts under control. I've only just seen this woman, who must be at least fifteen years older than I am, and I'm having fantasies about her. You're a married man with children; control yourself. He looked around in a panic, seeking Jen to distract him from temptation. He couldn't find her in the crowd, talking and drinking and getting merrier, no matter how hard he looked. Assisting Aunt Pippa with the food, he guessed, or doing something for someone else, eternal helper that she was.

Jennifer. His wonderful and oh-so-suitable wife, a prominent figure within their village community, and then some. Always obliging, no task too much, she accepted whatever she was asked to do with a smile that reached from her mouth, with its white and even teeth, to her dark eyes, and with a toss of her long, black and always-tidy hair. Kate Middleton before anyone had any reason to notice Kate Middleton, apart from her family and friends. That was his wife, the perfect partner for a doctor and respected member of the small and close society of which they were a part.

She was busy, she'd said when Matt had told her about their expected attendance at this party, smiling as ever to take the sting out of her words, what with looking after two children, not to mention her various roles and duties within the community. Her position on the parent-teacher association of the local school, the Women's Institute, the upcoming fête for which she was on the committee, the campaign to raise money to restore the church steeple, not to mention another to prevent a planned bypass of the twenty-mile-distant city from coming too close to the village. The list was endless, and Jen was in the thick of every activity. Too occupied on that account to attend this party which, she'd reminded Matt with a somewhat guilty smile, was after all to be full of his parents' old friends, people who Matt himself barely knew. It was no place for his wife when she had so much to do at home; but she'd make the time, she told him, and he'd smiled with relief at her willingness to do what she accepted as her natural duty by coming and supporting her husband. She was indeed the perfect wife.

His eyes reverted back to the mystery woman who,

although he tried hard, he couldn't prevent himself from assessing. He made a stab at keeping his observations on the surface, disciplining himself to focus on her face and to not speculate on the invisible. Not a single stroke of make-up; her skin was clear and natural-coloured, glowing too, from the sunny weather which they were experiencing. Either that or she'd been on holiday, the idea supported by the light tan of her limbs, well-exposed by the simple T-shirt dress she wore. Close-fitting, in a purple colour which suited her, it showed a figure slim yet curved in the right places, with well-defined muscles visible in both arms and legs, which extended bare from the short sleeves and skirt of the dress. It was clear she exercised, and Matt presumed she watched her diet; and if her limbs showed wrinkled skin in places, it was a minimal amount. Her neck, often a clear age giveaway in women of a certain age, showed no sign of "turning turkey," as had so many on show around her.

She had the beauty of the natural, he decided, and he appreciated that. Better to grow old gracefully than try to deny the passage of the years. He knew bodies, he'd seen all sorts, enough to know that this one had something special. What she must have been thirty to forty years ago! She intrigued him. He had to talk to her, and made his way across the room to where she stood, chatting and laughing. But then he saw Jen, and straightaway felt guilty. He wasn't being fair on her, thinking about another woman. She was wonderful for coming today, it being the school holidays and their young children, Sarah and Toby, having to be farmed out to friends while Jen was here with him. She hadn't complained but had taken time out to come and support him, and for that he felt blessed. He owed Jen his loyalty, and needed to stop this wondering about an unknown woman.

It didn't work. He still couldn't prevent himself being interested. She'd be nothing like Jen, he was sure, and the idea appealed in some strange way. An idea occurred then, as to why she seemed familiar, but his thoughts were interrupted by Pippa, who appeared and buttonholed Joe, who also seemed lost in thought.

'Joe, why don't you put on some different music? This is supposed to be a party, not a wake, and people are beginning to look bored with all this standing around to slow music.'

Matt agreed with her, glad of the distraction, so accompanied his friend as the latter went to attend to the matter. They settled on a Spotify playlist which Joe had compiled, an assortment of tracks from the seventies up to the present day. Something for everyone there, they hoped. A few of the older attendees obliged them by beginning to dance, and the atmosphere lightened; but it bothered Matt that his woman had been asked to dance by another man.

He had to make her acquaintance, and that wouldn't be easy, now that she was dancing. He'd intended to find himself next to her by "accident" while she was talking. It'd be difficult to catch her between dances, and he couldn't very well ask her to partner him while they were strangers. It'd seem a bit obvious, and with his father, Pippa and Graham present, not to mention Jen, he couldn't chance anything so bold. He wondered yet again what he was thinking of, but he couldn't help himself.

He watched her, as discreet as he could be, as she finished dancing and moved to the sidelines of a group not far from where he stood. She stood quiet, modest, nodding and adding the occasional remark to the general conversation. Without any conscious thought, Matt moved towards them, trying not to appear too keen, making a friendly remark to one of the men better known to him than others. A conversation ensued, during which he was more aware than ever of her presence; and then, miracle of miracles, those standing between them moved away, and it wasn't difficult for him to end up standing next to her, despite the fact that she was speaking to the woman to her right and unaware of his existence.

Matt kept his attention on the man to his left, who now launched into some old story about when he'd been serving with Frank in the Middle East. All he needed was the occasional nod and some light comment, "Really?" or "I had no idea," to keep him in full flow. Matt's attention was fixed on the perfume of his right-hand and so-interesting neighbour; a light, floral fragrance, not heavy and cloying like that of some other women, the type which gave him a headache if exposed to them for too long. He felt that somehow it was mixed with the woman's own natural scent. He could detect it, although he couldn't put a name to it. He just knew he'd recognise it again.

His luck was in. The man with whom he'd been speaking—or pretending to do so—made some excuse and went to the bathroom, or to get another drink, or both, for all Matt knew or cared. He turned in her direction, casual, not looking towards Jen, who out of the corner of his eye he could see advancing across the room. But just as he was about to make some casual remarks and ease himself into conversation with his woman, his wife took him by the arm and moved in close, speaking in a low voice so that only he could hear.

'Trouble, I'm afraid.'

Before she could say more he heard the voice, too loud for good taste, attracting the attention of almost everyone in the room.

He recognised it, glanced in the direction from which it came, and prayed for the floor to open and swallow him. He'd thought of her and she'd appeared. His mother, Penny.

2: PENNY

The front door was on the latch, so she'd let herself in; but on seeing the crowd of people enjoying themselves inside, her mood turned from nervous and hesitant to belligerent. Drinking always had the ability to change her attitude with lightning speed, and she'd been drinking today.

Why shouldn't I be here? I'm one of Graham's oldest friends. I know why they had me over for dinner a fortnight ago. They thought it better that Frank and I weren't here together, and I did too, at the time. But why the hell should I give place to him, why should I be banished from the party? Most of these people are my friends too, or they were, before Frank convinced them he was the perfect husband and I was the bad one for running out on him. Perfect husband, like hell. They weren't there, inside our marriage, in our house, our bed, our domestic sphere. What the hell do they know? Why should I not be allowed to come? It's my right, and I'm here to bloody well claim it.

She could tell Pippa was taken aback at the sight of her. She'd never be unwelcoming, she was too polite, too good a person, to ever look anything but pleased to see her old friend, even though Penny had turned up unannounced. She would've been too good-mannered to gate-crash, in the past, well-brought-up as she'd been—but the past was gone and this was now and she needed to see Pip, warm, comforting Pip, party or not.

'Penny! How lovely to see you! What a surprise! We weren't expecting you, but I'm so glad, and Graham will be too, that you changed your mind and decided to come and celebrate with him.'

A lie, and they both knew it was, but a face-saver for both parties. It'd been an unspoken but mutually-understood agreement that Penny, and her partner Ross, wouldn't attend the party, which would be full of old friends and close acquaintances of not only Pippa and Graham but of Penny's ex-husband, Frank, who she'd scandalously dumped in favour of another some years ago. The divorce had been acrimonious to say the least, and there was too much bad blood between Penny and Frank for them to sit easily in the same room, even one such as this with a large crowd of people; this crowd of people especially, sympathetic in a body to Frank, who was present with his second wife.

Pippa, being a truly decent soul, had managed to remain neutral and stay friends with both Penny and Frank while not bringing any animosity upon herself from either for her continued friendship with the other. Now she tried to avoid the problem which Penny's unexpected arrival might cause. People were already looking askance at the troublesome uninvited guest, before turning away so that she might not see and lip-read the whispered words which came from them, doubtless detrimental to her, whilst at the same time directing sympathetic looks towards Frank who, sitting at the far side of the room and engaged in conversation, seemed so far unaware of her presence.

'Come and get a drink.'

Pippa put an arm around her shoulders and guided her towards the kitchen, out of the gaze of the crowd. Without care the mood could turn hostile, not what she wanted or what Graham deserved for his big day. Penny, aware of the negative attitudes directed at her and defiant of them, nevertheless allowed herself to be led the short distance into the large kitchen-diner and, having ascertained that there was nobody else in the room, closed the door behind her to gain some privacy for the news she had to impart.

'Coffee?'

Without waiting for an answer, and hoping that Penny wouldn't insist on alcohol, it being clear she'd had enough already, Pippa busied herself with the kettle. She was flustered in spite of herself and forgot to take her friend's coat, which Penny removed and draped over the back of the pine settle situated to the side of the garden door.

'It's so good to see you. What have you done with Ross?'

Pippa hurried on as she tried to order her thoughts and buy time to deal with this unexpected hitch in the proceedings, but Penny moved the conversation in a different direction entirely.

'He's left me! Thrown me out! Oh, Pip—'

She burst into tears, at the exact same moment that Graham, having been appraised of his unexpected guest, came in through the kitchen door.

'Penny! What a surprise! I can't—'

He tailed off, at the sight of the ex-wife of his best friend sobbing in the arms of his own. He was loyal to Frank, always would be, and had mourned the demise of the marriage at which he'd been best man. It felt like a reflection on his skills in the role for which he'd been chosen, which he knew was stupid, the couple having clocked-up well over thirty seemingly-happy years before Penny had upped and left. But he had an affection for her due to all those years of friendship, and he'd never be so rude as to eject her from his house just because she hadn't been invited. He'd come therefore to welcome her and make the best of the situation, which it appeared was worse than he'd thought.

He stood helpless as Pippa, over the head of the woman who was now shaking in her arms, shook her own head at him, raised her eyebrows and gave a slight nod in the direction of the door through which he'd just entered.

'Get Matt,' she mouthed. 'Matt.'

She repeated herself, her lips exaggerating the word as Graham continued to look at her, uncomprehending. Then he got it, nodded, and made himself scarce in search of his nephew, almost colliding with Jennifer, as she made her own entrance.

She looked an enquiry at Pippa as she approached her mother-in-law, held firm in the comforting embrace of her old friend. Jennifer had always managed to get on with Matt's mother—just—but she'd never encountered her in tears, as now, so was cautious in her approach.

'What's wrong?' was the best she could manage, as she attempted a feeble pat on the sobbing woman's shoulder.

'It's Ross.'

Penny allowed herself to be helped to the shabby but comfortable old sofa located at the end of the room, an orangery-style extension which "brought the garden into the home," as the lifestyle magazines were fond of saying. Jennifer moved to get a glass of water, which she brought to the woman who, now a little calmer, was disengaging herself from the arms of Pippa, seated beside her. Penny waved it away, her disgust palpable.

Pippa tried her best, remembering her guests neglected in the next room, but being committed to dealing with the emergency which had arisen and gone to the top of her list of priorities. Penny'd always been mercurial in her moods, and now her tearful state looked set to change to one of irritation. Pippa didn't need a scene, not today of all days. She hesitated for a split second before offering the one thing that might placate her old friend.

'There's wine over there. Do you want a drink?'

'Please.'

Picking up on Pippa's approach, Jennifer managed to hide her feelings and fetch a glass; the smallest as she could get away with.

Penny accepted the wine, finishing it in two large gulps and waving the glass at her daughter-in-law for a refill. Jennifer had no option but to comply, and with something larger, of which Penny took just a small sip. She seemed to have calmed, to have collected herself, and then it all came out. The day after Penny had visited Pippa and Graham she and Ross had quarrelled—not for the first time—with Ross storming out—not for the first time either. This time it'd been different, however, this time he hadn't returned, contrite, apologetic, making it up with Penny before they'd carried on with life as it had been before the tiff.

This time he'd stayed away for two days, then returned, stony-faced and calm but chilling with it. This was the end, he'd told her. It was finished, over, and he wanted Penny to move out. She'd protested. What was she supposed to do, where was she supposed to go, especially at her time of life? She'd got grown sons, he'd pointed out, they could put her up and help her find alternative accommodation. She'd been stubborn. I won't do it, she'd insisted, I won't go.

"This is my house," he'd reminded her. "You don't own any part of it and you've paid nothing towards our living costs. I can get an occupation order, within a couple of days. Don't forget, my best friend is an experienced lawyer, I have expert help, and what do you have?"

She'd felt panicked, because he was right. She'd been so sure they'd marry, in time, that she'd done nothing apart from be a traditional housewife, and she was past the age to go out to work, anyway. She'd stuck out for her rights, however.

What if she refused to go?

He'd become threatening, putting his face close to hers. "I don't think that'd be a good idea," he'd said, his voice and eyes icy cold.

Then he'd relented. "Look, Pen, I don't want to be unreasonable, but it's over. We both have to accept that, and move on as quickly as possible. I won't put you out on the street, I'm not a monster, but you need to find somewhere else as fast as you can. Why not ring Matthew?"

He'd held out her phone, almost ordering her to take it, and she'd done so, trembling. She hadn't called Matthew; with his perfect life, perfect wife and two children she'd feel ashamed to admit another failure to him. "Not again," she could almost hear him thinking, even if he was too tactful to ever say it. Besides, he was so like Frank in many ways, it would've been almost like telling her ex-husband; and Penny had gone cold inside at the thought of what he'd say upon hearing of her not only being discarded by the man she'd dumped him for but by that man's successor too. She couldn't bear the idea of his laughter.

Instead she'd made a flustered call to Simon, her youngest and favourite son. She'd always seen more of herself in him, in appearance anyway, although he was an outdoor type too—at which she'd remembered that he was at present sailing a yacht around the Mediterranean. He'd answered, nevertheless, listened to her stark statement of need for somewhere to stay and then provided an immediate solution.

"You can stay at my place. I won't be back for a month, although I'll be right there if you need me."

That wouldn't be necessary, Penny'd assured him. She loved him more for not subjecting her to any questioning, above ascertaining that she was okay and unharmed. After a sleepless night, with Ross in the spare bedroom, she'd packed up enough things to keep her going and taken a taxi to

Simon's bolt-hole apartment, which by good fortune wasn't too far from Ross's place. Her now ex-lover had ordered and paid for the cab, and promised to send the rest of her belongings within the next couple of weeks.

So Penny had settled herself into her youngest son's flat. She'd already had a key, in order to keep an eye on the place whenever he was away. Then she'd gone to the village store for essential food items, returned to what was now her home, for the foreseeable future, anyway, and proceeded to sit in a daze, not knowing what to do or why. And then through her jumbled thoughts she'd remembered Pippa and Graham, the recent dinner she'd had with them; and the party to which she hadn't been invited.

Like the bloody twelfth fairy in *Sleeping Beauty*, or whatever tale it was, she'd thought, and had needed a drink to help her digest what that meant. A few glasses later and the tact shown by their oldest friends in keeping Penny and Frank apart had changed to disloyalty in her mind, and she'd determined to show them. Come the day she'd got herself dressed in her best and set out, but she'd needed a drink or two to keep up her courage at the thought of Frank and how he'd exult at her misfortune. A little nip every now and then from the hip flask she carried with her, just to top up the Dutch courage, and she'd arrived, somewhat the worse for wear.

Penny didn't give every last detail in relating her ills, just the bits she thought her friend needed to hear. It was enough, along with Penny's condition, for Pippa to understand that she wasn't in any state for company, nor to be left alone. She ought to stay the night, but that was a problem, because they had a full house. Pippa knew she needed to keep Penny close, until tomorrow when she'd have more time to help her friend.

Her forehead wrinkled as she looked up to see Matt, standing by the door where, appraised of the situation by

Graham, he'd entered during his mother's narrative, in so much silence that she, concentrating on her story, hadn't as yet seen or heard him.

'Can you sit with her while I sort something out?'

A slight inclination of her chin accompanied Jennifer's move to take Pippa's place beside Penny, who'd closed her eyes and leaned backwards in her chair as she'd finished speaking. She looked to be asleep, but Pippa wasn't taking any chances.

'You'd better come with me.'

Her voice was so low that Matt almost didn't hear her, but he obeyed. It wasn't until she'd led him down the passageway and upstairs to Graham's study that Pippa spoke again.

'I don't think she wanted you to know, from what she said. I'd hate to upset her further, and you can see how—well, she's distressed enough already.'

Matt was used to his mother being "distressed," so accepted his aunt's lead.

'I'll keep her here overnight—no, you and Jennifer need to get off, I know you've both got places to be tomorrow. I'll keep her here for, I don't know, a day, a week, as long as it takes, and I'll keep you in the loop. Before that though—.'

A phone call to The Crown Hotel, just over a mile away on the edge of the village, and Pippa had a lucky booking of the one room they'd got vacant; a single, as it turned out.

There was one problem, however.

'This is so embarrassing. I need to find Abby.'

She bustled off to the lounge, while Matt returned to assist Jennifer.

3: MATT

It was all arranged with speedy efficiency. Abby, a lone female guest, was located and informed of the situation by Pippa, while Matt sat with Jennifer and his now-sleeping mother. She'd agreed to stay at the hotel, rather than here at the house as arranged, and even offered to pay for her room, but Pippa wasn't having that. Abby was her friend and her guest, and it was the responsibility of the host to provide alternative accommodation now that Penny was to have the room allocated to Abby. The latter had removed her belongings to the conservatory, from whence she'd collect them when Harry and Sue, also staying at The Crown, departed, taking her with them.

Having helped Jennifer take his mother gently but firmly upstairs, Matt returned to the lounge and the party, which hadn't been interrupted in any major way by the entrance of Penny, so fast had Pippa managed to steer her into the kitchen. He needed a drink more than ever, but as he was driving he'd supplied himself with an alcohol-free gin and tonic before leaving the kitchen. Now he gulped it, trying to pretend that the fake was the real thing, as he scanned the room. There was his father, involved in a conversation and unaware it seemed of the arrival of his ex-wife, and there was Madge, his current wife. She seemed a little on edge, throwing occasional enquiring glances in the direction of Matt, who studiously managed to avoid catching her eye.

Blast it. He wasn't about to discuss his mother with the woman who'd replaced her. If Madge wanted to know anything let her ask her husband, who must have some idea of what was going on, despite appearances to the contrary. Wasn't it enough for Matt to come here to do the duty of a godson to Pippa and Graham? Wasn't he allowed to enjoy himself too? He went in search of the woman who'd interested him before.

He couldn't see her where he'd left her, but soon spied her on the edge of a group and paying close attention. There was a space next to her, and on the other side he was pleased to see a familiar face, Nick Osbourne, another friend of his father's with whom Matt was acquainted. Nothing more natural than to join the group, stand between her and Nick and strike up a conversation with the latter. He could bring her into the conversation, and if Nick went for another drink at some point soon, being a heavy drinker, Matt would have her to himself. Then what? He wasn't even sure what he was doing, but knew he had to do it, so made his way over.

Just as he was near enough to greet Nick, the woman was dragged away by another who materialised beside her, saying something like "Emily's here, do come and see her." The object of his interest let herself be led away to catch up with some other old acquaintance. Frustrated, Matthew contented himself with asking Nick about her.

'Who is that? She looks familiar, but I can't recall where I might have met her before.'

Nick was helpful.

'No, you probably wouldn't have. Her husband was in another outfit, and their postings didn't tend to coincide with ours. June and I only ever met them once, as did Pippa and Graham, I believe. They were good friends at that time, and Pippa kept in touch with Abby, which is why she's here today, I suppose.'

'Abby? Her name's Abby? And where's the husband?'

She was the one who'd given up her room for his mother.

'Abby Hamilton, short for Abigail, or Arabella, perhaps, and she's a widow now. Gerry passed away recently; it was quite sudden and unexpected. He could only have been about sixty-eight or nine.'

'Poor woman. How unfortunate.'

He didn't know what else to say, but was saved by Nick's wife June, who joined the group and greeted him. Matt turned the topic of conversation to the couple's grandchildren, a favourite topic with June and which could keep her going for hours. All that was necessary was to smile, nod and say something innocuous every now and then, while he kept a covert eye on Abby.

It wasn't easy, as more people were arriving, among them Jude and Bethany, who of course sought out Matt, and catching up with them took forever. Looking at pictures of Jude's children, who she'd sensibly left at home with husband Alistair, as well as others of Bethany's latest outdoor exploits, Matt lost track of Abby until what felt like an age later. By then the gathering had taken on a more party-like feel, and many people were up dancing. He couldn't see the object of his interest at first, but then the music changed to a Stones' classic, and she appeared on the dance floor from the other side of the room.

Some man was with her, but she seemed to be allowing him to dance opposite her more as a convention. She moved as if to herself, and in a way all her own, which was pretty good at that, Matt decided. He moved around, the better to watch her obvious enjoyment of the music. But then she backed into a man, a non-dancer standing at the edge of the impromptu dance-floor, watching the dancers with a glass in one hand which splashed some of its contents onto his jacket as Abby made contact with him.

It was Matt's father, and only a little of his drink was spilled. If only it'd been she who'd collided with me, thought Matt, remembering his own earlier gin-soaking. He saw Abby turn to face Frank as they collided, with an audible 'Oops, sorry' before she smiled, then whirled away in the dance. After watching her for some moments, whilst brushing the drops of liquid from his shirt, Frank returned to the people with whom he'd been speaking before going for a refill.

The music changed to something slow, and Matt could see Abby shaking her head and smiling a "No, thank you" to the man with whom she was supposed to be dancing. She left the floor, going over to the glass of wine she'd left on a sideboard, right next to where Matt was standing now. He took his chance.

'Hi.'

He smiled at her, and inwardly cursed himself for an idiot. Impress her, why don't you, for God's sake.

'I don't think we've met.'

Oh great, that really ought to do it, he told himself with savage sarcasm. He shut up, filling the silence with a weak smile.

'We have, actually.'

She smiled at him and he looked at her, enquiring. There was a nagging familiarity about her, but he still couldn't place it.

'You have me at a disadvantage, I'm afraid.'

'Oh, I wouldn't expect you to remember. You were only about eight at the time, or ten, or even twelve. I'm no good at telling children's ages, I never had any so I'm the one at a disadvantage there. But we did meet, at any rate.'

She grinned, a big sunny smile which exposed cream-coloured teeth; not the bleached teeth so common and so obviously false these days, Matt noted. Another indication of her naturalness, which lit up this room full of grey people.

He looked back at her, and didn't know what to say.

'Oh, yes?'

That was all he could manage. He wasn't winning any prizes for witty repartee, but was taking the gold, silver and bronze combined for making a prat of himself. His eyes met hers and locked with them, and for the life of him Matt couldn't drag his own away. He felt more awkward than ever and she seemed to sense this, moving her gaze off to the side so that he could look elsewhere. He dropped his eyes for want of any other direction and saw her body in the tight summer dress. Confused, panicked, he saw her wine glass, more empty than full, and focussed in desperation on that.

'Can I get you another?'

He gestured at the glass and she put her head on one side, quizzical.

'You look like you could use one yourself. Shall we go together?'

She set off towards the kitchen, expecting him to follow, which he did, obedient, like the little boy she'd remembered him as.

'Just something soft.'

He cautioned her as he followed her into the kitchen, where she was already searching the fridge, A carton of orange juice appeared in one hand, in the other a bottle of soda, which she waved at him with an enquiring expression.

'Yes, please.'

She found an empty glass and mixed the drink for him, then refilled her own and raised it.

'Have you come as the child you were back then?'

She was teasing, and smiled to take the edge off her

words.

'No, but I'm giving my father and his wife a lift. Designated driver, I'm afraid.'

Not true. Jen was also staying sober, and would drive them both home this evening, after giving Frank and Madge a lift to the hotel from whence they'd return home in the morning. Why had he done that? Not wanting to admit to having a wife? His conscience moved to correct the wrong, but Abby was already commenting, as well as frowning.

'Seems harsh, putting you on parade but not letting you have some fun. Why can't he do without for once?'

That seemed a bit severe too, Matt thought, but maybe she remembered his father's drinking habits from the past. He shrugged off the comment, trying to excuse his parent.

'He's not as young as he was, and he has health issues, so it's better if I drive for him. Anyway, I'm in surgery tomorrow, so it's better for me to stay off the stuff today.'

'Tell me about it. Don't we all have health issues? But I'll excuse you because you're getting yours attended to tomorrow. Nothing too bad, I hope?'

She was nothing if not direct, Matt thought, as she sipped her wine.

'Sorry, I should have said. I'm the surgeon, and I'll need a steady hand.'

'Okay, got it. So, tell me about your career. What made you want to go into medicine?'

Glad to change the subject he spoke, telling her about the interest that'd come to him whilst still very young, the desire when visiting the doctor to know about the whys and wherefores of treatments, the interest in biology in particular as a subject at school. All together these had culminated in Matt knowing that medicine was for him. He told Abby of his education, his university years, medical school and the further specialist training as a surgeon. The status of consultant he'd worked hard for and achieved, his hopes for his own private clinic now being realised.

She listened, seemed interested, made an intelligent comment from time to time and refilled their glasses when appropriate. At last he realised he was talking far too much and they had their own kitchen splinter-group going on; not to mention that it was all about him. Appalled by his own bad manners, he apologised.

'I'm so sorry. I've been banging on, all about myself, boring you and never even asking about you. I don't know what's got into me.'

She grinned.

'That's okay. Nothing much to tell, really.'

She was giving him a get-out, which he didn't want. To stay here and hear about her, that was what he wished for; but he offered her a similar exit.

'I'm sure you'd rather go and catch-up with—'

The people of your own generation, he'd been about to say, but that would never do, apart from the fact that he wasn't sure his father's friends were her generation. She seemed much younger somehow. He cast around in his mind for a suitable description of the other guests, but could come up with nothing.

Her smile widened as she watched him.

'The other old fogies?'

'No, no—'

He tailed off, and she shrugged.

'I only know a few of them. I'm here for Pippa and Graham, and I'm staying over; well, in the village, at all events. Which means I get to drink,'—taking a gulp of her wine—'but I think I've had enough now. I don't want to disgrace myself—I mean—'

She'd realised her gaffe, but he knew it wasn't intentional, and liked the fact that she could be discomforted too. He helped her out.

'Too much is bad for you anyway.'

She put out her tongue at him, in a way he found fetching, in an odd sort of way.

'No lectures, please, Doctor, I don't do it all the time. I have to watch my weight, but I'm taking a few days off and I intend to enjoy them. I'll be back on the diet soon enough, not to mention taking exercise. Talking of which, I need food now. Coming?'

She headed back into the lounge, on the way to the dining-room and the buffet laid out on the table.

Matthew followed, but got waylaid by some of his parents' old friends and had to go through the usual repertoire of questions and statements, I can see your father in you, all grown up now, I knew you when you were just so high, doing so well, all that research you've done, your father was telling me, he's so proud, a credit to your upbringing, etcetera, etcetera, etcetera. By the time he'd extricated himself, there was no sign of Abby in the dining room. He sought her in the lounge, where he saw her in a corner, talking to a woman he didn't know whilst drinking orange juice, he noted with approval. As he made his way to her, however, he was waylaid by his father.

'I'm afraid Madge is rather tired, so I think it's time to take her to the hotel. Jennifer's looking a bit done in too.'

Glancing across to where his wife was keeping up a polite front, Matt recognised the tell-tale signs of weariness in her posture. Yes, they ought to leave, get home and have a good night's sleep before the busy day that awaited them tomorrow. He felt disappointed and deflated, asking himself why that should be the case. What was this woman Abby to him? His feelings notwithstanding he went to collect his wife, to give thanks and say their goodbyes to Pippa and Graham. Jen agreed rather too fast, confirming her tiredness.

'I need to visit the bathroom first.'

Leaving her to go and do the needful, Matt went over to Abby, deep in conversation.

'I'm sorry to interrupt, but I have to be going now.'

Her companion waved her empty glass and headed for the kitchen, leaving them together. Matt stood awkward before Abby's enquiring expression. It was now or never, and he went for it.

'I'd like to talk to you again. Maybe when I can have a drink too?'

She raised an eyebrow, but thanked him and suggested he call her. One minute later her number was stored in his phone and she resumed conversation with another guest as Matt walked to the door, and didn't break off when he glanced back before going out to his car.

4: ABBY

She awoke after a good night's sleep, better than the four to five hours which'd become usual for her over the last few years. The bathroom beckoned, and she was out of bed and on the way before she realised she wasn't at home, nor at Pippa and Graham's as planned, but in the hotel in the village, about a mile away. She scrabbled around in the dark for the light switch, then found her way to the bathroom. Afterwards she opened the curtains a crack to ascertain whether or not it was yet light, which it was, but all was quiet outside so it must still be early. Her room overlooked the car park, with no more than four or five cars, but not her own. That was up at the house, in accordance with the original arrangement, and she'd have to walk back to collect it later. She checked the time on her phone. Seven-thirty.

Faint and distant sounds told her people were up and about, preparing breakfast, as the chink of cutlery and china suggested, and all of a sudden she was starving. The food on offer at the party had been okay, but not enough to sustain her for long. She wasn't ready to go down just yet, so switched on the kettle to make coffee, noting the little packs of biscuits provided. They'd keep her going for the time being.

While waiting for the kettle to boil she opened the curtains to let in the daylight. Her room wasn't overlooked, so with the ceiling light switched off she'd have privacy. As she did so the door from the reception area opened and two people emerged; she recognised Frank and Madge. She watched as they put their overnight bags into the boot before getting into the front, Frank as driver, Madge as passenger, then pulling out and driving off.

Her eyes narrowed, but she grinned. Designated driver my arse. He'd been lying, maybe to hide the fact of his little wife, doing her duty of polite conversation with unknown-and-no-doubt-boring old friends of her in-laws. Did he think Abby hadn't noticed her, helping him cope with his inebriated mother, getting her upstairs and away from making even more of a spectacle of herself? Didn't he consider that over the years Pippa had shown photos to Abby, including those of Frank and Penny's grown sons, and in Matt's case the wife and grandchildren? Along with Pippa and Graham's brood they'd been the youngest people at the party, and it'd been clear they were together. A liar, and not a good one, but with those parents he hadn't stood a chance in the honesty stakes.

Enough of him. Abby sat on the bed and drank her coffee, eating the biscuits and thinking back over the previous day.

It was a bit of a pain she'd had to stay here overnight, but the hotel wasn't a bad one, small, family-run country-village type of thing, so at least she ought to get a good breakfast before leaving. Why shouldn't she treat herself? She only needed to shower before setting out on her journey, which was just an hour-and-a-half. It was Sunday, and there was no one to miss her back at home, so what the hell if she took her time? She had to try and let go, to take things easy, now she was on her own and learning to get back to life in the mainstream. There was no rush for her to return, nobody to get back for. She could take her time and do things in a more leisured manner. She needed to learn to loosen up.

As things turned out it was better she'd come here, she

decided, to help out her hosts. Penny turning up like that had put additional pressure on them, and Abby didn't think she'd have liked to be there this morning to witness her inevitable embarrassment. Far better to be long gone by the time Penny surfaced, which Abby guessed wouldn't be until about mid-morning, given the amount she appeared to have put away. It was so sad to see what she'd come to, but Penny had been in the best possible care last night. Pippa and Graham wouldn't let her drive home until she was as sober as could be, and it was probable that they'd keep her there for lunch, even another night; without alcohol, of course.

More relaxed approach or not, Abby decided to collect her car sooner rather than later. She finished her coffee and showered, then removed the chair from before the door and went down for breakfast. It being Sunday, and most other guests taking the opportunity for a lie-in—along with the fact that this was a small hotel, a dozen rooms at most—meant she had the restaurant to herself. A lone waitress was clearing the used dishes from one table, presumably that which Frank and his wife had used prior to their early departure. She smiled at Abby and waved her to take a table, indicating that she'd come and take her order as soon as she'd carried the used dishes away.

Abby treated herself to scrambled eggs on toast. There was a lot more on offer but she didn't eat much for breakfast at home, never cooking anything more complex than toast, heated croissants, pain chocolat or crumpets, for special occasions; most days she just had cereal. Breakfast eaten, she returned to her room to collect her things, paid her bill and set off up the road to collect her car. She only had a small overnight bag and it wasn't a long walk, so she made it in about twenty minutes, looking back over her shoulder at regular intervals. All was quiet around the house, and Abby was careful not to make any noise getting into the car, not wanting to disturb anyone or bring them out of the house to speak to her. She'd spent the evening with these people and they were her friends, but yesterday was past and she wanted to leave as soon as she could and move on.

She drove slowly through the village, seeing no one else up and about, then increased speed as she moved out onto the larger A-road before joining the dual carriageway for the majority of her trip home. Her eyes and ears paid necessary attention to the road as she drove, but her thoughts wandered into their own path, prompted by the memories raised on the following evening.

Matthew. Frank and Penny's eldest son. A grown man in his forties now, a doctor of many years' experience and senior consultant in his hospital department. Quite incredible, when Abby remembered what he'd been the last time she'd seen him, so many years ago. The last time she'd seen them all, apart from Pippa and Graham. It'd been interesting, going back into the past, seeing those faces, some changed beyond recognition by the passage of time, some not at all, bar a few wrinkles.

They weren't all good memories, but that was life. No need to do any of that again. Time to put it all behind her.

She focussed on getting home, to her own place, her safe space; she pressed the accelerator harder, the better to get back there sooner.

5: FRANK

Making good speed through the light early-Sunday-morning traffic, Frank couldn't help thinking about Penny, both as she'd appeared yesterday and in the past. Madge, bless her, dozing on the passenger seat beside him now, had urged him to help, when his previous wife had arrived, and in such a dishevelled condition. She knew he'd do nothing without her say-so, knowing he wouldn't want to seem disloyal to her, good woman that she was.

"She was your wife. She's still the mother of your sons."

He'd had a quiet word with Graham, who'd suggested that Frank keep well clear. Penny'd had more than enough to drink, besides being in an emotional condition—nothing to do with Frank, he'd hastened to add—and was in that volatile state where her mood could shift as fast as a light switch.

"Best to avoid an ugly scene. Let Pips deal with it, eh?"

So Frank had retreated to join a small splinter group in the garden, the better to maintain a distance from both Penny, should she reappear in the lounge, and the comments which he knew the others present wouldn't be able to help making, friends though they were supposed to be. Madge, dear tactful creature, had appeared at his side after a decent interval, claiming tiredness but in reality giving him a plausible excuse to leave.

So goodbyes had been said all around, with promises to keep in better touch and a firm invitation to Graham and

Pippa to visit when a mutually-convenient date could be found. Frank was looking forward to that, but also couldn't help looking back to yesterday. For two pins he wouldn't have attended the party, but Graham was his oldest friend and there was no way Frank wouldn't have been there for him. In reality, however, he hadn't needed the last stand of the old and bold, the memories of what they'd all been in their youth and the visible signs of what they'd become in their declining years. It was enough that Frank had been feeling tired in recent months, lacking in energy and a bit short of breath on occasions. The doctor had pointed out that he wasn't getting any younger, which wasn't helpful, before he'd diagnosed anaemia and prescribed iron tablets. Nevertheless, the patient couldn't say he was feeling that much better, and seeing so many old acquaintances well on their way into God's waiting room, so to speak, only served to remind Frank of his own mortality. All in all it hadn't been the most fun he'd ever had even before the unexpected appearance of his ex-wife.

Penny. She'd left him for another man, and he'd been shattered. It wasn't like fidelity had always been his middle name; he'd had his moments and he wasn't proud of that. There was no way he'd ever have left Penny and the boys, however. He'd made vows and even if he hadn't managed to keep to all of them he'd been emphatic about the "Till Death Do Us Part" bit; so when out of the blue she'd announced her love for another and told Frank she was divorcing him, it'd hurt more than he could ever have imagined.

It was strange, how they'd known each other in childhood, lived in the same place, gone to the same primary school. Frank had pulled Penny's pigtails, when the adults weren't looking, as he'd sat behind her in church, and she'd kicked him hard on the shins later, by way of repayment. Two years they'd been there together, living almost next door to each other, and then his father had been posted overseas and they'd gone their separate ways. For Frank it was boarding school, then prep school, then military school before he'd entered Sandhurst, to follow in his father's footsteps. He'd been homesick at first, desperate for his mother, then hardening and getting used to it, giving as good as he got when the bullies moved in on him. He'd given another boy a broken nose, and gotten caned for fighting, but he'd ensured they gave him a wide berth in the future.

And Penny? He'd lost track of the little tomboy he'd played with as a child, until by one of those strange chances of life he'd encountered her again. There she'd been, grown up and grown beautiful, a charming young lady, no hint of the former hoyden to be seen. He'd fallen in love, and fallen hard, and it wasn't too long before he'd asked her to be his wife, and she'd accepted. It was soon after his passing-out that they'd married, and she'd accompanied him in his career as his mother had followed his father. In due course the boys had been born, and grown, and at length gone away to school in their turn, and God had been in his heaven and all right with their world, and over thirty years had passed; and then Penny had met *him.*

How Frank had loved her. She'd been the woman with whom he'd wanted to spend his life, and they'd been happy; which didn't mean he didn't still appreciate female beauty. He'd always had an eye for women, his love for Penny notwithstanding, and you didn't go blind just because you were married. He more than anyone knew he wasn't perfect by a long chalk, and there'd been times when he'd been sorely tempted. Military life took him away, as many other men like him, from family and home for long periods, and it wasn't always easy to resist temptation. But when his will had failed on occasion he'd always been discreet, and careful, making sure he wasn't taking anything unpleasant, medically-speaking, home to Penny.

She'd never questioned him about what he might have got up to whilst away. He'd never been subjected to the third degree on his return, like other men he'd known with jealous wives. If Penny ever wondered she never gave any indication. It was as though she accepted that life doesn't always follow the path we'd like it to, but that there was no point in making a fuss about it. Her husband was still just that, and had come back to her and their children. What happened on unaccompanied tours remained there and didn't come home with him. So Frank had stayed with Penny, which was where he wanted to be, and had envisioned their life together, when at length he retired. Somewhere in southern England, near sports facilities, their grown children visiting at times and bringing their grandchildren.

And how had she repaid him? By going off with bloody Jeremy, that's how. He'd been shattered when she confronted him, told him of her feelings for the other man and how she wanted a divorce. He'd been unable to believe it, asked her to reconsider. He was willing to overlook the affair she'd been having; he hadn't been a model of fidelity over the years, so he understood. She'd been left alone often enough, raising the children by herself. It was bound to happen that she'd meet others and be tempted, as Frank had been in his time. But Love! Divorce! That was something else.

She'd at least had the decency to wait until the boys were grown, finished at university and established in their respective careers, before she'd hit him with the bombshell, and he wondered how long she'd been seeing *him*. Nevertheless, he'd got her to agree to giving their marriage another go, of finishing her affair, and to this she'd agreed, after a struggle with herself. So they'd tried, but it was soon clear that it wasn't going to work. Divorce had followed, and maybe Penny had been carrying around an inkling of what Frank had got up to when away, and resented it, because she took him to the cleaners in the settlement. It was harsh, even by the standards which allowed a military wife a generous settlement in lieu of the employment opportunities she'd missed over the years spent following her husband. The solicitor she'd engaged specialised in representing women like her, and knew her stuff. Frank had been obliged to call Penny one day and ask if she wanted his blood too; at which point she'd seen enough sense to call off The Rottweiler, as he'd called her solicitor.

So there she'd been, settled with Jeremy before the ink was dry on the divorce papers, well off and doing very nicely, while Frank had little by way of savings and his military pension left to show for all his years of work and supporting his family. So when, after about ten years, lover-boy Jeremy had decamped and dumped Penny, Frank ought to have taken a grim satisfaction in her distress; but he hadn't. It'd hurt him to hear of her grief, how she was destroying herself by finding comfort at the bottom of a bottle. He'd followed the same route in the early days, until he'd realised the only person he was hurting was himself, and cut back on the stuff. He'd hated seeing the state of her yesterday, the plea in her eyes—because they'd met his for an instant, before Pippa had steered her out of the room—that it wasn't too late, they could still get back together. But it was too late, Frank felt, even had he not been married to Madge.

He remembered her then, asleep next to him in the passenger seat. They hadn't needed to leave for home quite so early. It was Sunday after all, they were both retired, able to do things at a more leisurely pace; but Frank had wanted to get back, to distance himself from the old crowd and the reminder of his ageing, and Madge had fallen in with his wishes, bless her. He felt disloyal to her in thinking about

Penny. She was a good woman, a good wife, she'd been there for him when his world had fallen apart. She'd chosen him when she could have had her pick of younger men, richer men, any man at the golf club and other places where she socialised.

He put a hand on her knee, giving an affectionate squeeze at which she awakened from the light sleep into which she'd fallen and turned on him a sunny smile. Frank replaced the hand on the steering wheel, the better to overtake the rather slow car in front and get them home as fast as safety allowed. But his thoughts went unbidden into other long-neglected areas of his past.

6: MATT

Matt was alert the moment he opened his eyes, a habit he'd acquired as a medical student, working night shifts and often being rudely awoken to help deal with an emergency. It'd followed him all his life since, so that even today, after arriving home late last night, he was alert and ready for the many tasks ahead of him.

He checked the clock. Early indeed, at only 4.30 a.m., and as he had things on his mind he decided to treat himself to another half-hour before throwing off the duvet and getting down to it. He turned over and checked Jen, still unconscious at his side. She'd be busy too, once awake, but at least her load was lightened today by the kids having stayed over with friends last night. They'd be taken to school without the need for Jen to ensure they got there in safety. Today that was somebody else's issue, so Matt decided to let her sleep. They both deserved a lie-in.

As his thoughts arranged themselves bit by bit, he remembered leaving the party, and the drive home with Jen. She'd looked weary, when they dropped off Frank and Madge at the village hotel, so he'd taken the wheel himself.

"God, what a bloody mess, my mother turning up like that. Thanks so much for dealing with her, Jen. D'you think she'll be okay?"

"I'm sure she will, Philippa'll look after her and get her

home tomorrow. I'll ring in the morning to make sure all's well. Will you be okay if I shut my eyes for a bit? I'm rather tired from it all."

"Of course. I've got the sat nav for directions and the radio for company. Go ahead, you've earned it."

She'd shut her eyes and dozed to the smooth classical music, leaving Matt with his thoughts; and home was at the forefront of them. He'd been glad to get back there, to his and Jen's haven, their comfortable house, their two children, the dogs, the cat; all part of their safe place in which he was awakening now.

He remembered the party, Abby, and his strange attraction to her. Why was that? Because he liked older women, he supposed, and even Jen had a few years on him. Perhaps it was due to his having been sent away to school at the tender age of eight. Far too young, he felt, and although he understood the concept of getting children used to flying the nest and standing on their own two feet, he wasn't about to send his own pair away until they were much older, if at all. Maybe a year boarding at a good school before it was time for university, to ease them into the almost-adult experience. Whatever. Matt himself had been sent to an all-boys institution with Matron the only comforting female presence available. She'd seemed so much older, to the eyes of an eight-year-old boy, but in retrospect she must have been in her twenties, and attractive. Matt had looked at females nearer his own age as he'd grown, of course, but somehow he'd always looked for that added extra something, a "motherly" aspect, which came with the lady in question being his senior, even if by just a few years.

He looked across at Jen, still fast asleep, her breathing almost inaudible. For some reason he felt irritated by her, and that wasn't fair. When he'd met her he'd been sure she was for him, good-looking in a way he could only describe as wholesome, and flawless in all she did, in his eyes. Once they were married she was the perfect hostess to those with whom they socialised, his professional colleagues and their friends, giving drinks and dinner parties which went off without a hitch. She never looked red-faced and flustered from preparing and presenting food, whether just canapés for drinks or full dinners of several courses. To their two children she was a model mother, spending time helping them with homework and being tech-savvy enough to keep an eye and make sure that they didn't venture into the dark side of social media and the internet.

She was also a member of both the PTA and the Parent Council at the nearby private school, well-up in the league tables and in high demand with those who could afford to pay the fees; which was why their daughter Bella was a pupil there, with younger brother Toby having just joined her this school year. In addition, Jen was an active member of several women's groups in their village, near enough to the hospital to make Matthew's commute as easy as possible, with the amenities of the city close by yet far enough away to guarantee some peace, quiet and countryside in which to walk their two dogs, Duke—a labrador—and Prince—a retriever. Jen organised visits to the vet when required, much as she arranged doctor's and dentist's appointments for the children. She employed and supervised a cleaner for the house—she couldn't do everything, after all—although she drummed into her husband and the children the need to keep the place tidy; no lazy "leave it for the cleaner" attitude in Jennifer's house.

"Cleaning isn't the most pleasant work, and there's no need to make Mrs J's job harder than it has to be."

She also did the shopping herself. Matt had pointed out that she could order this online and have it delivered, but his wife had been firm.

"It's important that I'm seen around the village, an active member of the community, not hidden away at home behind a screen and keyboard."

As part of her social presence she baked cakes for the village fête and other charitable functions, as well as a thousand other tasks which all contributed to the ultra-smooth running of the household and the lives of the family members who lived therein. Her home and larger sphere of activity ran like clockwork, leaving Matthew to get on with practising surgery untroubled by the distractions of life which bothered so many of his colleagues. He wanted for nothing, it seemed to those associates. He was living the dream, and yet—

There was one thing wanting beside which the perfections of the rest of his life paled into insignificance; Matt's otherwise wonderful wife was no longer his dream lover, although it hadn't always been so. Granted, she'd never been a sensual, sexual siren, as seen in films and on TV, but then neither had any of his girlfriends before he met her. He doubted that many such women existed; it was either that, or for some reason he always went for the wholesome, fresh-faced, girl-next-door types. Jen had been the cream of the crop, and he'd known without thinking that he wanted her for his wife from the moment he'd met her. Their sex life had been fine, with good, clean, unambitious love-making, nothing bizarre or kinky and no weird sex aids. They'd been happy with each other, but the births of Toby and Bella had changed things.

They'd put off having children for a while, Matt wanting to get established with a good salary behind him before undertaking the responsibility of more mouths to feed, and Jen had been nothing loath. It was understandable therefore that they didn't have as much energy as when they'd been younger, and tired more easily. It wasn't unusual for parents of any age to be exhausted for most of the time, in the days of night-feeds when the babies came, and both Matt and Jen had been walking around like zombies, with dark circles under their eyes. Jen, however, was too tired, too often, and since she'd become a mother she seemed less inclined to be a wife, in the sexual sense. Again, that wasn't uncommon. With children around the house the spontaneity of the act was lost, plus the energy expended in caring for these small people meant that sleep followed fast upon heads touching pillows. These things could pass, with time, when the adults involved got used to the new task of parenting. For Matt and Jen there'd been other things, however—

His thoughts were interrupted as she stirred beside him, stretched, then put out a hand to check the time on her phone.

'Oh hell. Time to get moving.'

She pivoted to a sitting position, then stood and went on auto-pilot to the en-suite, without even the usual perfunctory kiss which started their day. Matt sighed, throwing off the covers and heading for the family bathroom down the corridor. His musings were forgotten, as preparation for the workaday week took over.

Time for normal service to be resumed.

7: ABBY

She sat on the small balcony which opened off her bedroom and sipped her coffee in the peace and quiet of the early morning, enjoying the view of the fields which lay before her, and over which the sun had not long risen. She always sat out here, when the weather allowed. It was at the back of the house, away from any prying eyes, looking over open countryside, so she'd see anybody who approached from that direction. It was one of the things which'd influenced her to buy this house, and she'd been happy here for some time now. There was a decision to be made, however, and she'd been pushing it to the back of her mind for a while; but this morning it'd forced its way to the front, and she couldn't put it off any longer.

It was a difficult choice to make. She loved living out here in this tranquil, rural, idyll, and she'd always been good at being on her own. Even as a teenager she'd go on long walks just to be alone, and after she'd married her husband had been away on occasion, meaning she'd had the luxury of time to herself. She wondered if it was a healthy way to live, now it was just her on her lonesome in every sense. Was she going to spend the rest of her life in total isolation? She might have thirty-five years or so left to her, and while it wasn't exactly her whole life before her, it was still a considerable period of time.

She needed to get out there and meet a few people. Or did

she? She wasn't sure. Getting back together with Pippa and Graham was a start. They were about the only old friends with whom she was still in touch, and there was no family anymore; Abby was alone. That was a downside of a travelling lifestyle. You made friends of those people with whom you got on best, and they didn't necessarily come from the same place as you. Plus they didn't always get the same postings as you, or not at the same time, so you didn't see them for years at a stretch. You kept in touch, but somehow that whittled down to the Christmas card and round-robin letter, and even that could fade away at some point. It was the same when at last you retired and settled. Everybody tended to return to their areas of origin, or even somewhere else altogether.

Look at Frank. He'd been an Army brat—his words—Abby remembered him saying so. He'd been born in Hong Kong, but his parents had moved away when he was still very young, meaning he had no memory of the place and no family there or anywhere else his parents had lived to return to and settle with. He'd been packed off to school at a ridiculous age, and grown up into a travelling life of his own. Upon retirement he'd settled in the last place he'd been working, and even bought the rented flat he'd been living in. He'd met a local woman and married her, Abby'd discovered, but he still had to travel a distance to see his oldest friends.

Which brought her back to her own situation. She liked the upside of being alone, doing just what she liked, with nobody else to consider and no compromises. If she wanted to watch TV at 3 a.m. whilst eating cornflakes, she could; or if she wanted to take herself off on an away-day at a moment's notice there was nobody to stop her. Drive somewhere else, see the sights, eat and drink whatever she liked and stop over. She could do it, and be answerable to no one.

On the other hand, it might be a good idea in the long run to find a flat, a retirement apartment maybe, in a place closer to amenities and people; something in the small market town not too far from the village where she lived now, and which she visited once a week at least. It had enough shops for necessities, plus coffee shops and eateries, a pleasant park in the centre with a swimming pool nearby. There was a theatre, run by volunteers, which hosted visiting dramatic, opera and dance companies, celebrity speakers, all kinds of performances, and showed films and live screenings at other times. They even had an arts festival in the summer. Abby could imagine building a life around those things; an early swim a couple of mornings each week, out for coffee and cake, going to the shops to pick up a few bits and pieces, volunteering at the theatre a couple of nights a week, joining a book club perhaps. Forging social links, maybe even making new friends, and the rest of the time reading and writing and doing whatever else she pleased at home.

The problem was, she liked where she was now. The quiet village suited her, and it wasn't far to drive to Broxton if she wanted a bit more bustle and activity. Her current house was rather too large for her, true, but Abby was a firm believer in not rocking the boat. If you were in a place that suited you, why change it? The encroaching infirmities of old age might oblige her to go into a care home at some point, but she wasn't keen. Carers on tap treating her like a child, trying to persuade her to go and socialise with the other geriatric residents in the communal lounge? No thank you. Abby wasn't there yet, and even when she was she'd rather die alone and unattended in the comfort of her own home.

That settled it. She drained her coffee cup, then sat and looked about her, at the trees, the flowers, the fields, the birds. The early-morning song of these latter was pleasant, so she closed her eyes and drank it in, achieving an almost trance-like state until the silence from which the trills and warbles emerged was compromised by another, far less welcome sound; the distant rumble of traffic, as the morning exodus of commuters hit the highway and the sounds of the countryside became subsumed in the distant, single-note drone of vehicles going about the business of keeping the economy afloat. By no means was it Piccadilly Circus, Abby admitted, far from it, but when you've become used to something, anything which detracts from it takes on a disproportionate level of blame for the disruption.

She got to her feet. The rest of the world was rising and so should she, retired or not. A shower, a stroll to the baker for fresh-cooked pastries, and a decision. Have them there, with a cappuccino in the adjoining coffee shop, or bring them back to eat in the peace and privacy of her own conservatory? One of the big decisions of her life now.

*****

The coffee shop won, in the event. First thing in the morning it wasn't busy, custom in the main being locals who had to drive to work in Broxton, wanting coffees, teas, chocolate, whatever, to take with them. Abby took her time, enjoying the morning sun on her face before paying the bill and taking an unhurried stroll to the grocery store, to buy a few necessary bits and pieces. The village was in full bloom at this time of the summer, the flower beds and boxes a splash of colour, the sun glinting off the river which ran through the centre, the gentle quacking of the ducks which glided along the water or sat on the banks rising to a crescendo when a woman began throwing bread for them. The resulting stampede was captured on camera by a couple, tourists from the hotel by the look of them, the entire scene taken in by Abby as she passed, following the road which led out of the centre to her home on the outskirts.

It was as she walked up the lane that she got the most curious sensation, for all the world as though she was being watched. Stopping, she looked around, back the way she'd come and forward towards home. Nothing. Nobody. Those who were going to work had gone by now; the mothers who'd taken children to school were back at home clearing up from breakfast and enjoying a blissful coffee on their own before they commenced the daily grind of cleaning and ironing and shopping.

She started off again, this time with one ear cocked for the sounds of anybody following, whether innocently or otherwise, but she heard nothing more. It must have been her imagination and, shaking it off, she turned her thoughts into more productive channels. Listen to some music, read a book, try to write one of her own? There were many ways to pass the time, and plenty of time to be passed. There was laundry to be done, but that could wait. The joys of living for yourself, with nobody depending on you doing something by a certain time. A book on the balcony, she decided, and went inside to select something suitable from the extensive bookshelves, first making sure that all external doors and windows on the ground floor were closed and locked.

Alone again, naturally. Preferable, but not always comfortable.

8: PIPPA

Pippa stared unbelieving at the message on the paper she held before her. There were the beginnings of tears in her eyes as she slammed it down on the worktop with uncharacteristic force. Throwing back her chair and standing, she made a determined effort to compose herself, wiping her wet cheeks with the back of one hand and blowing her nose. Committing the used tissue to the bin, she straightened and got on with making lunch, although she soon stopped and stood, considering.

'Is that toast burning I can smell?'

'Oh, God.'

She hastened to flip the switch on the toaster as Graham entered, moving over to catch the slices as they flew into the air.

'No harm done. Just a bit of charcoal around the edges. Good for us, or so they say.'

'Yes.'

She busied herself with the poached eggs, while he placed the slices on the plates sitting ready. Eggs added, they moved to sit at the island.

'Pip, what's wrong?'

'Nothing. I'm fine.'

'No, you're not. I've known you too long and too well. You could cut the atmosphere in here with a knife. Darling, what is it?'

Pushing his almost-untouched food aside he moved across to her, putting his arms around his wife and hugging her to him, before pulling back and looking into her once-more moist eyes.

She leaned against him, enjoying the comfort he never failed to provide. Pulling away at last, she reached for the offending document, handing it to her husband for his perusal.

'This came in the post.'

His eyebrows drew together and his eyes narrowed as he read, before looking at her with enquiring expression.

'Is this some sort of joke, d'you think? Because if it is it's a bloody poor one.'

'I don't think so. A joke shouldn't fill you with fear, and that's what I felt. What I'm still feeling.'

Her cheeks were wet.

'But it's laughable. I mean, look at it.'

He brandished the paper.

'Those letters, cut out of newspapers, stuck on like that. It's like something out of a bad film.'

She shook her head, unable to speak as the tears welled once more.

He sighed, reached out and drew her against him. She gave herself up to his embrace.

'Whover this —creature—is, they don't know us at all. Dan and Simon are middle-aged men. Does this piece of scum honestly think we're unaware of their relationship after all these years? Whatever they're after, they're barking up the wrong tree. They've got it sadly wrong, ignorant bigot that they are.'

'I know. It just makes me so sad that there are people like that out there. Deliberately trying to upset people they don't know, and for what? Some sort of sick enjoyment at others' expense.'

'Don't take on over it, Pip, or they'll have won. Just be glad we're happy, and healthy, as are our children and their families.'

She leaned further into the relief that only he could give. Lunch abandoned, they moved as one to the sofa which looked out to the garden through the glass patio doors. Soothing his wife, his arms around her, Graham gave thanks for Pippa. They were blessed in each other, and in their children. There were an open family, no secrets kept, everything told, discussed and solved when a solution was required. He marvelled at her naïvety, her continued belief in the goodness of the human race despite so much evidence to the contrary, including this malicious message just received. Notwithstanding his outward equanimity, however, he was troubled. Was it some anonymous troll, as Pippa'd said?

Or someone known to them?

Whatever it might be, he'd take it down to the police station this afternoon. He doubted they could do much. Whoever'd done this had probably worn gloves, and posted it at a distance from where they lived.

Pippa's thoughts concerning the perpetrator mirrored those of her husband. She loved him dearly, always had, always would, and she never wanted to be without him. The letter had rattled her, however. Somebody, motivated by malice, had tried to unsettle them through the disclosure of information they believed unknown to both husband and wife. They'd got that wrong, so no harm done, and that was what Pippa needed Graham to keep on believing. She must never let him know, even by the smallest sign, that she was still worried; because what if they'd got that other information, the secret she'd carried for all these years, that thing which Graham must never know.

What if they knew of it? And what if they were saving it for a later date?

9: JENNIFER

She pushed her way through the kitchen door, talking into the phone squeezed between one cheek and a shoulder, simultaneously manoeuvring the two carrier bags held in one hand and balancing a cake box in the other. Kicking the door shut behind her, whilst warding off the loud and affectionate greetings of Duke and Prince, she managed to deposit the box and bags on the table, careful not to squash the one with the others, then concluded her conversation while turning around to pick up and sort through the envelopes which lay on the doormat.

'Six o'clock then. Absolutely. See you there. Bye for now.'

She swiped the screen to end the call, kicked off her outdoor shoes and clicked on the kettle. The cake box she deposited in the fridge, then opened the back door to let the dogs into the garden before dispersing the contents of the carrier bags in the pantry and spooning coffee into a mug to be dissolved in the water poured from the now-boiled kettle. She sank onto one of the oak chairs, leaned on the matching table and took a long pull from her mug.

She relaxed against the chair back, eyes momentarily closed as she savoured the flavour of her favourite beverage. Grateful for the rest, she enjoyed the peace of time alone, unencumbered by those others who peopled her life and their never-ending needs.

She sighed. It wasn't easy, being her, although if she told

anybody in the small village community within which she occupied a prominent position they'd look at her in astonishment and then laugh, no doubt. Mrs Perfect, ideal wife to Doctor Perfect, a surgeon and consultant who worked long hours at the hospital in the nearby county town, but was never too busy to attend to any neighbour who might be taken ill outside the local surgery's hours. His easy bedside manner extended to everyone, and he took as full a part in community activities as his busy schedule would allow, most notably in sports. Whatever he was unable to fulfil in the village his wife had covered; the PTA, various other committees including both wives' and mothers' societies, the book club, the choir, organisation of the summer fête and the Christmas market as well as other fund-raisers to "Save the Steeple" of St Peter and St Paul.

Whatever occurred, both Matthew and Jennifer were involved somehow, and to the wife fell the lion's share. They were well-liked, and well-respected, yet there was a price to be paid for the regard in which they were held, and with increasing frequency Jennifer felt she paid the larger part of the bill. Take today, starting with the school run. Despite the fact that her own Bella was into her teens now and capable of walking to school, parents needed to be watchful, even in this village. Dubbed "one of the prettiest in England," with its local-stone buildings and "tweeness," it bought in tourists all year round, as well as others, less desirable. A complaining Bella had to be dropped off therefore, along with ten-year-old Toby, before Jennifer moved on to her next duty. Today it'd been a meeting—with coffee, thank God—to discuss the fun-run being organised for next weekend. Then the aerobics class, of which she was a stalwart, the wife of a doctor having a duty to lead by example in the cause of fitness and health.

She'd had a little time to herself afterwards, to pick up some necessities from the small supermarket, not forgetting to collect and deliver an order that'd been phoned in by Alicia Thorn, at present housebound with a broken ankle sustained through a trip over an uneven paving stone; in the nearby town rather than in the village, thank goodness, or Jennifer would doubtless have had to get involved in forcing the local council to fix the pavement. Alicia was having a good day, the painkillers doing their job, so she'd been baking, in slow time, and had pressed part of the results of her morning's work on Jennifer. Hence the eclairs reposing in the fridge, towards which the doctor's wife now looked with longing.

That was another difficulty, a part of keeping up appearances in every sense. Jennifer was of a slender, willowy build; she'd been likened to the Princess of Wales, née Kate Middleton, yet nobody understood how hard she had to work to maintain her figure. Life was a constant diet, low fat, high fibre, sweets and cakes a definite no-no, although she was expected to play her part in the regular bake-sales held to fund-raise for the various local causes in need of finance. Her baking, all her cooking, in fact, was held by the community as second to none, yet nobody appreciated the torture involved in baking all these cakes without eating them. And now here was Alicia, pressing those bloody eclairs on her as a thanks for everything Jennifer was doing for her in her hour of need, etcetera, etcetera, and refusing to take no for an answer.

She looked once more in the direction of the fridge, and sought desperately to distract herself. Some demon had it in for her today, however, as her gaze fell on the wine rack in the corner, kept for guests at the dinner parties which she and Matt held most weekends. Jennifer never drank on those evenings, needing a clear head to hold it all together and serve each course at the appropriate time, unlike some households to which they'd been invited, with food overcooked due to the hostess indulging too freely in both wine and conversation and leaving the dinner to manage itself. Not in this household. Jennifer'd have a drink when the guests had departed, when Matt had gone to bed, after an offer of help which she'd refuse, on the grounds that he'd had a long week and needed his sleep. She'd pour herself a large glass of wine and sit savouring it in an armchair, before leaving everything as it was and going to bed herself. If Matt ever noticed in the morning that nothing had been cleared away from the night before he kept quiet about it, although it was possible that he didn't, always being up and gone early to the gym, grabbing breakfast at the coffee shop there to give Jennifer more time to cope with getting the children up and organised.

Now she averted her eyes from the wine, refusing its blatant invitation. She fancied a drink more often than she cared to admit, but she needed to watch her intake. It was one of several reasons why having Matthew's mother to live with them after the end of her disastrous relationship with that awful man Jeremy hadn't worked out. Penny thought they didn't know, despite the fact that she was clearly unsteady on her feet on more than one occasion when she came in for meals; that and the fact that Toby had one day asked at breakfast, in all innocence and a loud voice, why Grandma was "speaking squiggly." Jennifer had fudged her answer, because she couldn't explain to her young son that his grandmother kept alcohol in her room and was knocking it back at all hours. Penny was also prone, when under the influence, to lurch into a drunken diatribe on how badly life, and those people who ought to know better, had treated her. She always ended up in tears and had to be guided back to her room, with tender yet firm hands, to be put to bed and left to sleep it off. She'd been a bad example for the children. She'd had to go.

Jennifer felt weary. It took it out of her, all this caring for others, and she wasn't getting any younger. It'd seemed like a good idea at the time, not having children straight off, especially for somebody who suffered from iatrophobia; Greek for fear of doctors, Matt had informed her, when she'd told him, and they'd both appreciated the irony of that, for a doctor's wife. It hadn't changed the fact that she'd had to suffer the nightmare of childbirth, even if alleviated by home births and an epidural for both. That had happened after a number of years, when Matt was established and earning a good salary, but it meant she was that much older as they grew up and became more, rather than less, demanding. The strain was beginning to tell and Jennifer was finding it all a bit much, maintaining the illusion. She was well into her forties now, her birthday only a couple of months ago, yet all those around her took it for granted that she'd continue to help them, as she'd always done. But what did she get out of it?

She remembered when she'd met Matt, and how they'd clicked right away. She'd recognised in him a steady man, serious about his intended profession, upright, respectable, made to be a pillar of whichever community was lucky enough to claim him. Good looking too, in a dark and well-built way. He worked-out regularly at the gym, ate healthily, didn't smoke and drank only in moderation; he aimed to be an example to the patients he was to treat.

What had he seen in her, when he'd first encountered her at her place of work? He'd told her later, when they were together. A young woman, albeit a few years older than he, organised and tidy in both body and habits, slender yet shapely, neatly-dressed. Diligent in her work too, as he'd observed while stealing glances at her, and he'd fancied that she too was watching him, with the occasional upward flick of her eyes in his direction from under her long lashes. At some point he'd had to leave, but he'd returned at the same time the next day, and the third day too. That had been a Friday, and Matt couldn't be there on the Saturday. It was now or never, he'd decided, so took the plunge and waited for her to leave, departing himself at the same time and managing to collide with her, accidentally-on-purpose, to initiate a personal conversation.

They'd never looked back. Jennifer had seemed the perfect wife for a doctor, active in the community and attaching credit to her professional husband, and it had gone on like that for many years. They were both admired and looked-up to in the village—but Jennifer was becoming tired, of being the wife, the mother, the perfect example of domestic goddess held up before the community. If only they knew what had gone before—

She felt resentful. She wanted something for herself alone, something she could enjoy, here and now. Not wine, she had to drive later. She arose and approached the fridge.

*****

The eclairs were divine, every morsel of chocolate, cream and pastry. Every last one.

All of a sudden, Jennifer felt ill. She ran for the bathroom.

10: FRANK

He awoke to the slow realisation that he wasn't in his usual narrow bed, in his windowless and darkened cell, as the dawn breaking outside made abundantly clear. From what he could tell the room around him was glass-walled on three sides, rather like being in a goldfish bowl—although he'd bet it could be darkened at the touch of a switch. Or it was like those mirrored windows in police stations, where people outside could observe the interview being conducted inside, without themselves being seen by those within—although here it was those inside who could see out.

'Are you sure you'll be okay? Only I'm going out with Joanne, and we're due to meet at ten.'

She was ready to go, Frank could see, dressed in one of the outfits she favoured for her regular shopping trips.

'Go, go, I'll be fine.'

He shooed her towards the door.

'I've left out your cereal, bread for toast, and there's—'

'Don't worry, my dear, I survived well enough before I met you.'

Until he'd had his accident, he didn't say, but the knowledge of it was there between them.

'And will you—'

'Of course I will. Stop worrying and go have a good time.'

'See you later then.'

He kissed her on the cheek and waited at the door, waving

her off as she backed down the drive and pointed the car towards the town centre, all set for a morning at the shops. She hadn't asked him to accompany her. She'd learned early on in their marriage that, in common with most other men, including her previous husbands, hanging around while she tried on clothes, or shoes, or hats or whatever didn't interest him in the slightest. He ought to be grateful that she was so understanding about it, he supposed, and he was. But—

He returned to the kitchen, poured himself another mug of coffee and sat at the island, thinking. Madge was usually up and on the go early, but Frank liked to take things more slowly, given that he didn't always feel too good first thing in the morning. He'd have a couple of coffees, eat breakfast, smoke his first pipe of the day. He favoured an aromatic tobacco, which Madge was okay with as a smoker herself. He was glad she'd gone, because he wanted to be alone to rethink the party. *She'd* been there, arousing confused feelings about her on his part, and he gave his thoughts over to her and the changes he'd experienced in life since he'd left the Forces all those years ago.

This wouldn't do. There was no way to change the past, and brooding over it wouldn't help. He had plans for today, although there was no rush. Madge wouldn't hurry, she was meeting a female friend for lunch as well as shopping, and they'd have oodles to talk about. She wouldn't be back until mid-to-late afternoon, and he'd do what he needed to long before that.

He put his mug and bowl in the dishwasher—he hadn't bothered with more than cornflakes—collected his coat and keys, locked the house and took his own car in the opposite direction to that taken by Madge. He made a quick trip to the golf club, to collect a cardigan his wife had managed to leave behind yesterday. She hadn't missed it until she got home, and phoning to enquire had learned that somebody had found it lying in the corridor and handed it in to the office. Madge must have dropped it on the way out, and Frank had offered to collect it today, as he was going in that general direction and she wasn't.

'Morning, Frank. How's things?'

'All good, thanks, Cary. Yourself?'

'Same here.'

And with a nod to each other they went their separate ways. Frank wondered idly, as on previous occasions, what the other man's real name was. Somebody had once pointed out, in the bar, that he bore a distinct resemblance to Cary Grant, and from then on he'd been called Cary by one and all. Frank didn't know him well, just a passing acquaintance, so it wasn't really an issue, just a source of slight amusement.

The reclaimed cardigan deposited in the boot, he got back on the road and before long was pulling-up outside the residential block situated alongside the river. At one time the most desirable in town, these once-smart flats had seen better days when Frank had purchased his over fifteen years ago. He'd hit pay dirt with the first-floor river-view one-bedroomed place he'd found and rented at first.

The town was a little further than desirable from friends and family, he knew. His sons and brothers had told him so often, whenever they'd made the trek to visit him, or vice-versa. Why don't you move, had been their frequent refrain, closer to us, so we can all see each other more? But he'd resisted them every time, and wondered why they didn't get it. The bottom line was that he couldn't afford to move back to the more expensive area within which they all resided. He'd arrived where he was because it'd been his final posting before he'd resigned his commission, at around the time Penny had announced that she was leaving him; not that she'd been with him that much, having announced her intention of staying in the house which Frank had bought in preparation for retirement, She'd had enough of moving around over the years, she'd informed him, the boys had been gone for some years and were now settled in their own lives, so it was time for Penny to do what she wanted for a change. So Frank had been working and living away, while she was seeing *that man* behind his back, eventually moving in with him before the divorce had even gone through. Due to his senior rank, Frank had been allowed to live out, rather than in the Mess, and had found this flat, for which the rent could be paid from the allowance made to him. When his time was up and he retired from the service, it had made sense to stay where he was. He knew the area, had joined the golf club and got to know people, including the neighbours in the residential block. He'd taken over the rental of the flat, and made it known to the owner that if he was ever of a mind to sell, then Frank would like first refusal; and within a year it'd happened.

Of course, the day after he'd completed the purchase, the bottom had fallen out of the housing market. So, all these years later, the property was worth little more than he'd paid for it; or would have paid, had he bought it outright. But no, he'd had to take out a mortgage, which he was still paying. A mortgage, in his sixties! There'd been no choice, however, Penny having cleaned him out in the divorce. Jeremy, being a legal bloke, had known exactly who in the profession was cut-throat enough to screw Frank for every penny, and that's what it'd turned out to be, just about. Every penny for Penny. She hadn't left him with a great deal, while she and that asshole were rolling in it. Not a lot to show for a lifetime of service. Frank had never been lucky with money.

He'd known Madge from the golf club, where she'd been a popular member, always with a coterie of men around her at the bar. She never had to pay for her gin and tonic, or light her own cigarettes in the elegant gold holder which was a fixture whatever she was wearing. She was attractive in a well-groomed way, hair and make-up always immaculate, smart and well-co-ordinated clothing, well-spoken and mannered. She'd been the wife of a medical man, before his unfortunate demise. She was a good catch, able to take her pick of any of her followers; so why Frank? He didn't know. He'd always had a way with the ladies, but at the time he was down on his luck, ageing and losing his physical charm through a reddened complexion and some weight-gain due to heavy drinking in the wake of the divorce. He'd been flattered that she'd chosen him, he supposed.

Then there'd been his accident. A drinks party, at the Mess, a farewell for somebody, and Frank, still hurting from the divorce and drinking too much, had been the life and soul. He remembered getting into a taxi, but nothing after that until he awoke in a hospital bed, feeling lousy. When he hadn't turned up for work the following morning his adjutant had come to the flat, as he couldn't raise Frank on the phone. He'd got one of the neighbours to let him into the block, when ringing the entrance door-bell had elicited no response, and found the front door to Frank's flat ajar. Inside, he and the concerned neighbour had found Frank out cold on the bedroom floor, in a pool of blood and with a nasty gash to his head. He'd remained unconscious in hospital for three days, and they'd thought he was a goner, summoning his sons to his bedside.

Frank was made of stronger stuff, and recovered. He'd also stopped drinking, well, cut back on it, at least, and started working harder to eat more healthily and get fit. Madge had been there for him, when the news of his mishap reached the club. He'd needed a bit of help, at first, and she was there as an angel of mercy to cook for him, organise his cleaning and laundry, shopping, whatever needed doing in a housekeeping sense as well as a personal one. She cossetted him, looked after him with a concern which was touching and seemed genuine. As he felt better for her care, and as it was well-known that she was in the market to accept a marriage proposal from whichever man appealed to her, Frank did the decent thing. Why wouldn't he? She'd made him feel loved at a time when he was at a low ebb in many ways.

They'd married, and she'd declined his suggestion of living in his flat, which to be fair was too small for more than one person anyway; and Frank had no issue with moving into her luxurious house backing onto the golf course. The problems had set in on the wedding night, after the quiet registry-office ceremony followed by a restrained reception at the golf club—where else?—attended by Matthew and Simon as joint best-men, with a host of club regulars. Frank hadn't attempted to anticipate the wedding-night with Madge. She was an old-fashioned woman, and a lady, she'd have everyone know, and Frank was a gentleman and wouldn't have dreamed of forcing the issue. It was only after he'd put the ring on her finger, therefore, and they'd been declared lawful man and wife that, in the Lake District hotel to which they'd gone for their honeymoon, he found his new wife to be cold in bed.

She was dutiful, of course, and was perfectly agreeable to carrying out her wifely duties, but these were of a perfunctory nature. There was no passion, no cries of love, no thrashing around, no suggestions of alternate and more satisfying positions. Such had been the case in Frank's first marriage, and he couldn't believe he'd found another not-interested-in-sex wife. In truth, however, what else had he expected? He was in his sixties, Madge too—although she only admitted to forty-five. They were no spring chickens, no teenagers discovering sex for the first time. But Frank felt something missing, even though he had no grounds to complain that Madge wasn't doing what she'd contracted to. She was, even if in a cool and passionless manner.

It wasn't enough.

What kind of a marriage was this, he thought now.

A mistaken one, that's what.

He stuck his cold pipe into his mouth as he negotiated the traffic, his forehead wrinkled. He still had the flat, rented out to a reliable tenant and providing Frank with an income over and above his military pension; he needed it, after Penny had cleared him out. Recently, however, and after much thought, he'd given notice the tenant, who'd found alternative accommodation and moved out last week. On to stage two of the plan then; Frank was moving back in there himself. He'd tell Madge gently, and he dreaded the thought of what he had to do, but it just wasn't working. Look at this morning. He hadn't even given her a kiss before she left, and she hadn't asked. He'd be better on his own, and then he'd have no constant nagging feeling of guilt towards her.

*****

He unlocked the front door and walked down the hall to the lounge, standing in the doorway and surveying the room before him. Not too bad, considering some of the bad tenants he'd heard of. The curtains were the original drapes he'd bought, maybe in not too bad a condition he thought, checking them over, not too faded. Maybe an in-depth professional clean would render them still usable. He looked at the carpet beneath his feet. Threadbare in places, and dirty; it'd need to be replaced. There was a discount carpet warehouse out of town, Frank passed it most days on his way to the golf club. This wasn't a large flat; he ought to be able to pick up a good-quality offcut for a reasonable price.

It brought to mind his friend, Martin. They'd met not long after Frank had bought this place, when he'd encountered Martin struggling down the stairs with a tatty old rolled-up carpet. He'd pitched in and helped, and as they'd deposited the thing into the skip waiting outside they'd got talking. Martin owned one of the upstairs flat and rented it out, living with his wife not far away in another, larger, apartment. The tenants had left when their contract ran out, and the place had required a full renovation.

Which is what this one needs right now, Frank thought, returning to the current time and place. First take down the curtains, get them to a cleaner and see what could be done with them. Get rid of all the rubbish, the carpet, bits and pieces of old, tired furniture which he hadn't wanted and left for the tenants. A thorough clean, get in a team of experts to do that, fumigate the place if necessary. Change the kitchen and bathroom? The bath, basin and loo were in bad shape. He'd need a full refit in there, but maybe some of the kitchen could be salvaged. The oven and hob would have to go, and the fridge-freezer, but the cabinets could do with a thorough clean and have new doors fitted.

He'd have to see. A good paint job throughout, new carpet and some furniture would be needed. Frank still had some of his old stuff, in his den at Madge's place. It would be make-do-and-mend where possible, doing things himself where he could but replacing where he couldn't. He wasn't made of money, even with his pension and the rental income, which had now ceased. He had very little in savings. Penny had seen to that.

Determined to take his mind off the past, he unfolded the stepladder he'd brought from the car and began to take down the curtains.

11: THE PAST (1)

The English rose, everybody had always called her, the smooth skin, the strawberry-blonde hair, the rosebud lips and the sweet smile of innocence. She'd always been such a well-behaved child, obedient at home and at school, sweet-tempered and pretty; with a wild streak, however, not exactly rebellious but an occasional crazy need to take risks which even she couldn't understand. Challenged to climb a tree, or cross the stepping-stones over the river at the bottom of the meadow when there'd been heavy rain and it was dangerous, she'd always be there and do what was suggested; fortunately without ill consequences, or her parents finding out, which came to the same thing, really.

She'd been the pride of the pony club, the steadily-growing collection of rosettes in her bedroom a testament to this. Put on a pony at an early age, she'd been a keen and fast learner, excelling at every discipline. Dressage, show-jumping, she took the prizes at the various competitions more often than not. Her favourite was the cross-country, racing at break-neck speed along the stretches of the course between the fences, then encouraging her mount to negotiate these with the correct measure of care to get around without mishap and speed on their way to the next. She wore a hat, of course, it'd be too dangerous without, but in her mind she could feel her hair blowing free in the wind. This was her freedom, her passion, and she loved it above all else.

Until she met Jed, that was. Perhaps, given her reckless streak, it oughtn't to have been a surprise when she found another passion for this dark and handsome traveller, hired as a hand because the stables were short-staffed due to a flu bug that was going around. He'd been passing through on his itinerant way, and happened to enquire about the possibility of work, for the shorter or the longer term, relatively-speaking. He wasn't a stayer, wasn't looking for permanent employment, which suited the stable manager who was expecting the return of his permanent staff when the sickness had passed. Jed wasn't in any hurry to leave, and was happy to stay on for an indefinite period even when the regular staff returned, because it soon became clear that he knew a great deal about horses, as well as being willing to work for minimum wage as long as he was provided with three meals a day and a roof over his head for the duration of his tenure. The tack-room provided him with a sleeping place and basic shower facilities, while the manager's wife had four children and found it easy to prepare food for one more. Jed was content.

He also knew a great deal about women, and the mutual attraction-at-first-sight between him and this rosebud of a girl was soon being consummated in the straw as often as was possible. She, startled by her own unsuspected capacity for physical passion, was in the habit of staying late to care for her horse Clover, so her parents suspected nothing, until the fateful day when her mother picked up on a certain air about her daughter, as well as a noticeable gain in weight. Tests were done, a pregnancy confirmed, and then all hell broke loose; in the civilised manner of the British upper-classes, that is.

"How could you? A roll in the hay with an itinerant stable-hand, like something out of a cheap airport novel."

Her mother's lips had curled into a sneer, as she looked down her long, aristocratic nose at her daughter, before she swung into action. Harsh words were exchanged between her and the stable owners, who were equally keen to hush up the matter; members of staff seducing underage female clients was bad for business. The gypsy was sent packing and the daughter dispatched to a private nursing home on the coast, the recurrence of problems caused by a heart murmur she'd had since birth was the reason cited to her school and to family friends. If any of them had any suspicions about a baby born to her during her extended trip to the seaside, they kept these to themselves. The child was promptly taken away for adoption, with the young mother not even allowed to hold it.

Pale, silent and grieving, she was collected by her mother, who laid out the future which awaited her unruly daughter. A finishing school, private, all-girls, with no male members of staff whatsoever. A year there, and she could be launched onto society, there hopefully to find a husband who'd know nothing of her—aberration—from the behaviour expected.

It was made clear that what'd transpired would never again be referred to, not in words, at any rate. Nevertheless, she often felt her mother's eyes upon her, and returning the look she'd find the scorn and disapproval etched in them, as well as all over the older woman's face. In her turn, she was thrown into confusion by the entire episode. Her sudden passion for Jed, the discovery of her pregnancy, the dispatch of her lover to who-knew-where without so much as a goodbye, her own removal to the nursing home, where they were kind, in a brisk and matter-of-fact fashion, but hardly the sort of people to whom she could open her full and troubled heart.

It was too much, all at once, and she hadn't coped well. She'd centred her thoughts on the life growing within her, once ensconced in the pleasant room with a view of the gardens and the sea in the distance, as a way of avoiding having to cope with everything else. When the baby had been taken away—and she wasn't even told whether it was a boy or a girl—her heart had broken. She'd loved the unknown child, had loved its father, and look what love had brought her to.

She was glad when the time came to take up residence in the new school. Under the veneer of a return to normality she'd learned to cope by locking up her feelings and behaving as her mother wished. Chores were done without her being bidden, and her performance of not speaking until she was spoken to would have done credit to any child who'd been obliged to live by that creed in the nineteenth and early-twentieth centuries. She couldn't even confide in her brother, who was away studying and unaware of the events which had overtaken his younger sister back at home.

Once at the school she realised she could relax; only she'd forgotten how. The teachers were kind—for that level of fees they could afford to be—and the other girls pleasant. She interacted with them as expected, being friendly and obliging in all things. A model student, it was agreed by all, but on the inside it was a very different story. Although outwardly agreeable, she never got close to any other girls. Getting close did you no good, she'd learned, in a very hard lesson which was to stay with her for the foreseeable future.

Even after she was married.

12: MADGE

She placed the carrier bags in the rear of her Audi Q8 Sportback e-tron, then took her place in the driver's seat and checked her make-up and hair in the mirror. All good. She fastened her seat belt and reached for the ignition, but then thought better of it and leaned back against the seat, taking a moment before setting off home.

She felt better for the shopping trip she'd just enjoyed with Joan, as well as the late lunch with which they'd topped-off their meeting. These outings always steadied her, the enjoyment of finding new clothes to add to her already-extensive wardrobe, plus something cooked for her by somebody else, washed down with one long white-wine spritz. No more than that when she was driving, besides which any more would be hell for the figure she tried hard to keep in check. That issue notwithstanding, her mood had improved at this latest manifestation of being settled back into her normal, everyday life.

There was a reason shopping was called retail therapy, she supposed, and therapy of a sort was what she'd needed after their recent trip away, back into Frank's past with his old friends and work colleagues. Not having been a part of that meant she never felt quite at ease in the company of such people. She tried to fit in, of course, but at some point in the conversation somebody would mention something that reminded somebody else of an occurrence of their shared past, and then they'd be back there, in the land of "do you remember that time when?" with Madge an outsider, not privy to the historic happenings which bound them all together.

It made her feel insecure, and she didn't like that. Madge knew who she was, an upstanding and respectable senior member of a community within which she'd lived for many years. A woman ageing but still well-turned-out, admired and respected at the golf club, a place of which she'd been a member for almost as long as she'd lived in the area. Many of the other members remembered her from when she'd been much younger, much more desirable, and they still desired her now, twice-widowed as she'd been. She'd had her choice of them, and she'd chosen Frank, a relative newcomer with an irresistible charm about him which had drawn her to him like a moth to the proverbial flame. Not that she'd let him know that, of course. She'd played it cool, let him do the running, alongside the many others who'd been keen to make her their wife. Nothing less would do; she had her standards and anybody who didn't share them had no chance. She'd always known she'd marry Frank, however, and in time he'd come to think the same. Why wouldn't he, when she'd been there for him through his bad times, sympathetic, looking after his needs, letting him know through actions rather than words that she was the one to make his life easy and stress-free?

She didn't need a man, of course. Madge wasn't one of those women who needed a male partner to validate her existence. She'd been left very comfortable when David, her second husband, had died suddenly. She had their house, detached, four-bedroomed, backing onto protected woodland—which could never therefore be built upon—in a desirable top-of-the-market area, as well as a small fortune invested in sensible funds which didn't give top-rates of interest but were far less likely to lose the savings she'd entrusted to them.

Yes, Madge was doing very nicely indeed without a man who'd treat her like a child, or an idiot, or expect her to dance to his tune; to control her, in fact, and Madge didn't like anybody trying to control her. She preferred to be in charge of her own sphere, which was why she'd insisted on Frank moving into her house when they'd married. It hadn't been difficult, his tiny flat being only just about big enough for one occupant, never mind two, and he hadn't had a problem with moving to her place. He'd been sensible, not expecting her to share her assets fifty-fifty with him or vice-versa, and they'd had watertight legal documents drawn up before the wedding to make sure of that. He'd kept ownership of his property, into which he'd put a tenant whose rent gave him some income over and above his military and civilian pensions. He contributed to the household costs of Madge's place, because she wouldn't want him to feel like a kept man, and honour was satisfied on both sides.

The truth was that she liked having someone around, for various reasons. The house really was too large for one occupant alone, and it could be a bit creepy at night, especially with the woods to the rear; but the presence of another person removed that sensation. On the positive side, the size of the place meant they never had to feel they were living in one another's pockets. Madge could be on the phone to a friend in the lounge, while Frank did whatever he liked in his den. Then there was her social life. Madge enjoyed eating out, or going to the theatre for plays, opera, music, ballet, whatever was in town. There was no fun in doing these things alone. Sitting in a restaurant trying to avoid the looks, surreptitious or otherwise, of others who she knew were pitying her for being alone. It wasn't to be borne, and Madge scorned to read a book while she ate, the better to ignore them. She didn't need their pity, but she did like somebody with whom to share the pleasures of the table, or the theatre, or whatever else. She wasn't the only one who felt that way, and she'd be damned if she stayed home just to avoid such awkward situations.

It was fine her being at the golf club alone, of course, she being a long-standing and well-known member; but since David had passed-away she'd run into the issue of men plying her with too much gin and tonic and then offering to take her home. No way. Once they'd parked outside her house there'd be the expectation of coming in for coffee, and she wasn't about to go there. Not that Madge would've had any problem with refusing their requests, graciously, with a plea of tiredness, but they'd have known they were being fobbed-off, and she preferred to avoid any bad feelings when back at the club.

No, all around it was better to have a partner, a pleasant and charming man who'd escort her where she wanted to go when she wanted to go, and who wouldn't necessarily be in her face the entire time. Frank had fit the bill to perfection, she'd decided as she'd got to know him. Hurt by the demise of his first marriage, he was more than willing to enjoy a close relationship as a couple without being joined at the hip. To live and let live, in fact, and for most of the time it worked very well indeed; but the party, and other occasions when she was obliged to journey with him into his past, tended to unsettle Madge.

She knew as well as anybody, better than many, that people forming new relationships in their middle years, as she and Frank had done, were always going to have baggage. Ex-wives, husbands, partners, children and even grandchildren issued from those relationships, and there was the inevitable requirement to be in contact with the ex in matters concerning those offspring. There were also friends and acquaintances, although Frank had a multiplicity of these latter, which given his previous mobile lifestyle in the Forces was to be expected, she supposed. She hadn't anticipated quite so many, however.

She needed to be reasonable. It wasn't as if there were reunions every week like the one they'd just attended. Those were few and far between, but they made her uneasy nevertheless. Maybe it was because she had nobody from her past around, a few friends like Joan, the golf-club crowd, but nobody close, no family, to balance things up, to make Frank feel as awkward as Madge could never help feeling when around his people. She had an uneasy sense that, if it had been the situation, he'd have managed it with ease. Given his inexplicable charisma, he'd have had them eating out of his hand, impressed that Madge had landed such an attractive man. Whereas with his bunch, well, they were all very pleasant, but she couldn't shift the feeling that they tolerated her, for his sake. For his sons she'd always be second-best to their mother, although how he could ever have been attracted to the hopeless drunk who'd shown up last week she'd never work out. And then there'd been others, old friends sizing up Madge, trying to work out what on earth Frank saw in her.

She took out her phone, found a number and made a booking, then leaned forward and started the engine. Dinner out tonight, at a fine-dining establishment where she was a well-known and respected client. That should restore the status quo, not to mention her somewhat bruised ego.

No more gatherings like that one if she could help it.

13: MATT

'Here you go.'

Matt removed the blue safety helmet and passed it to Malcolm, the site manager, who in turn gave it to a passing apprentice sporting identical headgear. It seemed strange to Matt that they still had to be worn, given that the building was over ninety percent ready by now, but rules were there for a reason and he'd be the last person to break them.

He considered the irony of that when he'd shaken hands with Malcolm and the latter had departed to organise whatever came next in his schedule, leaving his client to contemplate from a safe distance the almost-completed structure which had grown up out of the ground over the last half-year.

His clinic. At last. The project of which he'd dreamed for so long, and finally been able to bring to fruition, making the dream into the reality which stood proud before him now. An impressive structure, steel and glass plus brick, in a roughly forty-sixty ratio; it wouldn't do to frighten off prospective clients by making it too "out there" and modern. Matt was no expert on the subject, and had been more than willing to take the advice of the architect who'd come well-recommended.

"People who need frail bones fixed, or replaced, don't want anything too *avant-garde* in the structure where their surgery's to be performed. If the building's too experimental that might suggest your skills are too. Solid and dependable fits the bill far better, with some modern touches to show that you're up to date, rather than stuck in the past, but tempered by a good firm foundation."

That sounded logical to Matt, and between them they'd come up with a design that worked; and with Malcolm and the team in place it'd taken physical form. The Highview Clinic. A good name, given the hilltop location, with a breathtaking view spread out before and below it. The glass-and-steel sections of the build had been kept in the main to this side, meaning clients could drink in that stunning vista, whether in their own rooms, sitting on the terrace in good weather, or undergoing physiotherapy in the treatment rooms on the ground floor. The administrative office and surgeries had been placed on the other side, where the car park sat at the end of the long and winding drive which led through beautifully-landscaped grounds from the impressive wrought-iron gates which fed out onto the main road.

It wasn't to be all about money either. The pressure on the NHS was well-known to everybody, and Matt was there to help ease it. So many were in need of surgery, and yet the waiting lists were so long. The elderly, in pain and in need of hip replacements, were those for whom Matt felt the most, and it was these who he intended to assist. Why shouldn't he help out some the most desperate NHS cases, treat them at his clinic and have the cost covered by those who could afford private operations? Not only that, but he'd come to a financial arrangement with Jeff, his plastic-surgeon friend, who thought the location would be ideal for some of his patients who'd want to recuperate away from the prying eyes of their acquaintances until their visible scars had healed.

Matt felt his chest swell with pride, unable to tear his eyes away from the embodiment of his vision, the pinnacle of his success, the end-product for which he'd been aiming for all this time. It'd taken hard work and dedication, but at last all the effort had paid off. Success.

Why had he felt the need for this token of accomplishment, and such satisfaction now that he'd pulled it off? It wasn't as if he was a working-class-boy-made-good, who'd dragged himself up by his bootstraps from a council estate somewhere to riches beyond his wildest imaginings, and lord of all he surveyed on an extensive private estate. Far from it. His roots were firmly planted towards the upper echelons of the middle classes, through the Army officer and his lady who were his parents. Up near the top of the tree, although it had to be admitted that his father had started out much further down. Frank had made no secret of the fact that his own father had been an ordinary bloke, although a brave and resourceful one. A wartime commission had lifted him to the officer class, and at length his son had occupied a place several rungs further up the ladder. He'd worked hard to consolidate his social status, and wasn't about to hand everything to his own sons on a silver platter.

Matt and Simon had been expected to make their own way in the world, earn their place in society without too much by way of handouts from the parental purse. Frank hadn't been delighted by his younger son's wayward choice of lifestyle, although he'd accepted it, as long as the boy didn't come to his parent with his hand out; and Simon had obliged. Matt had been a different matter, deciding from an early age to be a doctor and single-minded in his determination to achieve his aim; although he wasn't proud of the circumstances which had driven him to be the best possible.

Enough of that. Matt didn't want to go there right now, or ever, if he could avoid it. He'd done what he'd done, he was where he was, and he had the right to be self-satisfied about his achievements. A model wife, two wonderful children, a high standing in his community. A senior consultant in the NHS, a surgeon, in demand to give talks at universities and elsewhere; and now with his own private clinic, which he'd also use for philanthropic purposes in helping those of lesser means.

Matt was riding high.

14: MATT/ABBY

By Thursday he'd got through the busiest part of his week and had time to breathe, to take time out and think. There'd been surgery, some unexpected complications to cope with, although all had worked out well in the end. A meeting with his accountant, a few tax issues to iron out, a check on the health of his bank balance and a meeting with the architect to discuss and finalise the finishing of the clinic. A parents' evening at the school required his attendance, for although Jen would be there for the kids it behoved Matt as a good, responsible father to attend too, and he wouldn't have dreamt of doing otherwise.

With no surgery scheduled until next week he decided to take a well-earned afternoon off and fit in a trip to the gym. It was a thrown-together, last-minute thing, with one of the professional club trainers to put him through his paces; but they were used to that with Doctor Matt, and happy to oblige. He felt better for the exercise, and as the weather was good they finished up with a jog in the fresh air, followed by a drink—two, in fact, fruit and protein smoothies—in the café attached to the gym.

Sitting contented with the healthy concoction, Matt remembered Abby and his request to have a drink with her. That wasn't quite true. She'd been in his head ever since the party, and her number was in his phone. Pete the trainer having departed for a session booked with another client,

Matt was alone, the few other people in the café sitting too far away to hear his conversation. He took his courage in both hands and made the call.

It took several rings, yet he still wasn't ready when she answered.

'How about that drink?'

Nerves rendered him unprepared, and he plunged in with no introduction. Her reply was not encouraging, which might have been expected in the circumstances.

'Who is this?'

He could sense the frown between her eyebrows, the unconcealed forehead lines converging in perplexity above the perfectly-upturned nose.

'It's me, Matthew. We met at the reunion.'

He felt the eyebrows relax, the lines moving sideways and becoming less pronounced.

'Oh, right, yes. How are you?'

They exchanged polite questions for several minutes, after which Matt returned to his subject.

'We were going to have a drink, if you still want to.'

There was a pause.

'Yes, if you like.'

Even less encouraging.

There was silence, so he asked where she lived, and when she told him he knew they were meant to be. It wasn't too far from a university town, that of his old medical school, where he'd been asked to give a lecture a fortnight from now, the first in a term-long series, which meant he could see Abby each time too. He decided not to tell her this, not yet, didn't want to jinx himself by jumping the gun; and then he did, to his own great surprise.

'That's great. You're not far from my old university, and I'm giving a lecture there in a couple of weeks. I was going to stop over, so maybe I could meet you somewhere in the area. That's if you're free, of course.'

She was silent for a moment, and when she spoke she sounded doubtful.

'What date?'

He told her.

'I'll have to get my diary. Hang on.'

He did, and she seemed to take an age, taking her phone with her and treating Matt to the sounds of her digging through a drawer and rustling papers before coming back to him.

'Yes, that works. I've nothing else on.'

'Fine. It's a date then. Where can we meet?'

'There's Broxton, that's not far, and there are plenty of places. Or you could come here, there's a pub in the village. You could get a room in either place, if you're intending to stop over.'

Her words sounded flustered, coming out in a rush before she tailed off into an awkward silence in which Matt joined. He couldn't help but ask himself what exactly his intentions were, yet it wasn't something he wanted to confront just yet. He dismissed the thought, squaring away his conscience with the knowledge that she was an old friend of his parents, an acquaintance anyway, a figure like Aunt Pippa, and old enough to be his mother, which made it okay to visit her. He broke the hiatus.

'I'll come to the village, meet you at the pub. I won't book anything, in case I have to get back for surgery the following day.'

That wasn't what he'd said at first, but she let it go.

'Oh, of course. Yes.'

She confirmed the name of the pub, they fixed on a time, and it was a date.

'See you then.'

'Yes.'

Her tone suggested she was relieved, which was strange, but then Matt felt rather odd himself. A brief goodbye from both sides and the line went dead.

Matt wasn't feeling the euphoria he'd been expecting. He stood looking at his phone, wondering what he'd just done.

*****

After she'd disconnected from the call Abby sat, forehead creased, looking at the screen, at Matt's avatar. She hadn't expected him to call, having taken his suggestion at the party of meeting for a drink as one of those things people do in the moment and then forget all about when they get home; but it was clear now that this wasn't the case. Her frown deepened. She was angry with herself, because in her surprise at him actually calling she'd become flustered, lost her cool and fluffed the whole thing; and what was that "thing," exactly? Did he just see her as an old friend of his parents, whose company he enjoyed and with whom he'd like to be friends? Come on, Abby, you know that's not the case, you've lived in this world long enough to know how things work. It was obvious he was interested; she could remember the look in his eyes. Doubtless if he'd video-called she'd have seen it again; but she hadn't been expecting him to follow up on his offer.

It was all very flattering, considering she had to be at least fifteen years his senior; but would she really have an affair with Frank and Penny's son, if that's where he was heading? He was a grown man now, of course, and rather good looking in his way, but he'd been only twelve years old when she'd first met him, for Chrissake, and Abby wasn't sure she could get that image out of her head. It'd still feel like cradle-snatching, and that wasn't her thing at all. She considered ringing him back and cancelling, but she wasn't quite ready to do that. Give it a few days, let him down gently? Or wait until the day before? It wasn't like he was making a special trip just to see her. He'd been clear that he had a professional engagement nearby and was tagging her onto that, rather than vice-versa.

She started as the phone in her hand buzzed with an incoming email. Nothing important, just some company trying to sell her something. She deleted it, and simultaneously put the conversation with Matt out of her mind. It was in her diary; she could deal with it closer to the time.

Now she needed wine. It was almost five o'clock, the phone display told her, so it was legit. She made her way to the kitchen, and the fridge, then moved to the sofa to sit, observing the view from the window and brooding about Matt, the past and the present.

For some reason she remembered the time Penny'd broken her back. She was lucky to be alive, Abby'd been told; an inch closer to her spine and then, well, death, if she was lucky, or paralysed from the neck down if not. Frank had been so good, doing everything needed to get his wife back to health, and it was lucky the boys were away at school at the time. Friends had rallied round to help, but nobody could have done more than Frank; and despite that, some years later, Penny'd left him, run off with some other man who'd deserted her in his turn.

People were strange, Abby thought. Maybe it'd been the near-death-or-worse experience that'd caused Penny to realise the fragility of life, how we're all living on the edge, even if it doesn't feel like it. Just one mishap and goodbye Charlie, as Gerry used to say, and he'd gone far too soon himself, from natural causes. So Penny'd taken her chances and it'd paid off for a while, before she'd been the loser in her turn. What goes around comes around, apparently. That was the big question we all had to decide, Abby supposed. Do we owe it to ourselves to live the best lives we can, hurting those close to us in the process of doing so? Or do we compromise our own happiness out of a sense of duty to those we're already with?

She was darned if she knew any more than that she was a widow now, needing to please nobody but herself. On that thought she drained her glass, then headed back to the fridge for a refill.

15: JENNIFER

She burst in through the kitchen door as usual, overburdened as always, with bags and books and a head full of what needed to be done, as ever. The children followed, fresh from school, which they were eager to put behind them in favour of more agreeable pursuits.

'Okay, shoes off. I mean it, Bella. Then up and get changed, quick now. Tea, and then homework. No moaning, you know it has to be done, Toby.'

'Will you—'

'Yes, I'll help you with your decimals, Toby, it's easy once you get the hang of it. Upstairs now, quickly, both of you, and leave the phones here. We've a lot to get done, I don't need you sidetracked, sitting in your bedroom Facetiming or whatever. Go on, now.'

Complaining, but doing as they were told nevertheless, her rebellious offspring disappeared in the direction of the stairs, their voices raised in a quarrel getting fainter as they moved further away.

Jen got to work, kicking off her own shoes in the general direction of the door, letting the dogs out and the cat in, unloading a bag of books beside the laptop before putting groceries in both pantry and fridge, simultaneously taking out items needed for the children's tea as well as that of the pets. When they returned ten minutes later she already had baked beans on to heat, bread standing ready in the toaster. Toby preferred spaghetti hoops, but beans at least were rich in fibre, the toast wholemeal, rendering this once-derided staple a healthy meal, not to mention fast to make.

When they'd eaten—their mother making do with tea and a couple of biscuits, because she'd be eating with Matt later—they helped clear the plates and bowls into the dishwasher, then at Jen's behest got their homework from their school bags. Bella didn't have any problems to need help with, apart from not wanting to do the work but to get to the TV and all the games and social media notifications on her phone, but Toby was having problems moving from fractions to decimals. That worried Jen. He'd been doing this for a while, and ought to be proficient at it by now. Was this new teacher any good, she wondered. How were the other children in his class coping? She resolved to find out, quietly, from other parents. This was a good school, the fees were high enough, anyway, and the teaching staff ought to be the best to be had. Jen knew how hard you had to work to get anywhere in life, she didn't need either of her children at a disadvantage from the outset. Now she did her best to fix the issue, checking the book Toby was using and raising her eyebrows as she did so.

'Okay, the book doesn't explain it very well, so let's stop using it.'

She closed it with a snap, throwing it aside with a sharp gesture.

The large square divided into one hundred small ones wasn't great for a child to relate to.

'Right. Let's think of it in terms of money. Where's my purse? Here we go.'

She deposited a pile of change on the table, grateful that actual cash still hadn't gone the way of the dinosaurs.

'Right, find a pound coin. That's great; now find the penny. D'you know how many pennies in a pound?'

'A hundred.'

She moved with him through the coins, twenty-pence pieces, fifty-pence, how many in the pound and how that worked as both decimals and percentages. Jennifer was relieved that he had no problems, when money was the medium for teaching it. He used it all the time, he could relate to it. There was nothing wrong with her son, she realised with relief, just a badly-thought-out book.

'I wish I'd had you when I was learning that.'

This unexpected accolade from her teenage daughter, who'd been listening in unnoticed, brought a sense of pride in her own achievement to Jennifer. Homework concluded not long afterwards, she released them to the freedom of their bedrooms, there to indulge in their favoured leisure pursuits. She checked the clock on her phone. About an hour before she had to get started on dinner, the better to have it ready to go when Matt arrived home. Time enough to sort out her own form of homework.

Switching on her laptop, she made another coffee while it booted-up, putting biscuits on a plate for good measure, then signing-in to several social media platforms to check notifications and make postings on the various community groups of which she was admin. She sipped and munched as she worked, getting everything tidied and organised, then realised as she put out a hand that there were no more biscuits. She'd eaten the entire packet.

She hadn't meant to do that, and felt guilty at once. She'd have to cut back on something else if she didn't want to get enormous. Frowning, she opened another tab to check her email. She didn't use it that often nowadays, WhatsApp and Messenger having become her apps of choice, but some members of her groups were old-fashioned, or not tech-savvy enough, to use those, so Jennifer kept the email going for their convenience.

Now she worked her way through the list of messages, answering, saving or deleting: and then she came to one with an unfamiliar address, which she treated with caution. It hadn't gone into the spam bin, but it ought to have. She had to open it, in order to mark it as spam and delete, but as long as she didn't click on any links contained in it she should be fine.

The message opened, the contents making themselves known to Jennifer.

Her mouth dropped open and she sat, unable to do anything but stare at what sat before her.

Her coffee and biscuits curdled in her stomach. She had just enough time to close the lid and send the machine into hibernation, in case the children should pass this way, before she bolted once more for the downstairs loo.

*****

'Mummy, I can't find my charging cable, and I need to do my phone. Bella says I can't use hers, but I have to. Come and make her let me.'

Jennifer didn't hear him, slumped in her seat and gazing unseeing at the screen as she was.

'Mummy. Mummy?'

His tone aggrieved, Toby tugged at her sleeve, impatient. She came out of her trance all at once, shutting the lid with a bang and turning so fast he was taken off guard, almost falling as he jumped backwards to avoid her bumping into him.

'What is it?'

He wasn't used to abruptness and sharp words from his mother. He lowered his voice.

'I need Bella's charging cable. I can't find mine.'

'Well, go and tell her I said to let you use it. For heaven's sake, Toby, can't you sort these things out without bothering me? I'm busy.'

He didn't argue but retreated upstairs, throwing a wide-eyed glance over his shoulder as he went. He was back within minutes, his sister by his side.

'He can't use it because—Mummy, are you alright?'

'Of course I am. Why wouldn't I be?'

She was trying to pull it together, but not doing a good job. Bella peered at her.

'It's just—Toby said—you've gone really pale, Mummy. Are you ill?'

Jennifer made a superhuman effort, dragging out every resource to form some semblance of a smile and going forth to put an arm around each child.

'I'm okay, I'm just tired, and hungry. I've been doing too much. I'll be fine when I've had a sit down. Toby, go and use Daddy's cable, on the desk in the study.'

He went, grateful to be out of the room. Bella still looked concerned.

'Can I make you a cup of tea, Mummy? You can sit down while I do it.'

Jennifer was touched, and made a supreme effort.

'We'll do it together. Come on.'

While her daughter found the mug and added sugar and a teabag, Jennifer filled the kettle. Her thoughts were far away, however.

Who? Why?

16: MATT/ABBY

He lay awake in the early hours, looking at the sleeping woman by his side and going back over the evening they'd spent, which had culminated here, together, in a situation for which he'd been hoping but hadn't dared expect.

She was an experienced and accomplished lover, and he didn't have a problem with that; after all, he hadn't been expecting a virgin. Yet she brought a freshness and a passionate enjoyment to the act of love which enchanted him while he hated himself for comparing her to Jen, the latter losing in the assessment. It was clear that Abby'd never had children, and he couldn't deny the extreme intensification of his pleasure through the physical manifestation of this. Jen, unfortunately, had lost much through the birth of two children, including suffering some internal damage giving birth to Toby. Nothing huge, but she claimed it made matters a little painful when making love, and although Matt had a connection with a cosmetic surgeon who was top in his field and would have been glad to correct the damage, Jen wasn't keen to undergo it.

"It's unnecessary. Most women have babies and don't have surgery afterwards. It's a natural part of life and we oughtn't to worry too much about it."

"But we have the means to do something about it, and if it would make our love-life as it was before the babies, why not?"

Nevertheless she was adamant, and despite being married to a highly-successful surgeon she was frightened of undergoing a general anaesthetic "unless it was absolutely necessary." There were horror stories of things going wrong, with people dying on the operating table. "Not mine," he'd told her, "I've never lost a patient yet." She wasn't having it, however, and that was that. Subject closed, and their love-life got worse instead of better. She didn't deny him, Matt had to give her credit for that, in all justice, but it'd steadily become as though she were conferring a favour on him, enduring an act she'd rather not because it was an unnecessary nuisance as she wanted no more children.

Who could blame him then, for looking elsewhere? Although were Jen to find out about his affair—because that was what it was, not just a one-nighter, of that he was determined—she'd be surprised to say the least if she found out who it was with. Horrified, more like, and Matt blenched at the thought. Men, in Jen's opinion, had affairs with younger women, when their wives were getting middle-aged and over-familiar to their husbands; which was why she, and her peer-group of women in the village, took steps to keep in shape, to keep their skin soft and as unblemished as possible. If this meant expensive pills and potions, well, their husbands could afford it. Cosmetic surgery, however, was a step too far in Jen's opinion, and in a way he admired her for her refusal to risk an anaesthetic for what she saw as trivial reasons.

Given her obvious non-use of make-up and other artifices such as cosmetic surgery and the like, Matt guessed that Abby felt the same way. However, she had a naturalness about her that Jen couldn't aspire to, not to mention a never-been-used birth canal that won the prize as her best feature over face and figure, although he had to admit that those were in pretty good condition, especially given her age. Whatever, Jen would never understand his having an affair with Abby; and

Matt aimed to see that she never found out.

Abby stirred beside him, rolled over towards him and opened her eyes. He put his thoughts aside; he had over twenty-four hours more of playing truant, and he intended to make every moment count.

*****

He'd set off to give his first lecture at the university while the rest of the family was still getting up. Early-morning starts were a regular occurrence for him, although needing to be out the door by seven in the morning was rare. He could've left it later, granted, because he wasn't due to start until eleven, and the drive was somewhere between two-and-a-half to three hours, depending on the traffic. He'd need time to find the department, meet people, talk a few things through beforehand, of course, so he aimed to be there by half-ten at the latest. As organised as his wife in his own way, Matt believed in always leaving time for possible unforeseen mishaps.

The one that'd caught him out today was even more unpredictable than anything he could have thought of. Nine-fifteen, and the phone rang. Matt answered, his eyes never leaving the road.

'Doctor Fairfield? It's Professor Grove. I'm afraid we've run into a bit of a problem.'

'Can I call you back in a few minutes? I'll pull over somewhere.'

'Right you are.'

Matt ended the call. Despite the hands-free facility, he never liked speaking whilst driving. Divided attention meant accidents, in his experience, and he'd attended in his professional capacity to too many of the resulting injuries; those which hadn't proved fatal at the scene, that was. He spied a small petrol station up ahead, the sort found on the type of minor B-roads along which he was driving at present. He could make the call, and get a top-up too; not fair to use their forecourt without giving something back. He parked to one side, out of the way of the pumps, then hit the call-back.

'I'm terribly sorry for the late notice, but I'm afraid the lecture's off; not just yours but quite a few, all over campus. One of the unions called a wildcat strike first thing, and now half the teaching staff's out on strike, striding around outside the Senate, the library, all the office buildings, brandishing placards. Sorry to mess you around, but it literally just sprang up this morning. Most lectures are cancelled, and Dr Thompson, the member of staff under whose auspices you'd have been speaking, is on strike, and we couldn't possibly let you loose on the students without his introduction. He's deeply embarrassed, about it all, but couldn't go against the union—'

The Professor continued in the same vein, appalled, so sorry, embarrassed, etcetera, etcetera, etcetera, until Matt managed to cut him off as politely as possible.

'Please don't apologise any more. It's hardly your fault. You've been put on the spot and in a difficult position.'

Thus far Mr Nice Guy. Now the not-quite-so-accommodating part.

'You'll understand, however, that I'll need assurances that this situation won't re-occur in the future, should we have a future. I've a busy schedule, many patients depending on me, and colleagues who've rearranged their own timetables to take on my cases. You'll appreciate that I can't ask that of them too often. The NHS has enough problems already, without me adding to their backlog.'

He listened as the man at the other end spoke.

'Yes, that's understood. I'll be remunerated as arranged. My main concern, however, is not having this situation repeat itself. Should it do so, I'd have to reconsider my involvement.'

He listened again to the reassurances of the other, then finished the call and sat, uncertain, his fingers tapping on the steering wheel. He was much closer to his destination than to home, and was reluctant to waste the day by just turning around and going back. There'd be no time to accomplish anything at the hospital, and Matt never enjoyed days when he didn't achieve something. Besides, he'd arranged to see Abby this evening, and he didn't want to bail on her. Not that she wouldn't understand, she was most understanding, he was sure; but he wanted to see her.

He checked the time. Nine-thirty. Far too soon to call her; for all he knew she might still be in bed. He was about an hour out from the university, and from there it was another half-an-hour or so to the village where she lived. He could be there by eleven, all being well; and then what? Call her, explain what'd happened, throw himself on her mercy and suggest lunch instead of evening drinks. He decided to go for it.

*****

In the event it was just past eleven-fifteen when he entered the village square, at which point the satnav promptly fell out and refused to take him to the exact location he required. No problem really, as he couldn't just show up on the doorstep. He needed to phone first, and all of a sudden he felt nervous. What if she had other plans for the day? In that event Matt supposed he'd have to buy a sandwich in the store he could see on the other side of the square, drive back to the woodland picnic area he'd seen on his way in and eat a lonely lunch before reclining his seat to catch up on some sleep; five-thirty in the morning was too early even for him. He gathered his courage and called her.

'Hello?'

She answered on the third ring, sounding cheerful and sunny.

'It's Matt. Are you busy?'

'Oh, no, it's fine. I wasn't expecting to hear from you until later. Is everything okay?'

'Well, the thing is, I've been cancelled. They just rang me—'

He managed the white lie without faltering.

'There's been a wildcat strike called, so my lecture's been cancelled.'

'Bummer. They could have let you know sooner. All that way for nothing.'

'It is a pain, but I'm stuck with it. I'll have to find a way to kill time before this evening, that's if you're not going to cancel me too?'

'No, of course not.'

She was silent and he waited, hoping that maybe she'd save him the embarrassment of asking.

'Okay, well, how about we meet earlier? I'm not doing anything much else today, nothing that won't wait.'

Thank you, God.

'I was going to suggest I buy you lunch, but I thought you might have other plans.'

'No, no, lunch will be fine. Where are you now?'

'In your village, car park opposite the Black Swan. The satnav's refusing to show me your place.'

'It always does that. I'm a black hole as far as the satellite's concerned. At least I'll be undetected if an alien invasion occurs. Why don't you come here, and we can walk back in to eat. Lunch at the Mucky Duck okay with you? I can phone and book now.'

'Is that another pub somewhere?'

'No, silly, local lingo for the Swan. Anyway, drive up the road with the pub on your left, then there's the church further up on the right. Turn right down Church Lane—'

She issued instructions which he committed to memory; there weren't many of them. Her house, when he reached it, was at the end of a narrow lane, a good thirty yards at least past the previous house, with no other buildings that he could see beyond it. She was standing at the end of the drive, gesturing him to park there.

'You're well out of the way here. Are you the last house?'

He got out of the car, hesitant. How to greet her?

She solved the problem by taking his hand and giving a brief squeeze.

'Yes, it's just fields up there. It's kind of isolated, but I like that. Suits my situation.'

He gave the house an all-encompassing glance as she led him inside; modern, yet built in an old-farmhouse style. From habit he removed his shoes once inside, earning her approval.

'A man after my own heart. I hate when people bring whatever dirt they've walked through into the house. A bit OCD, I'm afraid.'

'Nothing wrong with that, same here. Goes with being a doctor, I suppose, in my case, at least.'

'Being a bit of a screw-up and grumpy old lady, in mine. Birds of a feather, for whatever reason.

'Anyway, you've been on the road a while. D'you want to freshen up?'

She indicated the downstairs cloakroom.

'Please.'

He headed towards it.

'Tea, or coffee? And how soon d'you want to eat? I can give them a call now.'

'Coffee'd be great. What d'you think? Half twelve, one? I had breakfast about six-fifteen, so sooner, maybe?'

'Half twelve it is.'

*****

Abby relaxed and sipped her wine, listening to Matt as he enthused over the plans he had for his new clinic. If the day had started on a somewhat awkward note, much earlier than intended, it hadn't stayed that way for long. She'd been considering the evening they'd planned ever since he'd phoned, humming and hawing about it all, more than once picking up her phone with the intention of phoning and calling it off, then abandoning the idea and deciding to go with the flow. They'd made the arrangement, might as well see where it led. She wasn't usually so indecisive, but there was something about Matt which intrigued her; and then he'd called early and caught her on the hop.

They'd had coffee in the kitchen, making light conversation concerning the house, how long had she lived here, had she done much to the place since she'd moved in, that sort of thing, and then it'd been time for lunch. They'd walked in, the weather being fine and it only taking about fifteen minutes to get into the village. Then there'd been deciding where to sit, risking the garden as there was no rain forecast, finding a table sheltered by a sun umbrella. What to drink, what to eat, starters or straight into mains. Nothing too heavy on account of the weather, but nothing too light either. Abby wasn't keen on salads, except as a side garnish, so in the end she opted for lasagne as a happy medium while Matt settled for a steak with salad and a side of fries.

Then there was the wait for food, and the first time they'd

had nothing to do to cover the wondering on both sides about what the hell they were getting into. The usual sort of conversation-openers ensued, nice pub, do you come here often and so forth. The old cocktail party gambits of Forces life came back with ease—well, they'd both been doing them for long enough—and it didn't take much time before the ice was well and truly broken and Matt was holding forth about his life. He seemed quite happy to talk, about his work at the hospital, his clinic project and how it'd enable him to help more patients to be seen sooner, his new weekly lecture at the university.

He didn't mention his family, his two children and his wife, and she wondered if he would. It depended on his intentions, and the "whether or not" issue should give her some indication of those; but if he started on the "my wife doesn't understand me" act she'd be out of there, metaphorically-speaking. He could come back to her place, have coffee and rest a while on the sofa, and then she'd send him on his way. He was drinking alcohol-free, keeping his options open perhaps, so it wouldn't be difficult. And then? He'd either get the message that there was nothing there for him more than a drink and a chat now and then, or he'd be persistent; in which case she'd block him, and then he couldn't fail to understand.

She had to admit he didn't seem the type to come out with the usual tired clichés, but what exactly was "the type?" There just wasn't any knowing with people.

'More wine? Or pud?'

'I'm not big on sweets. Well, I like them but they don't like me, if they contain cream, which they mostly do. But you go ahead, don't let me put you off. I can have another glass, to keep you company.'

'I'm good with that. I need the bathroom; I'll catch a waiter on the way.'

She emptied her glass as she watched him move across the room, his walk a carbon-copy of his father's, she noted, and fell to pondering the likeness in other ways. He was only a few years younger than Frank had been the last time she'd seen him, the recent party excepted. A certain squareness around the jawline, plus the dark hair. The eyes were dark too, and she wondered where they came from. Not from Penny, who shared blue eyes with Frank, and Abby couldn't see much of her in Matt. The younger son had been more like her, she recollected, her fair hair at least.

Matt returned, to consume the cheesecake of the day—white chocolate and raspberry, with extra cream—while Abby drank another glass of Pinot and teased him about such an unhealthy choice for a man of medicine.

'I'm escaping from the doctor for the day. Besides, I had a healthy main, and I'm not drinking alcohol.'

'All the more for me.'

He insisted on paying, in cash, she noted. All the better for wifey to not find any suspicious items on the credit card statement?

Whatever. They idled back up the road, she putting on the kettle so they could lounge around, side-by-side on the sofa, drinking coffee and watching TV. It was on a radio channel when she turned on, with 'Nessum Dorma' playing, to which Matt had hummed along without thinking.

'You like opera?'

He had to confess he didn't. He only knew this aria from the 1990 World Cup, and didn't know anything other than the tune and the title; and as he didn't speak Italian he didn't understand the words. He didn't add that he'd been about fourteen at the time.

He was willing to learn, he added, if it pleased her. It did, it seemed, because she proceeded to take him to the opera there and then, in her lounge. She put on a DVD of *Turandot,* which had subtitles, thank goodness, and they could pause it when required, and therefore miss nothing.

Matt had enjoyed it, much to his surprise, although he wasn't sure about the ending. It didn't seem right that Calaf should end up with the cruel princess Turandot, while little Liú, who loved him selflessly, had been tortured and then killed herself in order not to betray him. Had there been perhaps some mistake by those who finished the opera after Puccini's untimely death? Could they have misinterpreted his wishes for the piece?

'Many people feel the same way as you, and I'm one of them. But no, the man who finished it—I forget his name—had the detailed notes left by Puccini, and it seems this was what he wanted.

'I suppose it's not that far removed from real life. People often end up with the wrong person.'

She was silent, immersed in her own thoughts, and Matt wondered if she was speaking about her own life; but he refrained from comment and she continued.

'The thing is, people want a happy ending, love, and all that goes with it. Turandot doesn't come across like that, but as cold, and hard. In actuality she's frightened of marriage and all that entails, being obedient to a man and being controlled by him; and then of course there's sex. She's terrified of that, because her ancestor the Princess Lou-Ling was taken prisoner and killed by an enemy prince, and it's not difficult to work out that he must have raped her too. It's frequently the fate of female prisoners in war; I must show you *The Trojan Women* sometime. It's been going on forever, and it's still going on today.'

So we're to have one more time at least, Matt noted. He nodded agreement and, taking that to indicate an interest, rather than just a polite pretence, Abby continued.

'Turandot's had a negative introduction to the idea of sex,

which is why she puts her suitors to an impossible test and then has them killed when they fail. Liú, on the other hand, is love embodied. She's a slave, and if a princess like Lou-Ling can be raped and murdered then nothing is off limits for a slave girl. Liú's probably suffered abuses we can only guess at, but she's survived, and with her ability to love intact, so of course we want her to get a better deal in life than she's had so far. But no, to those that have shall be given, so the Ice-Princess gets the man, who she doesn't deserve in my opinion, and the have-not slave ends up on the rubbish heap. The usual shit, sexual violence, women victims in the wars men create, and it's not going to stop any time soon.'

She sounded bitter, far more than a fictional story warranted. Matt didn't want to ask, not right now, so instead reached out and put his hand over hers. She didn't pull away.

'No need to go there, anyway. It's good to watch things together and discuss them. With most men it'd be turn up, have sex, leave with minimal conversation. But you and I are actually having a relationship.'

But not sex. Not yet. Maybe.

'I like to hear you talk, to hear the inner workings of your mind. I don't just want you for your body, I want your mind and personality as well.'

She looked around and met his eyes. He took her in his arms, and she relaxed into the comfort of his embrace, then kissed him full on the mouth.

'You're adorable. You make me feel good.'

'It's mutual.'

He returned her kiss, then stood, scooping her into his arms and carrying her upstairs. He had to be off early in the morning, and wanted to make the most of the time he had left.

Plus he didn't want to think about where this might be heading.

*****

This was the woman who slept beside him now, with whom he'd made love into the early hours, and who now, as if on cue, turned towards him and opened her eyes. He moved across to her, reaching out and stroking her hair, as if to make sure he wasn't still asleep and dreaming. She reached for him too, and matters looked to make a by-now-familiar turn; and then Matt's phone rang, the shrill tone destroying the lazy morning peace of the room. He picked up, spoke, listened, then sat bolt upright, his eyes open and staring as he spoke rapidly, leaping from the bed and looking around for his clothes.

He hung up, located his shirt, moving like a man possessed. Alarmed, she reached for her robe and went to him.

'What is it? What's wrong?'

'I have to go. As fast as possible.'

17: THE PAST (2)

I was well brought-up, by parents who were respectable members of the community and who taught me the difference between right and wrong. My father's work dominated all our lives, but that was the way back then; the patriarchal system with women as housewives and child-bearers, so I didn't feel deprived. My parents expected that I'd marry and have children as a matter of course, but they wanted me to have other options just in case. Hence my training for a secretarial career, and it was while I was studying that things changed.

It was Marcia, my flatmate, who started it. She'd been to a party somewhere and met this young man. They'd been attracted, and soon they were inseparable. I was happy for her, but it did get rather irritating coming home and finding them wrapped around each other on our sofa, or in the bedroom with the noises coming out telling me in no uncertain terms what they were up to. I had words with her about it, because it was my bedroom too. It was a small flat, only one bedroom with two single beds, so Pete, or whatever he was called, never stayed over; but I couldn't get into my own bedroom when I wanted to, and that wasn't acceptable.

Marcia started staying at his place, which was better, but it was clear she wanted to spend more time at ours. Whatever the reason, I'm sure she thought that if she could get me dating someone things would balance out and I'd spend time at the home of whoever I started seeing. I thought it presumptuous of her to imagine that I'd sleep with someone just like that, so when she suggested I go with her and Pete to a party I agreed, certain that nothing would come of it.

She was surprised when I capitulated so easily. "Really?" She couldn't believe I'd said yes as soon as she suggested it. I could see her preparing her "Go on, it'll be fun, you know you want to" speech, the one she'd had to use on me in the past and which was redundant now. It was quite fun, in fact, to see her surprise. But I'd agreed to go with her, so off we went.

Well, the god of chaos, or whatever, must have been listening, because that was the night I met Rod and really kicked over the traces. It was a different kind of party to those I'd been used to, bottles all over the kitchen table, some token snacks, crips and suchlike. The people were different too, long-haired hippy types, beads and kaftans and dancing barefoot to a very different type of music than the latest pop sounds you heard on the radio. There was a lot of smoking, and a strange smell which I deduced was marijuana because Marcia'd told me Pete had introduced her to it. I remembered that a part of his attraction for her, wherever she'd met him, was his absolute difference to any man she'd ever known before.

I was a bit unsure about the whole thing, standing uncertain on the sidelines, and then I noticed him looking at me from other side of the room. He was thin and wiry, long-haired and bearded like most of the other men, with a lop-sided grin which was not unpleasant to look at. It was his eyes which got me first. They were a light blue but glowing, with a directness of gaze which held me mesmerised. He maintained the hold as he crossed the room, and I think I was his from that moment.

"You look a bit lost, sweetheart. Shall I help you find your way around?"

He didn't wait for an answer but smiled, and if I hadn't fallen for him already that would've clinched it. He took my arm, gently, and led me to the kitchen where he managed to find a clean glass and some halfway-decent wine for me to drink out of it. Then we talked, about what I don't know, I can't remember, but I do know that the party and everybody in it ceased to exist as I sat and listened to him, speaking in my turn. It seemed the most natural thing in the world when he offered to take me home. I was certain I'd fallen for him but I wasn't going to ask him in or do anything intimate with a man I'd only just met, so I tried to avoid the issue.

"I have to wait for Marcia."

I didn't sound convincing, I knew, but I hoped it'd work.

He read my thoughts and laughed softly as he glanced across the room to where Marcia and Pete were wound around each other, as usual.

"I don't think she's likely to be going home just yet, do you? Where do you live? I'll take you in a cab, if it's far, or walk you, if it's close. But I promise I'll leave you at the door. Scout's honour."

He sounded amused, but not mocking, just humouring me as one might a young child. I felt the blush on my cheeks. I'm not usually embarrassed, I can give as good as I get, but I seemed tongue-tied with him. He smiled, to take the sting out of his words, and soon we were walking towards my flat, but in silence now.

"We're here."

I spoke at last, and with reluctance. I didn't want the evening to end, but I wasn't going to ask him up and dreaded him trying to force the issue, despite what he'd said. But he didn't.

"Well, then."

He was looking at me, holding me in that intense but gentle gaze, and I couldn't tear my eyes away.

"Can I see you again?"

I think I spoke, but I didn't hear my words. I nodded, almost imperceptibly, and he got it, because he leaned forward and kissed me, lightly, tenderly, not the tongue-in-the-mouth attack which I might have expected. I closed my eyes and savoured it. He pulled away, too soon for me, but I opened my eyes and those electric blues still held me.

"I'll call you."

Then he was gone, moving up the road away from me, back in the direction we'd come, and it was only when I was back upstairs and getting ready for bed that I realised he hadn't got my phone number.

He must have got it from Marcia, or Pete, because after I'd spent a restless night followed by an unsatisfactory day trying to learn shorthand, which I hated, I got home to find Marcia in a fever of excitement.

"Rod called."

She was jumping up and down with exhilaration.

"He was disappointed you weren't in yet but I told him you'd be here within the next hour. Hurry up and get changed, he's coming to collect you at seven, he's taking you out to dinner."

"What do you mean, taking me? He hasn't asked me and I haven't said yes."

I was insulted that anyone would just assume I'd agree.

"No, silly, I told him you'd go. I mean, why wouldn't you? Do go and change, he's gorgeous, a bit quiet and thoughtful but you probably like that. Go get ready!"

I was cross with Marcia for presuming I'd go out with this man. She must be anticipating me starting to have a steady date, being out a lot, meaning she could bring Pete home without any problems. I was just about to tell her what I thought when the phone beside me rang and I picked it up.

"I thought I'd better check we've got a date tonight. I wasn't sure you'd appreciate Marcia making up your mind for you."

He sounded amused and I laughed along with him.

"Absolutely. I was just going to tell her so."

"And when you've done that, will you come out for dinner with me?"

I waited a moment. It wouldn't do to appear too keen.

"Okay then. If you like."

"Miss Cool. Can I pick you up at seven?"

"That'll be fine."

"See you then."

The line went dead. He was gone, and I was glaring at Marcia even as I went to the bathroom to freshen up and sort out what I was going to wear. Nothing too smart, nothing too casual, I thought, as I rejected one outfit after another; and then the bell went and I heard the door opening, with the sound of voices in the lounge.

He was sitting talking to Marcia, but stood as I came into the room. I realised I'd hit the right note dress-wise with the floral kaftan-style dress and beads that complemented the clean, ironed denim jeans and waistcoat he wore with a cheesecloth shirt. He thought so too, from the look he gave me before he said goodbye to Marcia and led me downstairs.

"I thought we'd walk, if that's okay with you. There's an Italian I like about ten minutes away on foot, and I only live five minutes from here. But if you prefer we can drive somewhere else."

"No, I love Italian."

"That's great, because I like wine, and I don't drink and drive."

A sensible man, despite the hippy look, and I was happy to walk with him, although conversation was a bit stilted. He steered me down a side street a few minutes later, pausing beside a white van.

"Are you sure? We can still drive somewhere else."

The van wasn't quite what I'd been expecting, and I suppose it showed on my face.

"It's for my equipment."

I must've looked blank.

"I'm a photographer."

"Of course. And no, I'm fine to carry on walking."

I realised he must've told me what he did, at the party where we'd met, but I'd been so overwhelmed by his attention that I'd completely forgotten. I'd make sure to pay better attention tonight.

The restaurant was small and cosy, with quite a few people in already, which offset the nervousness I was feeling. I hadn't eaten out in a while and the food was good. With a drink inside me I thawed out, as we exchanged life stories over pasta and red wine.

Rod was from the north, which I thought I'd detected in his accent, although it was over-dubbed, as it were, with a southern inflection. From an ex-mining community somewhere, Cumbria, I think, and with very little available by way of work, he'd come south and made his way through a variety of jobs; bin-man, pizza delivery, hospital porter and so on. At last he'd worked in a shop selling photographic supplies and found he'd got a way with a camera. It hadn't been easy, but now he was set up in a studio and earning good money selling his pictures, and asking me to get involved in his work by way of letting him do a few portraits of me. I was happy about the idea, flattered even, especially as he told me he had a feeling I'd be a natural in front of a camera.

He asked me to share another bottle of red wine, which I was willing to do, and when we'd drunk that there was tiramisu, followed by coffee and brandy. He walked me back in the direction of our respective flats, kissing me long and lovingly on the corner of his street. He asked me to share his bed that night, and by then I was ready to do so, having fallen deeply in love and deciding to throw caution to the winds. I was enjoying life as I hadn't in so long, and didn't want it to end.

I was a virgin, and he was a gentle and considerate lover. By the morning I was even deeper in love than I'd been the previous evening, if that was possible. He made me coffee and toast while I showered and used his toothbrush in the rather-cramped bathroom of his small flat, then walked me home and kissed me at the door.

"Tonight?"

"Yes."

I didn't want him to go, and wanted to see him walk back the way he'd come; but he made me go indoors and didn't leave until I waved out of the window, so I was able to watch him from there. It was still early, and as I might have expected Marcia was curled up with Pete in our bedroom, as I found when I crept in and extracted some clean clothes from the wardrobe. I did a fast change in the living room; doubtless Marcia would want a blow-by-blow account of my night, and I wasn't ready to share even the details of the meal, never mind what'd happened to me at Rod's flat. I let myself out as quietly as I'd come in, going to a café not far from the secretarial school where I was a student and indulging in a large breakfast. Despite the toast I'd had earlier I was ravenous, and blushed internally when I remembered how I'd worked up my appetite.

*****

So began my relationship with Rod, the craziest part of my life before or since. I didn't move in with him, not straight off, anyway, although he did ask me soon after we got together. I got into the habit of spending my evenings at his flat, where he'd bring friends and associates, other guys in the business and their model girlfriends. We'd talk and drink, do a bit of puff; because I was using drugs by now, purely for recreational reasons, of course. I'd been hesitant at first, but I allowed myself to be convinced that it wasn't as bad as society made it out to be.

"Look at us," Rod *told me when he'd first suggested I might like to try a bit of grass, when we were with his friends and someone lit up a joint. "No one here's an addict. It's cool and so relaxing. Would I lie to you?"*

Of course he wouldn't. He *was so considerate of me, gentle, caring, in love with me, as I was with him; he'd told me so, and he'd never hurt the girl he loved. So I dragged on the spliff and coughed, of course, not being a smoker, and they all laughed, but not in a bad way, telling me how it'd been the same for them at first.*

One thing led to another, and soon I was having the occasional snort as well, and then there were the pills. It felt so good to let down the drawbridge, figuratively-speaking, and lose the last of my inhibitions, which had been well on the way to the door marked 'Exit' from the night I'd met Rod. *We didn't just experiment with drugs but with sex as well, and our love life got better, wilder, as I wondered at what a green girl I'd been on that first night.*

One evening we came home from meeting friends in a bar, the worse for drink and feeling very much in the mood for love. We'd hardly got the front door closed behind us before we were tearing at each other. We couldn't even wait to take our clothes off before Rod *had scooped me up onto the dresser against one wall of the living room and pushed my skirt up over my thighs as I fiddled with the zip on his flies. What followed was fast and frenzied and, when we were barely finished he reached out for a camera which was lying nearby.*

"Don't move. Stay just as you are."

I didn't have much time to think about it, as he moved away from me. His *now-flaccid organ was still hanging out of his trousers, making me laugh wildly as I thought about what he'd just done to me with it.*

"That's great, darling. Now, just move your left arm up, that's right."

Still very much under the influence of the drink and drugs we'd had earlier I obeyed him, smiling, amused by it all because pretty much anything would have made me laugh, given the high state I was in.

"Now, get up off the surface. Slowly does it, good. Now, reach around and unzip your skirt, not too fast, good girl. Let it drop to the floor, then lift your right arm, now the blouse, buttons, from the bottom up, slow now."

He had me remove my clothing item by item, except for the stockings and garter belt which I always wore when with him; without panties, I might add. It gave us both a thrill, to be sitting in a bar or restaurant and know that beneath my skirt the important areas were naked and available. More than once we found a doorway in a back alley behind shops and indulged in speedy sex, me up against the wall, legs around the waist of a rampant Rod.

Now, when I was naked apart from those items, he had me stand while he assessed every inch of me, with the lights on. He turned me every which way and observed me like that through the lens of his camera, then took even more shots before leading me into the living area and having me recline on a couch, to take even more pics. All the while he continued with the instructions, talking to me, encouraging me, telling me how good this or that was.

"Yeah, darling, that's good, that's gorgeous, just move your left arm up a little, let your fingers trail down your left boob, good girl, drop your eyes, yeah, that's very suggestive."

I noticed his manhood responding, coming back to life, and began teasing him about that, even as he clicked away. It wasn't long before he dropped the camera and was on me again, carrying me to the sofa and this time playing with me, teasing me, withdrawing himself and taking his time before plunging back inside me, making me beg him to continue. He must have been a gymnast, because he reached over for his camera and proceeded to take snaps of me as he brought me to a climax. He did put it down to concentrate on his own, however, when I'd arrived and was helping him to follow.

When we were tangled together, exhausted, he extricated himself from my embrace, reaching to put back on his shirt and underpants, then took up the camera.

'Come on.'

He moved towards the kitchen, which being rarely if ever used for food preparation—we tended to eat out or get takeaways—he'd transformed into a darkroom, small but functioning. I went to the bedroom and found a robe, then followed and watched as he began the procedure of developing the shots he'd taken.

'These'll take a while. Best get some sleep.'

He left the process to take its course, following me to the bedroom where we were soon crashed out; and by the morning I'd forgotten about them, having my secretarial course to go to.

A couple of days later Rod called me into the darkroom, where he brandished the finished pictures with a triumphant air, one at a time.

"These are great, darling, just look at you. Even though they can't see the rest of your body, or me, anyone would know you're coming, and then some. You're a natural."

"For photos or sex?"

I was high on the bizarre situation and the positive feedback, not to mention the joint which I'd been puffing when he'd called me through.

"Both."

He put down the pictures and reached for me, carrying me out to the sitting room and depositing me on the sofa. It was mad, bad, and wonderful, all at the same time. I was loving the craziness of it, kicking over the traces in every way possible as I indulged in behaviour that would have shocked me to my respectable core not quite a year ago. I hadn't felt this good in a long time.

*****

It was one evening, when we were at the flat and eating pizza he'd had delivered, that Rod made a proposition.

"What do you say to a bit of glamour modelling, darling?"

I didn't say anything for a moment, because it'd come out of nowhere and I was surprised, shocked, and speechless.

"Yeah, I know, it's the last thing you were expecting. The thing is,—"

He paused, and I felt he knew I wasn't going to like what he was about to say.

"I showed some of those pics we took to a guy, a business contact, magazine editor, you know."

My face must have shown my dismay, because he backtracked.

"No, not the really personal ones, I wouldn't show him those, just the face and upper-body ones."

"You showed him pictures of my boobs? Those aren't personal?"

I was angry and upset, all at the same time.

"Believe me, darling, they aren't, not in this day and age when half the female population sunbathes topless. It's no big deal, honestly, but you're carrying around a serious asset in there."

He reached out, his hand sliding into my unbuttoned-to-the-chest blouse and cupping one breast. I flinched away, but not too far. My head wanted to withdraw, my body wanted to stay and continue where I knew this was heading.

"Tony, the magazine guy. He wants some new girls on the pages, new faces, new bodies. There's nothing wrong with the usual models, of course, but the readership—yeah, I know—likes a bit of novelty."

He left it there, studying my face with an intense gaze. I'd stopped laughing now, at the idea of a bunch of guys who eyed-up pictures of naked women being a "readership."

"It'd be something new, darling, get you out of that office. You'd be wasted as a secretary, sitting on your gorgeous arse typing all day and having some balding old suit ogling your legs for nothing when he calls you in to take shorthand. Guys would be paying to see you in the mags,

and it'd be good money too, and useful. Let's face it, your little habit isn't cheap."

He did have a point, several, in fact. I'd made no secret that I found my secretarial course boring. I'd gotten into it at my parents' behest, because I hadn't known any better, but the longer it went on the more I was sure it wasn't for me. Was that all they'd had in mind for me? A "steady" office job, something to bring in some money and keep me busy until I met Mr Right and settled down to do housework and raise children, as my mother'd done before me?

Maybe that was why my use of drink and drugs had increased. The thought that, when I'd done my quota of learning my way around a keyboard at 70 wpm, or the minutiae of Pitman shorthand, or how to write the perfect memo, there'd be a bottle of wine waiting for me with Rod and his crowd, not to mention a smoke, or a few pills; well, more than a few, to be honest. Increasingly that was what got me through the day.

I had to face it. I was ready to ditch the secretarial course and go where the winds of chance, and Rod, took me. He'd been funding me, and supplying me, and I could hardly expect him to go on doing that. It was time for me to start work, in some shape or form, so why not model for photographs? It didn't sound like particularly onerous work and—I tried not to think it, but it would creep in—it was entirely probable that I could do a bit of stuff to give me that added 'oomph' in front of the camera.

I decided to go for it.

*****

It wasn't difficult to drop out from the secretarial college, or to move out of the flat I shared with Marcia either. In truth, I'd hardly been there for ages now. I'd pretty much moved in with Rod, and Pete had moved in with Marcia. They sounded like a pretty committed item, given that he'd left his old room, brought all his stuff over and taken on my share of the rent.

My parents were a different story, but I managed to convince them, with a little help from Marcia. She could seem very sincere when she needed to, having a sort of "butter wouldn't melt" quality to call on. Her sworn testimony that Rod and I were in a serious relationship helped get around their initial qualms about me moving in with him without being married. Living together was a thing of the time, young people were doing it all over the place, and although I hadn't exactly taken Rod to meet my mum and dad, they were willing to take my word for his honourable intentions. He was the man I was going to marry and have children with, as far as they were concerned; job done. After that, it was a simple matter to keep in as little touch with them as was necessary to keep them on-side, although I didn't need their financial support as I'd be earning money and could pay my way in the second-floor apartment I now shared with Rod.

I wasn't the only model he worked with, in fact, I wasn't a model at all. I was just starting out, whereas the others were already established, or on their way. But everyone has to begin somewhere, and although I hadn't been looking for a career in modelling, it brought in good money and gave me time to think about my future. I was only too aware that I was wandering, aimless, and needed to take some hard decisions about starting life on my own.

Modelling was okay, in the event. Looking down the lens of a camera wasn't quite the height of job satisfaction, but it beat the hell out bashing away at a typewriter or taking dictation about some dreary dental products or car parts. I mused about nothing in particular while I posed, because there's not a lot else to do except listen and do what the photographer tells you to.

Rod started me off with glamour shots, swimsuits, lingerie, that sort of thing, and the magazines ate them up. Then he moved me on to upper-body almost-nude stuff, hands covering nipples, pouty lips; you get the idea. Full-body shots too, just a pair of panties or bikini bottoms, playfully pulled down at one side to almost but not quite reveal something more, while the bosoms were still partially-covered by my hands.

The glossy mags couldn't get enough, and both Rod and I had more work offered than we could cope with. Life was sweet; but then he decided I could do more. Little by little the instructions from the other side of the camera changed.

"Open your legs a little, love, not too much, just get them excited."

Then it was,

"Remember the shots I took of you on that first afternoon, darling? I told you then you're a natural, you look like you're coming even when you're just lying there thinking about it. The punters love it; they want to be there giving it to you."

I opened my mouth to speak, but he rushed on and wouldn't be stopped.

"I'd love to pose you with a guy, I know one who'd be good with you. You'd look great together and I know you'd get on. Why don't we give it a try?"

"Rod—"

"Hear me out, darling, please. You wouldn't be doing anything, just lying on the bed. You'll both keep your pants on, of course, but we'll show upper-body stuff that suggests you're doing it, or you've just done it, or you're just about to do it."

I looked at him, not speaking.

"Please, honey, just give it a try. You know we're making much more from the tits 'n arse stuff, and this'll take it to a whole new level. The rent on this place isn't cheap, and you know the landlord's probably going to raise it next month."

He was right, so I allowed myself to be persuaded. I felt I'd earned the right to enjoy myself for a change, and this was an easy way to make the money to support my new lifestyle. In reality I knew it wasn't a good way to be going, but I didn't think about it too much and just went with the flow. Being with Rod was good enough, we had a connection and the sex was great; and in my naïvety I just assumed that good sex was the same as love. As time went on I learned through bitter experience that this wasn't the case. My situation felt, bizarrely, like water going down a plughole. The more water there is the slower it goes, but then it speeds up as the water runs away. That didn't make sense at the time; all I knew was that I was losing my grip, and my life was spiralling out of control.

I ought to have known.

*****

I made the most of the scene at Rod's place. It was easy going, fun, living in the here-and-now, so I put aside the question of my future because, after all, I wasn't exactly over the hill yet. I was only in my twenties.

When Rod insisted that nothing else would be going on—"Guaranteed, love"—I reluctantly let him bring in the male model, Jon. He seemed fine, friendly and reassuring, so we did some stuff, on the bed and standing, up close and personal and suggestive, but with absolutely nothing else happening. I did some more, with a couple of other guys, and then things took a downward turn in every sense.

"Just you on your own, darling, bikini bottoms, handbra, face the wall, turn away now, slowly, that's it, just one hand over your boobs now, drop the other one, yeah. Face the camera and think about doing it, I mean really doing it. Pull the bottoms away a bit, find your bush, stroke yourself gently—"

"NO WAY. What the hell are you asking?"

So we stopped the session and he went into talk-around mode.

"You're gorgeous, darling, but you can't keep on making these cheesecake pics. People want more, and I know you've done the stuff with Jon and the other guys, but they like you, you alone. All the blokes out there want to be with you, doing it for you. These are still shots, they won't see any action. There's only you and me here, so just do it for me, huh? Like I know you can?"

He started stroking me gently as he spoke, touching me in all the right places. He knew well which buttons to push, and soon we were making out on the studio bed. After that I did what he wanted, before we went back to his place and got mellow. We had wine, and pizza sent in, and Rod had scored some gear from his regular dealer earlier in the day. Our friends came round bringing speed, so there was plenty of everything and I didn't feel so bad about the pictures. Some of the girls talked to me, to reassure me, at Rod's behest.

"It's no big deal, you'll see that when you've toughened up a bit. Not everyone can do what we do, we're the lucky ones. We're making good money, so are you now. We're on to a good thing, so why blow it?"

I was feeling good, with the wine and the stuff, so I thought they were right, and why should I be so picky? I stopped the thoughts of why, gulped some more wine, dragged on some more weed and decided not to rock the boat. I knew I was behaving badly, however, and spiralling towards trouble; which came, in the form of Rod, as I might have expected. The work with Jon became more explicit, more suggestive poses, less clothes, actual physical contact, intimate even. We stopped short of actually doing anything, just about, although those seeing the pictures of me, naked, on my knees and back to the camera before a similarly naked Jon, standing, facing the camera, would have thought otherwise. Or me on all fours, Jon kneeling behind me—

Why did I do it? Maybe because by now I was off my head on drugs for most of the time, aided by Rod. I can't explain why, it just happened, I suppose. I felt so good when I'd smoked a joint, dropped a pill, had a snort or even used the poppers that Rod used when we were making love. It got so that I took drugs as casually as I'd eat toast for breakfast, or shower in the morning, or put on warm clothes when it was cold. They were just another factor of everyday life; and a threat to that life, as I was to find out.

One evening, when we'd just got back from the studio, sex was even better than usual. Rod was careful to make sure I was enjoying myself, took his time, encouraged me, praised me even more than usual and collapsed on his back when he'd brought us both to a more-than-satisfactory conclusion.

"I've said since the start you were a natural, darling, and you never

fail to prove me right."

I murmured something to the effect of him being not so bad himself. He put his arm around me and held me, caressing me gently, and it happened all over again. Afterwards, as we lay there smoking hash, it came out.

"I can't help feeling you could do more."

"What did you have in mind?"

I wasn't worried at this point, partly because I was relaxed on gear and partly because I didn't really see what more I could do.

"Well, can you act, for example?"

I thought he was joking.

"You know I went straight from school onto a secretarial course, so no, I can't act. Why're you asking?"

He hesitated.

"I've got a contact who's making a film, and he thinks you might be right for it."

I looked at him, quizzical. Did he really mean some guy thought I'd be good in a film, even though I couldn't act if my life depended on it? I waited, while once more he hesitated.

"It's—explicit," he managed at last, but seemed reluctant to say any more. The silence hung heavy between us as I sobered up, fast. I wasn't going to say anything, as I couldn't believe the explanation which was slowly dawning on me. After what seemed an age, Rod found his tongue again, and I couldn't believe what I was hearing.

He wanted me to make a porn film, to do it with some other guy, on camera, with the resulting footage sold on video, to whoever'd pay to watch it.

"It's great money. You could do well in the business, make a name for yourself."

I found my own voice, although due to the shock I was feeling it came out in a whisper.

"I have a name, Rod, but I don't want it known as that of a porn actress."

I looked at him, but he couldn't meet my eyes.

"I thought you loved me. Is this all I mean to you? A woman who'd have sex with a stranger, with other strangers watching and recording it all on camera?"

He got defensive then, and aggressive with it.

"You've all but done it with Jon, many times. Don't tell me you weren't begging for it, every time, all that bullshit about making him stop before. Why wouldn't you go that bit further? What'll you care if someone's filming you? You'll be off your face on shit and snow anyway."

I felt my world falling apart around me. I couldn't believe he'd say such things. Rod, who I'd thought I loved and who loved me, suggesting I'd do those things.

I didn't say anything. I didn't know what to say. As if sensing that he'd pushed me too far, he rolled over and walked out of the room. I could hear him showering in the tiny bathroom before he returned, towelling himself off. I watched as he dressed, without a word, then put his wallet and keys into his pocket and turned to me, sitting up where he'd left me and covered with a sheet. I didn't want him to see me naked again, which was ridiculous, I know, but things had changed.

"I've got to go meet Brad. I arranged it earlier. There's a deal to be done there. It'll give you time to think about things and come up with the right answer. We need the money, you know that. Don't force me to make your mind up for you."

He left without saying more and I sat, stunned by the last words he'd thrown at me. What did he mean? Was he suggesting that he'd force me to do what he wanted? He'd never been violent with me, but he'd never had to be. I'd always done what he wanted, with minimum persuasion on occasions. Too off my head, as he'd just said.

Survival instinct kicked in, and I knew I had to get out of there.

Where would I go, I wondered as I took a fast shower. There was no danger of Rod returning anytime soon; his 'meetings' usually stretched to some heavy drinking with more than a little drug use which went on late into the night. Nevertheless, I wanted to go as soon as possible.

Marcia. She was my only hope, and at least she'd let me sofa-surf until I could make other arrangements. I was a bit worried about Pete being there too, given that it was through his crowd that I'd met Rod; but as we'd never socialised with them since I'd moved in with Rod I was sure they weren't that close. Whatever the case, I decided I'd have to risk it; there was nowhere else, after all.

Dressing fast, I found a big old holdall, one that I'd used to move in with Rod. I threw in every piece of clothing I could. I'd bought more since I'd been here, and I couldn't fit it all in, so I just took the newest and best, plus some old favourites. A few bits from the bathroom and I was done, apart from raiding the pile of cash kept in Rod's bedside drawer. I had no qualms about taking every note—and there was a considerable amount—because I'd earned most of it through my efforts in front of the camera. He had a bank account, but there were certain purchases which were best done with cold, hard cash.

Which reminded me. I flew to access the stash kept in a secret little nook behind one of the bathroom cabinets. What I found there ought to keep me going for a while, although I didn't know what I'd do when it ran out.

I hung out of the window which overlooked the street, just in case. No sign of Rod. Good. I left the building with caution, then walked fast, trying not to look over my shoulder too much, but I was in luck. It wasn't far to the place I'd once shared with Marcia, and being summer it was still light.

I might have sobered up fast, but there was still a good amount of stuff in my bloodstream and I was freaking out with fear. Arriving at the flat I hung on the bell, causing Marcia's head to appear from the window upstairs.

"What the—"

"Let me in quickly, please! He might be here any minute!"

By now I was frantic, irrationally afraid that a vengeful Rod would appear around the corner at any minute and drag me back to the plans he had for me. Marcia took one look, disappeared back inside and within a minute was opening the door, pulling me in and up the stairs.

I was safe, at least for the moment. But that wasn't the end of my troubles.

*****

I suppose I was lucky in that both Marcia and Pete were willing for me to stay with them until I could make other arrangements. I had enough money, though not a lot, to pay something towards the household costs, even though I was sleeping on the sofa; but I was in no position to make demands. I tried to do a bit of tidying-up while they were at work, in a spirit of appreciation, but most of the time I'd end up just sitting, trying to work out what to do; which more often than not required a smoke, or a snort, to take the edge off my anxiety.

I knew Rod would come looking for me, and I wasn't wrong. Pete flat-out lied in denying my presence at the flat, and short of demanding that he be allowed to search the place, for which he had no legal right, there wasn't anything Rod could do. I suspect he kept watch, given that he lived so close by, to try to catch me going out or coming in; but as I never went anywhere he would've been wasting his time.

I was a mess, a bundle of indecision, and a great deal of credit goes to Marcia and Pete for looking out for me. Even had I wanted to leave the safe haven I'd found I was terrified in case Rod was on the lookout for me. In any case, where would I go? I had more pride than to go back to my parents, to admit that the living-in relationship I'd chosen had failed and, worse, for them to see the drug-addled disaster their only child had become. I had more immediate things to think about too, as the stash I'd taken with me from Rod's place was rapidly running out, and I had no way to replenish it. If I'd been able to go out, which I wasn't, where could I get a deal? Not with Rod's suppliers, unless I wanted word to go out that I was on the scene, and be set up with my ex in wait the next time I went to score.

I was getting ill, with withdrawal symptoms which I tried to hide from Marcia and Pete. If I stayed under the covers on the couch, pretending to sleep, while they got up and went to work in the morning,

I could then shiver and shake my way through the day, eking out what little stuff I had left so that I could put on a 'normal' front when they were home in the evening.

I was on a downward spiral, and reached rock bottom when Marcia came home one evening to find me pale, sweating and confused, clutching my stomach against the cramps which hit me at regular intervals while at the same time throwing-up into the toilet. She couldn't get any sense out of me, panicked, and called an ambulance. I was admitted to hospital, where they gave me something, methadone, I think, to help stabilise me before trying to work out what'd be best for me.

Marcia and Pete had to point out that their flat wasn't the ideal location for my recovery, with only one bedroom which they needed for themselves; also that I wasn't family, and they couldn't support me financially either. I didn't hold it against them; they'd done enough, and the information helped me, in the event. I claimed to have nobody in the world, only a little lie as my parents were a no-no; and as they couldn't put me out onto the streets I was admitted into a residential detox unit.

I don't want to remember that terrible time. Suffice to say I survived, to be discharged eventually into one-room accommodation at a halfway house for people like me. I hated it, being on my own yet surrounded by others, hearing them through the walls, some of them raving from their own withdrawal. I didn't feel secure there, but it was the best on offer. I looked into the tarnished surface of the mirror hanging there, the cheap aluminium backing missing in places, and saw the new me. Pale and thin, my previous voluptuous curves now non-existent. I'd lost weight due to frequent bouts of colds, coughs, flu; you name it, I caught it. My immune system had been weakened by the drug-taking, and although I was told I'd improve over time, if I stayed off the stuff, I never did manage to gain back the good health I'd enjoyed before.

I'd been assisted to find work too, and started out as a secretarial temp. Even though I'd dropped out of my course I could still type and take shorthand to a competent level. As they were desperate for temps, the wages not being great, the agency was happy to put me through their own tests to gauge the speed of my skills; and those clients to whom they sent me didn't need to know about my lack of formal qualifications.

It wasn't a great time in my life, but it was better than what'd gone before, and I even quite liked getting out of my dismal room and mixing with 'normal' people out in the real world. I'd learned a bitter lesson, and it stuck. I buckled down and did the work offered, determined to live my life differently from now on. Where there'd been chaos there was now discipline, while I rode out the time until my health recovered and I could likewise improve my circumstances.

And I did, when I met Him. And I've never looked back.

Until today.

18: MATT

It'd taken all his willpower to drive with care, but at least it was still early when he'd left Abby and the traffic wasn't too heavy at that time. As his journey progressed, however, the rush hour had commenced and the volume of traffic increased in proportion, meaning he got slower when he wanted to get faster. Frustrated didn't cover it, but Matt just had to go with the flow, slow as treacle as that might be. He drove with the windows open at first, the fresh air helping to keep him sharp, but as it warmed up he closed them and activated the air conditioning at a low temperature to perform the same function. He'd had coffee before he left Abby's place, and about an hour-and-a-half into the drive he'd have killed for some more, but he wanted to get there as soon as possible. Good sense won out, however, along with the need for petrol, so he bought a large take-away cup at the services and sat in the car park drinking and resting. Then it was back to the road.

If he hadn't known he was almost there he'd have known from the smell, faint at first but getting stronger, which found its way in through the air vents. Thank goodness the site was in a secluded spot, he thought, otherwise there'd be half the road closed off for the emergency services. As it was he could see the smoke from some way off, then what was left of the building, now a smouldering ruin. There was still one fire engine present, plus a police car, and Matt could see Malcolm hurrying towards him as he parked—not too close—and walked across.

He put his hand to his head as he contemplated the wreckage of his dreams. Charred brick walls surrounded by steel posts and girders bent and twisted by the heat, the whole thing decorated in bizarre fashion by fragments of shattered glass, ash from burned roof trusses and the discoloured debris of ladders and other tools of the building trade. There was a strong smell of burning, with embers still glowing in places, some hissing from the water which had been liberally applied and lay in puddles in places, the whole surrounded by a surreal cloud of steam and smoke. Several firemen in their signature yellow-banded beige uniforms wandered around the perimeter.

'Don't get too close. It's not totally out yet, and not safe.'

Malcolm accompanied his words with the offer of a hard hat, which seemed ludicrous in the circumstances, but Matt put it on anyway.

'What the hell happened? Don't tell me it was a cigarette.'

He made as if to run a hand through his hair, but encountering the headgear he dropped it to his side and stood, stupid, unable to think straight or address himself to what he needed to do now.

'No way. I've built this company on strict principles. Anybody smokes on site they're out on their arse. I've heard too much of that on other sites. We've earned a reputation for meticulous care, that's why you hired us. I know my workforce, they've been with me a while and I'd stake my life the lads wouldn't light up on the job. They know better.'

'What then?'

The other man hesitated.

'Well, the police think there might be arson involved.'

'What?'

'Petrol. You can smell it.'

Matt could. Not strong, but there. He looked at his site manager.

'Not us. We've no reason to have the stuff on site. They're waiting for it to cool before they can get the forensics team in.'

Matt ran his hands across his face, thinking with longing of his bed at home. It was all too much.

A policeman appeared at his side, addressing himself to Malcolm.

'Excuse me, sir. Is this the owner? We could do with a word, if you would.'

'Yes, this is Doctor Fairfield. Let's go into the office. That's still standing, at least.'

'Please.'

Desperate to sit down before he fell down, Matt allowed himself to be led to the portacabin to do the necessary.

*****

Later, grateful to be on his way home, he pulled into a convenient layby, leaned backwards and shut his eyes for a few moments. So tempting to just stay there, sleep, forget everything. But no, there were things to be done, and if he didn't do them nobody would. First he called Abby, who'd have been worried since he'd left so abruptly. She expressed relief he'd got there okay, and that nobody had been injured, but was concerned at the suggestion of arson. "Don't worry about keeping in touch," she'd told him before he could broach the subject. "Just get home, get some rest and get it sorted out. I won't expect to hear from you; you've got far too much on your plate. It was good to see you, but that's that for the time being."

He appreciated her understanding, if regretful that he had to put whatever they had on hold until better times. Then he called Jennifer. She hadn't a clue, of course, believing that even now he'd be on his way home from giving a lecture and spending a night in a budget hotel. He could have waited until he got home, but he preferred to give her time to digest the news before he got there. This way she had half-an-hour to process things and be used to the idea when he walked through the door. Matt couldn't cope with any more horror than she'd express in a phone call before he arrived home.

In the event she was suitably supportive, putting aside her own worry over the situation; and unlike with Abby, Matt chose not to tell her about the suspicion of arson. That could come later. First he needed to get home, drink more coffee and rest before considering the way forward.

Thank goodness he had the rest of the day off.

*****

Abby let out a sigh as she swiped to end the call. She hadn't been able to help worrying after Matt had left, even though she knew he had a drive of several hours ahead of him and calling her wasn't high on his list of priorities. She understood, of course, but was relieved that he'd let her know he'd got back safely, and that nobody had been hurt in the fire. The clinic was destroyed, the fire had taken a fast hold, and now he had to sort out the insurance claim, get the mess cleaned up when the investigation into how it had started was complete, then consider how to move forward.

Arson. It didn't bear thinking about, so she put the idea from her and recollected how things had been before the blind panic of his sudden departure. At least she'd managed to insist he have a quick shower before he rushed off, making him coffee and toast before he'd left, kissing her and promising to call her later, before he'd left for the building site where his dreams and clinic project had burned down.

Even though it was a dreadful thing to have happened, maybe it was best that he'd gone earlier rather than later. Abby didn't want to get too used to having somebody around; that way lay discontent with her usual isolated state. Perhaps next time, when she was prepared for his coming, they could do things differently. A lazy morning with coffee and croissants in bed, a long walk across the countryside and a light lunch in the pub, before more bed rest and a lazy lounge on the sofa, with bubbly and smoked salmon sandwiches when they got peckish—

Come off it, Abby. You've been reading too many books. Last night was a bonus, a result, an unexpected treat, a swansong. This can't go anywhere, so just take what you've had and don't expect any more. That way you won't be disappointed if there's no more, and pleasantly surprised if there is.

She breathed out, feeling the tension leave her body with the exhaled breath, then moved to the kitchen and returned with a large glass of chilled white.

Time to relax and consider it all.

19: JENNIFER/MATT

She thought she was going crazy, and how she was holding it together she didn't know. She hung on, however, tenacious, determined yet frustrated at her inability to act, to do anything, to even know what she should do. No further contact had been made, no demands issued, but the emails kept coming in an arbitrary fashion which slowly drove her to the edge of insanity. Every other day for a week, then nothing for ten days, which led her to hope. Was it over? Had they finished with her, whoever was doing this, had they had enough of their sick fun at her expense and turned their vile attentions to another? No, because she'd open her email and her stomach would drop at what she saw, and it'd begin again.

A month of this, and her health had begun to suffer. Even had she wanted to tell Matt—and no way would she do so—he had far too much to contend with at present, the usual pressures of his work compounded by the burning-down of the clinic and the fall-out from that. She had to try doubly hard to hide it from him, but the sleepless nights were affecting her; feigning unconsciousness until she was certain he slept, then trying to stay still so as not to awaken him, instead tossing and turning in her mind. Who? She thought she knew, but why, after all this time? Money, was the only realistic possibility she could think of, along with a bit of torture just to get back at her for good measure. They hadn't asked for anything yet, but what would she do if they did? There was no way Jennifer could pay them off without Matt noticing. They had joint accounts, being a trusting couple who'd never need to hide any financial transactions from each other; until now, she thought with bitterness. Even the shopping account, which only she used for ninety-nine percent of the time, was in Matt's name. He'd notice anything different on the statements, and then she'd be lost, even more than she was already.

Nevertheless she took measures, took to the internet herself, googling, scouring social media, hoping against hope; and then she found it, that one piece of information which sent her back to square one and her mind racing, asking again, who, who? She'd go about her daily schedule, trying to appear as normal, smiling and chatting on automatic pilot with the members of the community to whom she was a well-known figure, all the while thinking, was it you? You? You? Paranoia set in, the feeling that all eyes were on her as she walked down the High Street, around the Market Place, into the supermarket, checking the others in the aisles, at the tills, her thoughts spinning out of control inside whilst her body moved like an automaton through the landscape of Hell her world had become. Her mind felt like it was burning out, continually examining possibilities, motives, anything that could help her get out of this nightmare. She'd go through the motions, trying to grab a nap on the sofa whenever the opportunity presented itself, then fall into bed at night and still be unable to get more than a couple of hours of fitful, broken sleep.

Morning would come, and like a zombie she'd pick up the reins of her day, drinking more coffee than was good for her in an attempt to stay awake until her always-punishing schedule allowed her a brief respite. She'd just about manage to set an alarm for twenty minutes' time, then close her eyes on the sofa only to open them what seemed like seconds later as the damn thing went off, loud and jarring and jangling her already-shredded nerves. And then there'd been *that* incident.

She felt so ashamed, but she was exhausted, she couldn't help it. She'd slept through the alarm, and missed collecting the children from school. Mortified didn't cover it. Thank God it was just Bella and Toby, and none of their friends. You had children, you loved them, and you did everything in your power to protect them. Jennifer would never put them on the school bus; bullying had been known to occur there, and they didn't need that before they'd even arrived at school, where the staff were on constant lookout for such antisocial proclivities in their young charges. The parents' sharing scheme had seemed good, therefore, everybody taking turns and the pressure taken off from individual parents' shoulders. But then somebody had been late, forgotten as it turned out, distracted by some issues at work. No harm had been done, in the event; a member of the school staff had watched over the children until they'd been collected, but Jennifer had decided that she and she alone could make sure that Bella and Toby were safe. She'd taken over the school run for her own children, because she felt they were at risk within the parents' pool scheme; and now *she* was the forgetful parent!

Matt had noticed, despite all her attempts to hide it, because the school had phoned him at the hospital, when they couldn't raise Jennifer. He'd rung Mrs Jenkins, who'd just said "On my way" and gone straight there, calling Matthew as soon as the children were belted into the back of her car. She'd taken them home, as she had her own key, and found Jennifer unconscious on the sofa. Waking her with care, after having sent Toby and Bella to get changed, she'd made tea and sorted out the children's meal while Jennifer drank a large mug and came to.

Disaster averted, Matt had nevertheless come home earlier than usual, and took a closer than usual look at his wife. Why hadn't he noticed before? His conscience smote him for having been too bound up in other matters to pay more attention to his family. Yes, the fire was troubling, but he ought to have noticed the decline in his wife. The bags under her eyes, the dark circles, the lankness of her hair and dullness of her eyes, showed him a Jennifer he'd not seen before, one whose health was on a downward spiral; and he didn't even know about her new absent-mindedness, items forgotten from the shopping order, no money to hand when the gardener had to be paid, and a previous occasion when she'd slept through the alarm, fortunately being awoken by a phone call about something else entirely, which prevented her from being late collecting the children.

She couldn't explain what was wrong with her to her concerned husband, who examined her with professional thoroughness but couldn't find any physical reason for his wife's gradual decline.

"I just feel so tired all the time," she told him. It was true, and the only explanation she felt able to give without revealing the truth.

Exhaustion, Matt decided, brought on by her too-busy life, her too-packed schedule. He felt guilty, of course, but his life was demanding too, and he couldn't see any way in which he personally could lift any of the burden from her shoulders. There just weren't enough hours in the day. She'd have help, nevertheless, he decided, just not from his own hands. He arranged for Mrs Jenkins the cleaner to come in for a few more hours per week, to undertake tasks which Jennifer had previously performed herself, including walking the dogs. A quiet conversation over lunch with Elizabeth, the administrator for his department at the hospital who kept Matt's personal timetable and appointments in good form, and she agreed to take over the social media accounts for Jennifer's various community organisations. She'd need to be in email contact with Jennifer, to keep her in the loop, but it'd take the bulk of the mundane and routine from his wife's shoulders, and he would of course recompense Elizabeth for her time.

He also provided Jennifer with sleeping pills. A last resort, and one he didn't care for, but she was falling apart before his eyes, and a twenty-minute doze in the afternoon to which she'd confessed wasn't going to cut it. So she slept the sleep of the drugged each night and awoke nevertheless with a heavy head and a need for a gallon of coffee each morning.

Matt could only monitor her condition and hope for an improvement. He had so much on his plate, there was no way he could take time out, and what use could he be anyway? Then the brainwave hit him. His mother. Penny had little to do, left on her own as she was, apart from sitting around and moping about her situation. It'd do her a power of good to get out and involved in something other than her own woes. It could help her get over those issues, and Matt was convinced he could get her on-side.

Hoping that he was right, he determined to call Penny; but as he went to get his phone it began ringing, the display telling him that it was his mother. Very convenient. No time like the present, and time was of the essence in this case.

20: PENNY

Consciousness crept up on Penny slowly, and she wished it hadn't. The bright sunlight from the side window hurt her eyes, as she'd forgotten to close the curtains, and that pain was soon joined by the throbbing in her head. Wincing, she reached for the popular over-the-counter painkillers which always sat on the bedside table—and which needed frequent replenishment—and the bottled water which always accompanied her to bed. Two tablets washed down, she burrowed back beneath the covers, turned on her side and prayed for sleep to return and blot out the sharp, stabbing pain which had now taken over inside her left temple.

She was granted that, at least, awakening two hours later to a clear head with just a slight feeling of muzziness. A shower, coffee and toast soon removed that, and Penny was left to contemplate the day which stretched before her. The afternoon, more like. She hadn't awoken the first time until nine o'clock, and with the extra hours of sleep she'd managed after that, plus showering and eating breakfast, it wasn't far off midday. She hadn't bothered dressing; what was the point? Still in her dressing gown, she made more coffee and moved to the sofa in the lounge, there to contemplate the tempting array of activities available to her.

It was too late to go out for lunch, had she any friends with whom to do so, but alas, there were none. In cases of divorce friends tended to come down on one side or the other, despite initial attempts to keep in with both halves of the ex-couple. Social occasions were difficult, even in cases where the split had been amicable and mutually-desired. Old partners might be fine with their new situations, but new partners could be on-edge; or if one but not the other had formed a new relationship, jealousies or resentments could arise. Penny's split from Frank had been contentious to say the least, so having both under the same roof at the same time was nigh-on impossible, as Pippa and Graham knew to their cost. They'd tried to solve the issue at their recent party by having Penny over alone a few weeks beforehand, but she'd shown up at the party anyway, causing a delicate situation which had taken all Pippa's skills to manage.

Despite such difficulties, their oldest friends were the only couple who'd managed to stay friends with both Penny and Frank. The others had drifted away, or lived too far away to be handy for lunch, or coffee, or a morning of shopping; and indeed, Pippa fell into this category. As to new friends, so far Penny had made none. She'd been absorbed in her life with Jeremy, then Ross, having met the latter on her first attendance at a social club which Matt had encouraged her to join. She'd concentrated on him, rather than making any other friends, and had abandoned the group when their relationship took off. Now she was in a hiatus zone, recovering from her split with the latter whilst borrowing her younger son's apartment. She'd no idea what the future held, or indeed where it might take place. In this area, she hoped, as Matt lived nearby, with her grandchildren, who Penny thought might take the edge off the loneliness in her coming years.

Focussing on her more immediate problems, she considered what she might do to fill the afternoon. Shopping? There was nothing she needed, and anyway, it was raining. Go for a walk? No, also on account of the weather.

Read a book? She'd got far too much time for that, but was between books at the moment anyway and couldn't find another she liked the sound of. Daytime TV? Please no. Watch an old DVD, listen to music? Increasingly one of these two was her go-to option, although in general it worked best if accompanied by a bottle of wine.

Wandering down the hallway, she noticed a package in the cage beneath the letter box and went to retrieve it. She turned it over, examining it, as she walked back towards the kitchen. A jiffy envelope, just the address, no name on the typed label, postmark none too legible but not recognisable as anywhere in the immediate area. Too well sealed with tape to be torn open, so she took the scissors from the drawer and cut across the top, peering inside as she reached in—then dropped it as though burned and stepped backwards, eyes wide, nostrils wrinkled, before running for her phone.

Matt. Get Matt.

*****

'Calm down, please, Mum. I know it's horrible, but if you keep distressing yourself like this they'll have won.'

He'd been about to call her anyway, so had dropped everything and rushed over as soon as summoned.

'Who the hell would do a thing like this? Sending—excrement—through the post. It's disgusting. Thank God I didn't touch the stuff. Bloody cowards. Why?'

Her chin began to tremble. Matt took her in his arms.

'I'll call the police, okay? They must get a lot of this; there's too much hate going around these days. Maybe they got the address wrong. It's not unknown, and the sort who go in for this type of thing aren't noted for their intelligence.

Now, why don't you make us both some tea, while I make the call.'

She did as requested, still with a tremor in her hands, he noticed. It took a while for the officers to arrive, so they drank tea—the offending package placed in the hall, by the front door—while they waited. Matt attempted to distract his mother, raising the matter about which he'd intended to call her before her emergency had taken precedence.

'I'm sorry this has happened, Mum, but I was going to call you anyway. I'm afraid I need a favour.'

'I'm listening.'

'It might be better if we discuss it later, when the police've been and you've had a chance to get over it. How about an early dinner, tonight, if you'd like and if you're free.'

Free? Like she had a packed social calendar. She almost laughed, but controlled herself.

'I'd like that. Shall I book the pub? What time?'

'I'll collect you, say six o'clock? We can walk over, it's only ten minutes, if you don't mind.'

'Of course.'

Then the doorbell rang and the police were with them, asking questions, putting the package into an evidence bag, explaining that it was unlikely they'd find whoever'd sent it. Yes, it happened, more than anybody'd like. There were some right sickos out there, but too cowardly to do more than send anonymous packages like this one. The police departed, taking it with them, and then it was Matt's turn.

'Will you be alright?'

'Yes, don't worry, I'll manage. It was a shock, but I'll get over it.'

'You can come back with me if you want to.'

He felt he had to ask, but hoped she wouldn't take him up on it, things with Jennifer being as they were.

'No, you get off. I'm sure you've got enough work to do.

I might call a few people, have a chat, make me feel less alone.'

She winced as the words left her mouth. Wrong thing to say. She didn't want Matt thinking she was reproaching him for her solo state. If he thought that he didn't bite, however.

'Good idea. Take your mind off it.'

'See you later then.'

*****

After he'd gone she couldn't get on the phone fast enough. She hadn't spoken to Pippa in a while, and her old friend was just the right person to calm Penny's distress. It rang a few times at the other end and then was answered by Graham.

'Penny? Good to hear you. How's things?'

'They could be better, Graham, but I hope all's well with you. I was hoping to catch Pippa.'

'She's in bed, I'm afraid, and out for the count. She's not been sleeping well, been a bit on and off, so after lunch I persuaded her to take a pill and go to bed. You know what she's like about medication, so it shows how bad she is that she took this one without a fight. You'll have to be content with me, or I'll get her to call you back, probably tomorrow.'

Pleased as she was that Pippa was getting the sleep she needed, Penny wanted to talk to somebody now. Graham was as good an old a friend as his wife, so she proceeded to tell him of the anonymous package of unpleasantness delivered to her. He listened, then spoke. She could almost hear the frown in his voice.

'God, are you alright, Penny? Horrible. Thank goodness Matt could come over.'

He hesitated.

'I don't want to make something out of this that it's maybe not, but—. We got a letter recently. No, no, nothing as bad as what was dumped—sorry—on your doormat. A letter, one of those ridiculous things made up of letters cut out of newspapers and glued on a sheet to make words. I won't repeat it, all I'll say is it's homophobic, concerning Dan and Simon.'

Penny took a moment to digest this.

'But I'm living in their flat, and I haven't been there long. Good God, Graham, d'you think the two are connected? Aimed at the boys? Oh God—'

'Look, don't get worked up about it, when you've just got over it. Don't you worry about anything. I'll let our police know and call Matt so he can speak to them at your end. If the cops can speak to each other they might be able to tie things together—although I'm not hopeful. Try not to think about it too much, Pen, but be cautious. There's some bloody nasty types around these days.'

A doorbell was heard in the background at his end.

'Look, I'd better go. Keep calm and carry on, Pen, and I'll get Pips to call you tomorrow. Oh, and Pen, don't mention this to her, will you? You know how sensitive she is, and she's still bothered about that bloody letter we had. If you need to talk again you can call me on my phone. Right, must go. Take care, catch you later.'

He departed with a flurry of little kisses, and then the line went dead.

Penny put the phone aside and decided to watch an old series on TV, to keep herself occupied; a couple of episodes of a lifestyle programme, people downsizing from city houses to cottages in the country, although she couldn't concentrate. She was desperate for a drink, but contented herself with tea. She'd have wine with her dinner, and Matt wouldn't be pleased if he arrived and found her preloaded.

*****

A little doze and she went to prepare for her evening date, after a call from Matt to the effect that Graham had been in touch, and they'd both updated their local police forces. Penny felt better at hearing that. She'd rationalised the unpleasantness of the morning by now. The front door was solid, with bolts and a mortice lock for good measure, plus there was a security system with camera and alarm rigged to the local police. Should anybody come here—and there was no indication that they would, if they were the type who'd send packages from a distance—she'd be well-protected.

In the bedroom she draped various garments across herself, checking in the mirror. Such a change to get dressed up. She had some beautiful clothes but nowhere to wear them these days, so made the most of the occasion. Matt, on arrival, was impressed to see his mother putting the morning behind her and making the sort of effort she rarely if ever made these days. It boded well for his proposition, which he put to her when they were settled in a booth at the Rose & Crown, he with an alcohol-free beer, she with red wine, while they waited for their food to be bought.

'Jen's not at all well, and I can't find any reason other than that she's trying to cope with a far-too-heavy workload. I've arranged for Mrs Jenkins to come in for an extra couple of hours each week to help, and for John to do some extra bits and pieces as well as the garden. I'd like to offload the school run too, and I was hoping you might take it on.'

'I'm so sorry. What's—I mean, what are her symptoms?'

'She's tired all the time, and she's not sleeping, which doesn't help. She looks exhausted, dark circles under her eyes, and she's hardly got any energy. She keeps dozing off during the day, and she's forgetting things. She didn't collect the kids from school one day last week, and that's the worst. I want to give her time and space to rest, and someone else taking the kids to school and bringing them home later would be a huge burden off her shoulders.'

Penny put her head on one side and seemed to consider it. The waiter chose that moment to bring their food, so that gave her a few minutes while he fussed around warning them about how hot the dishes were, and whether they wanted any mustard, or ketchup, or whatever.

On the one hand she wasn't keen, disliking her oh-so-efficient daughter-in-law for exactly that reason. How dare she have such a successful and well-ordered life, when Penny's own was such a mess? Not to mention the grudge she still held over having been ejected from their home on the flimsiest of excuses, which had to have been Jennifer's doing. Penny could never believe that her own son would have thrown her out so heartlessly, conveniently forgetting that an inebriated grandmother at the table for breakfast and dinner was not a good influence on her young grandchildren.

She'd like to see those grandchildren however, she admitted to herself now. In her immersion in her own love-life she'd cut herself off from her family to a great extent. With romance now firmly consigned to the past, and with too much time on her hands, she thought it desirable to get close to them again, to avoid loneliness in old age as much as anything; and here was Matt offering her the ideal way back in, not to mention she'd be with other people, in company and feeling safe from attacks like that of this morning.

'Of course I'll help, darling. You should have asked me sooner. It's not fair on poor Jennifer, having to do so much. If there's anything else—.'

They agreed, over Boeuf Bourguignon for him and Coq

au Vin for her, that for the time being she'd take the school run out of Jennifer's too-full hands; call round for the children in the morning, deliver them to school and collect them in the afternoon, taking them back home and seeing if she could do anything else for Jennifer while she was there.

As long as she was sober, Matt stressed, and Penny rushed to reassure him. No way would she drink a drop before driving, she told him, then dropped her eyes before the rather hard look he gave her. She'd had time to re-evaluate things since her journey to Pippa and Graham's party, she insisted. She'd made a mistake, and been lucky. She wouldn't risk the children for anything, apart from the fact that she didn't need a conviction for drink-driving on top of everything else that'd gone wrong in her life. She'd still have a drink, but only when she was home with no need to go out again; but she didn't say so to Matt.

Her protestations won him over, and he allowed himself a smug inner smile. He'd killed two birds with one stone, got help for Jen and given his mother a reason to get out of bed in the morning and away from unpleasant memories.

He'd got it sorted. He thought.

Apart from the question of who was attacking them.

21: FRANK

Frank surveyed his handiwork with pleasure. The weeks of hard work had paid off. The place smelled of fresh paint, not unpleasantly so, and the cream-coloured walls, doors and skirting boards looked almost professional in their finish. The contract cleaners he'd hired had done a good job, so he'd had an immaculate surface on which to work. The curtains had come up beautifully, as had the brass rails upon which they hung, for which he'd used quite a few cans of Brasso. There'd been a couple of cracked panes in the windows, and while they were being fixed Frank had let himself be talked into upgrading the glass to a thicker, more insulating grade. Expensive, but worth it come the winter, there only being storage heaters rather than full central heating. The discount warehouse had come through with a good-quality carpet at a bargain price, even less than he'd expected, which offset the cost of the windows to some extent. Martin, good chap, had pitched in with fitting it. His DIY skills, acquired through years of being a landlord, were far and away better than those of Frank, whose life lived in married quarters hadn't equipped him for such things. If something went wrong in those you reported it to the Quartermaster, who sent someone out to fix it.

Be that as it may, Martin had got involved in many other ways than fitting the carpet. He knew where to get the best deals on kitchens and bathrooms, and assumed without having to be asked that he'd fit them. Frank was better at ripping out the old fitments, after which Martin would come in with his knowledge of tile grouting, plumbing, fitting cabinets and so forth. He knew a good electrician too. It made no sense to take risks doing dodgy wiring jobs themselves, so the new cooker and hob were connected by a professional before Frank helped Martin fit new worktops and doors to the old kitchen cabinet carcasses, which had cleaned up a treat.

So now it was down to furniture. Frank knew what he'd be bringing from Madge's house, meaning he just needed to buy certain items. The bedroom had a fitted wardrobe, with a mirrored door, so those wouldn't be needed. He'd been methodical with the rest, looking around town and treating himself to lights and lampshades, a coffee table and matching nest of three small side tables in a style modern yet retro, which suited his taste. He'd had some old pictures framed, from a calendar he'd been given years ago and which he'd liked enough to keep. Modern and mildly erotic, they now adorned the walls of the bedroom above the new brass bedstead with its crisp new blue-patterned linen which went so well with the carpet. Frank liked blue. No greens or browns in his life, apart from on the golf course. It was too great a reminder of a service life lived in khaki.

The place was looking good, almost ready to move into. He'd already been camping-out there for the occasional night when he'd forgotten the time and worked late, or because he wanted to get an early start the next morning. Come moving-in day he'd hire a van, and Martin would be on-side to help him move his furniture and personal effects out of Madge's house. Before that was the hard part. Madge. He'd told her the tenants had moved out, which wasn't a lie, but he hadn't told her that they'd done so at his instigation. She understood the need to do some work on the place before re-letting it, but she didn't know that Frank was to be his own tenant.

He'd break it to her gently. He was a gentleman, after all, and he didn't want to hurt her. She'd been good in so many ways, and maybe if it hadn't been for his accident he'd never have married her; but the fact was that it hadn't been working for Frank for some time now. He and Madge got on well, had a civilized relationship, and maybe that would be enough, very probably was, for thousands of other couples like them. But love? Passion? The latter, certainly, was present, but it was Frank's passion for golf, and Madge's passion for the golf club, the bar and the game, in that order. There was none for each other, and that wouldn't do, in his book. His sons would most likely scoff, if he told them. You're in your seventies, Pa, they'd say, what are you talking about? Passion? At your time of life? They wouldn't understand, not until they reached the same age and felt as he did. But Frank knew. He'd been living this half-life for far too long, and was determined to do so no more. He had maybe twenty-five years left, probably less, but still a lot of years. He intended to live them.

He considered. Madge had one of her book club meetings coming up soon; there was one each month. Why don't you have it on Zoom, he'd asked her once, given that you all live a distance from each other and it's a bit of a hike to get together? Because you can't have a pleasant pub meal and a good chat on a computer screen, she'd told him; from which he understood that the books, all lightweight romances, or so-called "chic lit," from what he could tell, weren't that important in themselves, but merely another excuse for a get-together, dinner, drinks and a good evening. Madge always stopped over, the better to drink as much gin and wine as she liked, and he didn't grudge her in the slightest. Let her have a good time, remind her that she had a life outside this house, away from Frank, as she'd always had before he came along and would still have after he'd left. Yes, he'd tell her when she came back from her meeting. He hoped.

22: MATT

It didn't take long before Penny was an established figure around the house, arriving to pick up the children for school after breakfast or sometimes before, preparing it for them and eating it with them if Jennifer wasn't feeling too great and had stayed in bed. She'd then collect them and bring them back in the afternoon, once more making their tea if Jennifer was having a bad day as well as staying on to prepare dinner. Often she'd eat with Matt—Jennifer having gone to bed early, if she'd got up at all—but only if invited. It was as though she'd ransacked some old files and brought forth the relevant one, because she slipped back into the habits of motherhood with ease.

That was strange, Matt thought, because apart from the age of nought to eight, when he'd been sent away to school, he didn't have that many memories of her doing the motherly thing. During the holidays, of course, but the rest of the time it was matron, at school, who provided the female figure in his young life, and in a place that never, ever, felt like home.

Home. A nebulous thing, for Matt, given that he'd been away so much. He remembered going back, after his first term, to a married quarter in whichever station his father was posted to at the time. Then he'd returned to school, and the next holidays he'd maybe gone to another house entirely in yet another place. It was less disruptive for him and Simon, he supposed, for their parents to move to a new posting during term-time, while the boys were away. Such a lifestyle meant their parents were "home" in themselves to the boys, the sole fixed and stable point to which Matt and Simon could return; which is why it'd been such a wrench when they'd divorced, Mum leaving Pa for that other one. Even though Matt and Simon were grown men by then, out in the world, forming their own families, they felt the wrench when the home of their childhood was torn apart, and Matt wasn't sure he'd quite forgiven Penny to this day. Nevertheless, he did feel sorry for her, because his father's successors had both dumped her, and she'd been left with nothing. She hadn't been able to claim any money or other assets from them, given that she'd been married to neither; not that she needed their money, rolling as she was in his father's life's earnings. God, he thought, what a bloody mess divorce makes, what a bloody load of unhappiness.

Nevertheless, she was here now, helping keep his home together when he needed her, and he warmed to her for that. It was important to him, the entire set-up, wife, children, even the dogs and the cat. Matt loved his work, but appreciated how he was enabled to perform well and professionally because he knew his home, his refuge from the world outside, was working like a well-oiled machine. It must have to do with his having gone away to school so young; but his parents had wanted him to have a stable education, not one that was disrupted every few years by changing schools, changing teachers. Some children could cope with that, although many had no choice in the matter, their parents wanting their offspring with them no matter what the consequences. Matt's father had been a boarder himself, and it having worked out for him, presumably, he was an advocate of his sons following the same path.

Matthew wasn't quite sure how his mother had felt about her children being sent away. She'd allowed it to happen, and he'd never heard her complain, but he'd never seen her cry either when he and later his younger brother had left; but then the archetypal stiff upper-lip was a part of her life. Do what has to be done and if you don't like it, don't display your negative emotions. The same code had been passed on to him, both overtly and covertly, so that at school he'd had to cope as best as he could; alone. It wasn't something he had any intention of inflicting on his own children, who were at an excellent private school not far from the family home.

Not for them the attaching to the school matron as Matt had, a sort of surrogate mother imparting feminine comfort when required. Matt's matron had always been ready to talk to and help the lonely eight-year-old boy when he was in need. In truth, he'd needed far more often than he'd sought the loving warmth which she could give, because it wouldn't do to get a name as a wimp, always crying for mummy. There were always bullies, on the lookout for those they saw as weaker, in whatever way, and he'd learned not to behave in such a way as to attract their violent and abusive attention. So he'd kept his tears for the night-time, crying in silence under the bedclothes, and not approached Mrs Lupton too often. He had positive memories of her from the times when he'd done so, however, and perhaps his attraction to Abby had something to do with these.

It hadn't been the same for his younger brother, because by the time Simon arrived at the school the older brother knew his way around and was able to look out for the younger in a way nobody had been there to do for him. He'd sorted out the bullies when Simon was threatened; and thinking of this, Matt realised with a jolt that he did remember Abby, and exactly where from.

They'd been back for the summer holidays, he must have been about twelve, and Simon nine or ten, and they'd been playing around with some other children on the grassed area near a married quarters patch. Another group had approached them, all boys, one particularly big and aggressive. Who were they? he demanded, because he hadn't seen Matt and Simon around before. When told he stated that he didn't like boarding school kids; snobs, think they're better than the rest of us. To emphasise his point he ran at Simon, the smallest, and made to hit him. Simon ducked, and the big boy missed, but then Matt was on him, because no one was going to beat-up his younger brother, as he'd made known to the bullies at school. They struggled together, but the boy was big even for Matt, who'd inherited his father's thick-set and stocky build plus his large hands, of which he made good fists; so even though he managed to bloody the big boy's nose—he'd broken it, he found out later, to his immense satisfaction—he himself sustained a nasty gash to one side of his face.

"Hey! What the hell do you think you're doing?"

They all stopped to stare at the woman who'd shouted, and who was walking towards them from the houses with a determined air. The big boy and his cronies took off, fast, pushing past another woman, who'd emerged from one of the houses. Matt's attention was on the first woman, because he recognised her. A few days ago he'd been going into the NAAFI shop with his father, and she'd been coming out. She and Frank had exchanged greetings, and Frank had introduced him, as "my eldest son, Matthew." She'd turned and smiled at him, which she did a lot, he'd noticed, and asked if he was having a good summer. He'd replied in the affirmative and she'd smiled again; then, with a few more words to his father, she'd gone on her way. She'd registered with Matt in that way the females of the species do, when boys are just becoming aware of them as interesting; and in some kind of acknowledgement of this he'd told his father "I like her, she looks nice." "Yes, she is," his father'd agreed, and they'd gone into the shop.

And two days later there she was, bearing down on them and checking the damage to his face.

"That looks nasty. Better get you to the Medical Centre. It's Matthew, isn't it? And this must be Simon."

Matt had nodded, unable to speak. She'd spoken to the other woman, who'd reached them by now, exclaiming over what a bully the big boy was. She knew who he was, they'd sort him out later. And Abby, for it was she, had asked her to phone and let Major and Mrs Fairfield know what'd had happened, and that Abby had taken their boys to the Medical Centre, which she'd proceeded to do, after taking them into her house to find a wad of tissues for Matt to hold over his cut. She'd fastened them into the back seat of her car, then waited with them at the Medical Centre until their parents arrived.

She'd sat outside with Simon while Matt's gash was being treated and stitched. He remembered the occasion as the time when he'd first shown an interest in medicine. What was the fluid the doctor had cleaned the cut with, and why were stitches also called sutures? Who'd thought up the idea of those little curved needles instead of the usual straight ones?

"You ask a lot of questions," the doctor had said, but he answered them all in a good-natured way. So Matt had been emboldened to ask more, about what it took to become a doctor, and the man had been very informative; so that when Matt returned to school he'd spoken to his teachers about his new career goal, and they'd made sure he was focussed on the correct subjects to get him there.

Before that, however, he'd emerged from the treatment room, cleaned, stitched and with a gauze pad under a large plaster covering one cheek. His parents had arrived by then, and he'd had to deflect his mother's distress by telling them he was okay, and they should see the other guy; at which his father had winked at him, man to man. They did see the other guy too, because the big boy—not so big now—was just then brought in by his father, which was how Matt found out he'd broken his nose. His father spoke to the big boy's father, just down the corridor where they couldn't be heard by the others present, and it seemed the other father had words with his son, who stayed well clear of Matt and Simon, and other boarding-school children too, from then on in. But before that, his parents had thanked Abby, who had made modest "It was nothing, anybody would have done it" comments before giving him and Simon her big, sunshine-like smile and leaving.

How strange life was, he thought now, that the years somehow lessened the gap in their ages: that a boy of twelve, with the passing of between thirty-five to forty years, could form an intimate relationship with a woman who'd been in her twenties when they'd first met. Older than him she might be, but he'd moved into the same zone as her, so to speak, through the inexplicable workings of time.

Talking of which, he had a meeting to attend. Time to get moving. There just was never enough of it.

23: PENNY

It was strange how things worked out, Penny decided as she grabbed her car keys from the hook in the kitchen and exited the apartment. She'd never been one of those grandparents who lived for their grandchildren, spending every pound possible in thoroughly spoiling them as though they'd got nothing else to do with their lives. Not that she was doing that, but the weekday school-run routine had given her something to get out of bed for, and she was even beginning to enjoy it. She felt guilty about that, because she oughtn't to be glad when her daughter-in-law was feeling so bad she could barely function, meaning that Penny fed Toby and Bella when she got them home, and sometimes prepared Matt's dinner too.

She could even feel sorry for Jennifer, for whom she'd not had much time in the past. Her daughter-in-law, Miss Perfect. Penny knew who'd had her turned out of the house when she needed shelter; her own son would never have thrown her out like that. She was letting bygones be bygones, however, because she could enjoy a certain sense of superiority in knowing that she, the mother-in-law, was at present keeping the household going.

She was early today, having bought some ice-cream for the children's tea, and wanted to put it in the freezer before continuing on to the school. Jennifer had ice-cream delivered with the rest of the shopping from the supermarket, but this was an artisan make from a farm shop a few miles out of the village, and young Toby loved it. She'd taken him and Bella back to her apartment on occasion; there'd been no repeat of the unpleasant anonymous package incident, and she'd relaxed enough over time to feel secure there. The children had tried the ice cream there, liked it, and requested more. She'd been pleased at their reaction, and it was only a short trip for her to buy it. Maybe she was spoiling them, but not too much.

Jennifer's car was on the drive when she arrived. Nothing unusual there; she didn't venture out any more than she had to these days. Penny had a key, but she rang the bell anyway. She didn't want it to seem too much like she was making herself at home, didn't want to upset her daughter-in-law and perhaps earn another banishment. When there was no answer she tried again, then a third time. Still no response, so she let herself in, intending to leave the ice-cream. She jumped back, startled, as Kit the cat flashed past, her fur brushing against Penny's ankles. Recovering herself, Penny went over to the freezer, calling out as she did so.

'Jennifer? It's only me, just dropping off some ice-cream on the way to the school.'

There was no answer, which was unlike Jennifer. Even if she didn't feel up to coming to the door she'd call out, in a weaker or stronger voice depending on how bad or otherwise she was feeling. Something felt off, so Penny went to investigate.

'Jennifer?'

The conservatory, lounge, dining room, study, even the downstairs loo; nothing, apart from Duke and Prince, who she discovered shut disconsolate in the study, which was strange; Matt didn't tend to let them in there. Fending off the rough tongues with which they greeted her she let them into the garden. Upstairs, to the master bedroom and en-suite, the children's rooms, the spares, and at last the bathroom.

What she found there horrified her.

24: THE PAST (3)

It was hard when my mother died, and it hadn't been an easy life when she was alive. I'd never known my father. He was long-gone by the time I was able to register the lack of him, and my mother never wanted to talk about him. "We're better off without him," was all she'd say when I pushed the issue, and I learned not to ask.

I had hazy memories of my early childhood, a vague idea that things weren't always bad. There were a few half-remembered friends, a red-haired girl, a boy who used to pull my hair. I was a good pupil, which continued as I grew up, and my teachers expected great things from me; but at some point I realised that academic excellence and all that went with it was a luxury I couldn't afford. We'd moved from the house and village where I'd been born, to a flat in a city, and I was out of there and working as soon as it was legally possible. We needed the money, my mother said, so it was shop work for me, stacking shelves in a supermarket and hoping for promotion to the tills.

Then my mother met Bryn, and everything changed. I disliked him on sight, and the feeling was mutual, I could tell, but Mum wouldn't hear a word against him. I didn't see a lot of her in those days. She'd be out living it up with him and I wanted to be glad for her, given that she never had any fun, working as a cleaner to bring in enough money to keep a roof over our heads. But I couldn't, because she was with him.

I started working extra shifts, when I could get them, so I wouldn't be around the flat when he came to pick her up, or have to go back and find him lolling on the sofa waiting while she got dressed-up to go to the pub, or to the cinema, or for dinner, or wherever he was taking her. I'd make sure I didn't come home until they'd gone out, and when they came back merry with drink and fell into her bed I'd be shut into my box-bedroom and trying to sleep, so I wouldn't have to hear the noises coming through the wall.

Despite taking my time, I got home one evening and found them still there. They were going out soon, Mum said, so I went to my room to wait until she'd gone and taken him with her. I heard the front door open and close, and then Bryn was in the doorway. I hadn't heard him approach and knew his presence signalled bad news.

"What d'you want?" I was barely civil with him, as was usual. "Where's Mum?"

"She's gone up to the corner shop. Needs new tights or something."

He was looking at me, his breathing heavy. I could smell his beer-and-fagsmoke-breath from a couple of feet away.

"Why didn't you go with her?"

He shrugged, and moved further into the room. I got off the bed, my instincts on full alert.

"We're all alone, just you and me. We can have a talk. You should be nicer to me."

He leaned in as he spoke, and I knew what he was going to do. My knee came up like lightening and connected with his groin. I wasn't one to take shit from anybody. He doubled over, groaning, and I took the opportunity to push him through the door. He staggered out and collided with my mother, who I hadn't heard coming back.

"What's going on?"

She took in the scene and worked it out for herself; then all hell was let loose. He was still winded and groaning as she hit him and screamed at him. I thought about trying to pull her off, but decided against it. He collected himself enough to put up an arm to ward off the blows raining down on him as he backed towards the front door, and then he was gone, out into the night and the rain.

I picked up his jacket between finger and thumb and threw it out after him, slamming the door. Mum and I looked at each other and she had a sort of lopsided smile, part pleased but part sad too. She'd liked having someone around to make her feel desirable, rather than a faded middle-aged woman with a grown daughter and a cleaning job to support us. She came into my arms and I held her until the sobs subsided. Then I made some tea.

*****

He was gone and it was inevitable that everything changed again. It goes without saying I was glad, but Mum was inconsolable, crying as she went around the flat trying to dust, or wash, or iron, or cook. I suppose she cried when she did her cleaning job too, but at least there was nobody there to see or hear her. I felt bad, and thought maybe I'd been too harsh in my judgement of Bryn. He hadn't beaten her, and I'd only ever heard sounds of fun coming from them when they were together. If he'd hit her when they'd been out I'd have known by her mood, and I'd have seen any bruises, our flat being far too small for privacy and Mum and I not having any secrets from each other on account of that. But then I remembered he'd tried it on with me, and that was unforgiveable. We were well off without the scum, and Mum would get over it in time.

It was a bombshell she found out she was pregnant. It wasn't unexpected, I suppose, given the sounds that used to come from her bedroom, but I'd assumed they'd taken precautions. Mum had, as it turned out when I questioned her, but these things aren't always one-hundred-percent effective, as she told me. I wasn't keen on the idea of Bryn re-joining our family, but I felt guilty that he'd gone on my account. He'd tried to assault me, so he'd had to go; nevertheless, I wondered out loud whether he ought to be made to shoulder his responsibilities. Mum wasn't having it. He was filth, and she had her pride, and she wasn't going begging to the likes of him. "Bloody men," she almost spat her disgust, "even your father could be a sod. Who needs the bastards?"

Not us, it was clear. We tried to carry on as we'd done before, whilst preparing for this unexpected addition to our numbers, because Mum never considered a termination. I started to mention it once, and the look she turned on me stopped me in my tracks. Instead she continued cleaning for as long as she could. It was quite easy as pregnancies go, she told me, but at a certain point she had to stop and prepare for the birth. She'd resisted knowing the sex, which was a good thing as it turned out because neither of us could build up a picture and make a small person with a name to attach to her bump.

Complications set in during the birth. Everything seemed to go on for too long, it seemed to me as I sat and held her hand. I had no experience of this process, and I'd been told it could take ages, so maybe this was normal. It wasn't. It went on and on, because the baby was the wrong way round in her womb and they couldn't right it, so an emergency caesarean was carried out—I'd been removed from the room by this point—and that too went wrong. My mother bled out there in the delivery room.

I was numb with shock when they told me, but I didn't have time to dwell on what'd happened. I suppose they thought it was some kind of consolation when they put the baby into my arms; a healthy, screaming and kicking little boy, who they told me was going to need his big sister more than ever now their mother was gone.

I couldn't grasp it. My life wasn't meant to be like this. It'd been bad enough before, insofar as we hadn't much money and a tiny flat, but we were happy compared to so many others. At least neither of us was a drug addict and we weren't living on the streets.

*****

I did what Mum and I had always done and just got on with it. The supermarket was very good about it, considering they hadn't been prepared for me to have what to all intents and purposes was maternity leave. They told me to take as long as I needed to sort myself out and my job would be there for me when I was ready to return. In the meantime there were other members of staff who'd be only too glad of the overtime to fill the gap left by my absence.

I went through the motions of what needed to be done. My mother's funeral was a basic cremation, no ceremony or wake as there was nobody but me to attend. I registered the birth, got all the visits and checks carried out at the hospital and by district nurses, or whatever they're called, as well as applying for allowances and benefits, given that I couldn't go out to work and support us both. Somehow doing all the official stuff took my mind off the business of caring for the child, to whom I hadn't warmed. He was a cute little thing, it has to be said, and being my mother's flesh and akin to myself made some kind of bond; but he was also half Bryn's, and I couldn't lose sight of that fact, try as I might.

My feelings about his father affected me as the child grew. I couldn't help seeing in his face the bastard who'd used my mother and tried to rape me, even though I knew it wasn't the baby's fault. Nevertheless I learned to bath and change and bottle-feed him. I plucked a name out of the air and came up with Robert, but I never managed to love him as I felt I ought to.

We muddled along somehow and achieved a sort of equilibrium, but it wasn't to last. At a certain point I had to go back to work, but I didn't see how I could manage it, working shifts at all hours and with nobody to mind the baby. The money I could bring in would give us a better standard of living, but not if I had to pay out for care, and I wasn't happy about leaving him with strangers, no matter how well-recommended they were.

I was mulling the problem over one afternoon as I cleaned the flat while Robert slept; and then I had one of those eureka moments. I remembered my mother telling me she used to work as a cleaner when I was a baby, and that she'd take me with her, asleep in my little carrycot, for most of the time, anyway. The woman she worked for was a teacher, so wasn't home while Mum was there, and didn't mind me being with her as long as her work around the house was done.

That was the answer. I could make some extra money and care for the baby at the same time if I got a cleaning job and took him with me. I started searching and soon had an interview lined up. I had to pay Mrs Papadimitris next door to look after the baby while I was gone, because taking him to a job interview wasn't a good idea and I didn't want to prejudice my chances. It wasn't a problem, in the event. My new employer, Mrs Farrell, went out to work herself, not having children of her own, and she'd no problem with me bringing Robert with me.

It worked like a dream, and it must have been meant to be, because things soon snowballed. I'd never been keen on housework, but being able to have my half-sibling where I could keep an eye on him made it the best possible option in our circumstances. I worked four mornings a week, Monday to Thursday, and Mrs Farrell was pleased with my work. Then a friend of hers wanted someone to come in on Fridays to clean up so the house would be in good condition for the weekend, and Mrs Farrell recommended me. I took it on, glad of the extra cash, and then another friend needed someone. Mrs Farrell didn't mind me working for others in the afternoons, so long as I did her house in the mornings. Before I knew it I was working a five-full-days week, and had a good amount of money to support myself and Robert.

Nevertheless, I wasn't happy. For so long I'd been head down, working at cleaning and being a mother to Robert, that I hadn't thought about anything else. One Friday evening, my week's work over and the baby put to bed, I sat with a glass of cheap red wine—my weekend treat—and thought about the future. All I could see was me cleaning other people's houses all week while raising my half-brother; it wasn't enough. It wasn't what I wanted to do with my life. I was nineteen, but I felt about thirty-nine with all the responsibilities I'd been shouldering. I deserved a life too, a love-life, a career, whatever I wanted, but it seemed I was chained to quasi-motherhood for maybe the next seventeen or eighteen years. It wouldn't do.

I couldn't think what to do about a better job at present; having a baby to care for put paid to that. I could have a bit of a social life, however; all work and no play, as they say. I needed a bit of leisure to relieve the tension, and that wasn't too difficult to arrange. I'd had to give up the supermarket job when I took on the cleaning, but I was still in contact with some of the people I'd worked with there. One phone call and I was sorted to meet up for a girls' night at a pub not too far from my flat. Mrs Papadimitris next door was glad to babysit Robert again, and she didn't want much for doing it. She loved children, she'd had six of her own, all grown and away now, which I suppose was why she was glad to have another baby to mother, and I could enjoy myself safe in the knowledge that my half-brother was well cared for.

*****

Unfortunately it all went wrong. Even before Mum had gone I hadn't had a social life to speak of, and now I had the luxury of some me-time I went for it. Friday night with the girls became a permanent fixture, and then Tina and Linda asked me to go late-night shopping with them. Soon visits to the cinema worked their way into what was becoming a rather crowded evening agenda. Of course I was spending money, but I cut back on my grocery budget to balance things out. I made sure the baby got all the required nourishment, that went without saying, but I was used to skimping on costs so I just managed to eat less myself, and of worse quality foodstuffs.

It got to the point that I was rarely home with Robert in the evenings. I told Mrs Papadimitris I was working extra hours, and I'm sure she didn't believe me; but she gave me the benefit of the doubt and kept Robert with her until whatever time I got in. On one occasion that was the next morning, as I'd passed out on Tina's sofa after a Saturday night binge. I charged home, when I woke up and realised where I was and what had happened. At least it was Sunday, and I didn't have to work.

I rang the bell and composed an "I'm so sorry" speech, but she wasn't having any of it. She'd had enough, and put her foot down.

"No," she told me with a hard face, so unlike her usual friendly self,

when I began to speak. I was yawning and dishevelled and not yet completely human.

"What?"

I didn't understand what she meant.

"You don't get to take him, not this way, not like this, coming home half-way through the morning."

Then she really let me have it, Greek-mama style. I was a disgrace, a drunk, an unfit mother unworthy to have a little angel like Robert. She was going to make sure the child was cared for and if I didn't like it I could call the police, which she knew I wouldn't do.

I was wide awake in a moment, at the thought that I might lose Robert. Remind me of his bastard of a father he might, but he was also a part of my mother, all I had left of her.

"You won't involve Social Services?"

I was horrified.

"No. You think I'm stupid? Send that sweet little thing to be put in a home, or fostered by God-knows who, to be abused? No, he stays with me, who've been more of a mother to him than his own mother, the Virgin forgive me for saying so."

She crossed herself as she finished, as though to apologise to the mother of Christ for mentioning her in connection with my sordid goings-on.

I didn't bother reminding her that I was Robert's half-sister, not his mother. I thought she was being unfair. She'd been paid to care for the baby, after all, and I spent all my days with him, not to mention my nights, even if I was working. It seemed pretty hard that I couldn't have a few hours off each day to look after my own welfare.

I kept those thoughts to myself, however, as I needed to get her back on side. I was suitably apologetic, assuring her that I'd clean up my act and start staying home, and she was mollified. She sniffed, gave me a hard look, but went inside and brought out Robert, washed, changed and fed.

"Just make sure you do. I'll be keeping an eye."

The door closed behind her with a resounding bang.

*****

I brooded on the matter as I worked for Mrs Farrell; Kathleen, as she'd told me to call her when our relationship reached a certain point. She worked as a teachers' assistant at a nearby school and was often home before I'd finished, making us both a cup of tea and spending her time playing with little Robert while I completed my work. I noted with irony that she displayed all the maternal qualities which seemed lacking in me, and yet she had no children of her own, the reasons for which I hadn't dared ask. That day she must have noticed that something wasn't right. I suppose I looked rather bleak.

"Is something wrong? If you don't mind me asking. You don't seem your usual sunny self today."

I put the ironing board away and sat with her, at her invitation, then took the plunge and told her my worries as I drank the tea she'd made for us both. She listened and then thought for a moment.

"What would you do? Left to yourself, I mean?"

"I don't know. I haven't had much time to think about it. University, maybe? Or some kind of training for a proper career? I mean, there's nothing wrong with cleaning, someone has to do it and I don't mind, but for the rest of my life? There has to be more for me."

She looked thoughtful and started to speak, but then little Robert clamoured for something and Kathleen attended to him, while I took the ironed clothes upstairs and put them away before packing up the baby and taking him home. The next day Kathleen once again made tea and picked up where we'd left off the previous afternoon. She couldn't have been that much older than me, ten or fifteen years maybe, but she was almost maternal towards me in her care, as much as she was to Robert. She got straight to the point.

"You need time out for yourself, and there's no shame in that, despite what your neighbour thinks. You've spent too long, from what you've

told me, on helping to support the family, first with your mother and now with Robert. You're young, with all your life in front of you, but you've no friends, no social life, no love-life and no career prospects beyond cleaning up after the likes of myself."

She was very direct, and it was clear she'd given the matter some thought.

"If you want to get out there and find those things before you're much older why don't you? I'll be more than happy to babysit, but you'd have to bring Robert here because Pat likes us to be home together in the evenings."

I was so grateful to Kathleen. I couldn't believe my luck, and I had no issue with taking Robert round and leaving him overnight. I trusted her completely.

*****

My life bloomed. I decided I'd like to become a teaching assistant, like Kathleen, and for that I needed GCSEs in English and Maths. I found a couple of evening courses, signed up, and then my own life got going at last. I enjoyed the courses, did well on them, and made friends too. A social life grew around me, and behind it all was Kathleen, looking after the baby and asking no payment above and beyond the joy of having him to herself.

One afternoon, a few months later, she asked me to leave the cleaning and sit down to have tea with her. She was awkward and hesitant, unlike her usual self, which made me feel nervous; but I waited in silence for her to speak.

"The thing is—"

She paused, then let it out in a rush.

"How would you feel if Pat and I adopted Robert? Please, let me finish—"

I was looking at her in disbelief.

"You don't have to answer at once. Take your time, think about it. I realise it must be a shock, coming out of the blue like this. I love Robert, so does Pat, and of course you do too, but he's not your child and you need your own life. If—when—you qualify you'll be working longer hours, and one day you'll meet someone and want children of your own. We can't have any."

She flushed at this, and wouldn't meet my eyes, from which I guessed it was she who was at fault on that score.

She hurried on.

"Robert spends so much time here anyway; it just seems the right thing to make it a permanent arrangement. He'd have a secure future and you'd be free to have a normal young person's life. You could keep in touch, that goes without saying; he's your brother, after all. And of course we'd make it worth your while," she added, as if it was an afterthought.

I didn't know what to say. Kathleen was right, it was a shock, something I hadn't seen coming. Or had I? It was clear how much she cared for Robert, and if in idle moments I'd fantasised about her taking him from me, well, I was justified, wasn't I?

My silence must have unnerved her, because she reiterated what she must have felt was her major bargaining point.

"Obviously we'd make a meaningful contribution to the future you deserve."

She drew a deep breath, having got everything out. We both sat silent while I thought it over. I couldn't take it all in, it being unexpected and such a big thing. I asked for more time to consider it, and Kathleen agreed.

I lay awake that night, partly because Robert was restive and kept crying, as though he knew his future was in the balance. I was up and down with him, but in between times I couldn't stop thinking about Kathleen's offer. I wondered what there was to think about, really. Here was a married couple, well-monied and well-set-up, with a luxurious home but no children to share it with. They knew Robert, who was used to them and their house and was still so young that he was bound to forget any vague awareness he might have of my role in his early life. What kind of life was it, in my scruffy little flat? I kept it clean, but couldn't do much about the general worn-out condition and the damp patches; the latter was a health risk, especially for a small child. And I'd be free, finally, to live life for myself at last.

On the other hand he was the only link to my mother I still had. We shared her blood, and if I let him go I'd be losing her too. I agonised over the issue, first coming down on one side and then the other. She'd want us to be together, but she'd also want the best for us both. Was that Robert being raised by me, in an uncertain situation, living a hand-to-mouth existence and not being able to think far ahead in terms of eating and keeping a roof over our heads? Honestly? I felt sure she'd be happy to see him with a prosperous couple, a man with his own business, his own property, his wife already adoring Robert and desperate to give him a future containing her love and all the material comforts she and her husband could provide. And the best for me surely didn't mean sacrificing my own life for maybe eighteen years, until Robert was old enough to fend for himself and I was middle-aged, past my best years.

I made my decision, and the deal was done soon afterwards. It wasn't a formal adoption, because when Kathleen and Pat had tried before Social Services hadn't been convinced they weren't still trying for their own biological child, which went against them. Some years had passed since then, so they could have applied again, but in the interval Kathleen had been involved in an incident at the school where she worked, that of a child with a grudge against the staff. Kathleen had been cleared of any inappropriate behaviour, but she was still worried that the accusation might go against her.

I was happy with the treatment my half-sibling received from the Farrells, and had no qualms about them taking over as his parents. I was stunned when they made their financial offer. Eighty-thousand pounds! I couldn't believe my luck. It was a considerable amount back then, and even these days it's a significant sum. Not only was Robert—who I was ashamed of not loving enough, given who his father was—to be taken off my hands, but I'd have a huge sum of money to kick-start a life of my own. I agreed before they changed their minds, and it was settled.

Left to my own devices I stopped cleaning for Kathleen and Pat, through a mutual agreement that it'd be best to cut close ties so that Robert could get used to my absence. I found a flat to rent in a better area and took it for a year, which I thought would be a good time-frame in which to map out a life-path. I didn't know what that would be, and decided to take a well-earned few months out to think about it when my GCSE courses finished the next month. I wasn't going to blow my new-made fortune, no way. I was far too careful with money, I'd always had to be, and I was aware it wouldn't enable me to live without working for the rest of my life. But I'd never had anything at all by way of a social life, until recently. I'd gone from school to working as a shelf-stacker to help Mum support us both, and then she'd gone and I'd been left holding the baby and working every hour I could just to keep the wolf from the door and give Robert a start in life.

I'd given him that now. Loving parents, a home in a prestigious postcode and the certainty that he'd never go short of anything. Patrick Farrell was a self-made man with a business he'd built from scratch after starting out labouring on somebody else's building site. If he couldn't have his own biological children he'd made up for it in material wealth, but now he and Kathleen had a son, who they'd love, and provide for in excess. Some might say I should've felt guilty for selling my own flesh and blood, but I didn't. Providing for one's own could come in more ways than one, I felt, and this was the way that had come to me. If Robert ever met and questioned me in the future I was confident I could look him in the eye and justify my actions.

In the meantime there was my own future to consider. I continued with my evening courses and social life with my new-found friends, plus I found work in a bar for several shifts each week. Nothing too strenuous, no waiting tables, just pulling pints, pouring wine and spirits, opening mixers and getting to chat to people as I did so. It helped pay the rent and kept me from dipping too deep into my nest-egg. Life was better than it had ever been, apart from when my mother was alive and it was just the two of us. Then, love had made up for the lack of money, and now I had the money but not the love. There was no such thing as the perfect life, I decided.

And then I met Him, and my new life took a different course.

25: PENNY

She'd never forget the sight that'd greeted her, of Jennifer slumped against the side of the bath, the empty pill bottle by her side. Penny hadn't hesitated, kneeling and shaking her daughter-in-law, shouting her name, willing her to respond until she groaned, her head lolling forward across her chest.

'Jennifer! Jennifer! Wake up, stay with me, come on now.'

The eyes tried to open, the irises rolling backwards to leave rather bloodshot whites on show.

'Jennifer! Tell me! You took these pills, didn't you? Didn't you? How many did you take? Was it a full jar? I need to know.'

'Ha—oooh.'

The attempt at speech didn't make it any further, the eyes closing and the head drooping to the side. Supporting her with one arm, Penny scrabbled around with the other, searching for her bag which she'd dropped in her haste. Groping around inside she located her phone, then made a fast call.

'Ambulance, please. Yes. Yes. Overdose, yes, I think. My daughter-in-law, I just found her, on the bathroom floor, and there's an empty pill bottle. I don't know how many were in there, but I don't think it was full. She can't speak to tell me. I've managed to wake her, but only just, and she's very groggy.'

More of the same, name and address given and

instructions given back. Then it was a frantic time, hauling the dead—please God, no—weight of Jennifer to her feet and dragging her around the room, keeping her shuffling around, the closest she could come to a walk after Penny'd unceremoniously stuck her fingers down her resisting throat over the bath, to bring forth a stream of vomit. A good thing in this situation, even if some of it had splashed back and over the arm supporting her head. No time to worry about that now, she'd clean up once Jennifer was in the hands of the professionals.

The children. Mid-stagger along the landing Penny remembered, so led her semi-supine charge back to the bathroom, leaning her against the wall and balancing her there whilst retrieving her phone, which she'd left on the floor whilst getting Jennifer upright.

'Hello. This is Mrs Fairfield—no, their grandmother—yes, that's right. Look, I'm supposed to be collecting the children now, but there's an emergency at home—no, that's alright, it's being dealt with. It's their mother, she'd been taken ill—no, please don't alarm them, just tell them there's been a road accident and I'm stuck in the traffic, something like that. Is there somewhere you can keep them safe, until I can get there? I'll be as fast as I can, but right now I'm waiting for the ambulance—A detention class? They won't like that, but it'll have to do. Perhaps they could do their homework in there? That'd be great, thanks so much. I'll call and update you when—another number? Yes, please, that'll be good. Could you text it to me, please? I hear the ambulance so I have to go. Thank you.'

It was true, thank God. The siren was getting closer, and then the reflection of the flashing blue light rotated against the window. She laid Penny down on the floor, sprinting down to open the door and admit the paramedics.

*****

Later that evening, Bella and Toby back at home, fed, watered and in bed, the dogs likewise and the cat beside her on the sofa, Penny lay back in the armchair and considered the frantic events of the afternoon. She was desperate for a drink, which was surely permissible in the circumstances, but she'd contented herself with coffee. She was in charge of the children, Matt being at the hospital keeping an eye on Jennifer. They hadn't wanted to go to bed, bless them, and she'd had a hell of a job to make them go. Despite the best efforts of the school secretary to whom Penny'd spoken, they'd been spooked by the whole thing, and no wonder.

After following the ambulance to the hospital—she'd wanted to go inside, with Jennifer, but realised the need to take her car—there'd been the rush beside the trolley on which they'd deposited Jennifer. The paramedics had done so much at the house, pumped her stomach, checked her vital signs and so forth, but she needed to be admitted. Matt had been waiting at the door. Penny had called him on the hands-free once on the road, trying to keep calm so as not to worry him too much, which he had good reason to do, his wife having just overdosed.

'What the hell happened?'

She struggled to keep up as he marched along, his hand on her arm, beside the trolley which bore Jennifer along.

'I found her on the bathroom floor. She must have taken the wrong pills. The prescription Paracetamol were there at the front of the medicine cabinet, but she must have picked up the sleeping tablets by mistake. You know how many headaches she's been having, and how out of it she is on occasions.'

A lie, of course, but Penny wasn't ready to tell the truth, now or perhaps ever. She'd need to think about that.

She felt his fingers tighten around her arm, saw his jaw lock before he spoke.

'I curse myself for giving her those bloody sleepers. I thought I was helping.'

They arrived at the door to the emergency room, stopping to let the staff wheel Jennifer inside. She touched his arm with gentle fingers.

'It wasn't your fault. She wasn't well, not sleeping was making her worse. You did what seemed best. She's alive, they're going to get her better. Don't beat yourself up, Matt, please.'

Words failed him. He leaned down and kissed her instead.

'Whatever. Thanks for being there for her. Now—'

He looked into the room, then back at Penny.

'Sorry to do this, Mum, but I think you'd better wait out here.'

'No problem. I need to go and clean up a little.'

She indicated a Ladies room across the corridor.

'Then I'll be back. And Matt—'

He turned, halfway through the door.

'Let me know as soon as possible. I need to go and get the children from school.'

'Jesus Christ, I'd completely forgotten them. What—'

'Don't worry, I phoned the school. They're looking after them, but I should collect them soon or they'll start to worry. They don't know what's happened; they think I was stuck in a major traffic jam.'

'Okay. Right.'

He closed his eyes, running a hand over his forehead and through his hair.

'Would you mind going for them now? I'll be here for Jen, you have your phone, so I'll keep you in the loop. Would you be able to stay, for as long as it takes? Sort them out, feed them, you know?'

'Of course.'

His smile was wan as he moved towards her, but she was already halfway to the toilets.

'Go, go. Jennifer.'

She blew him a kiss, then did what she needed in the bathroom. She was busting for the loo by now, and the wet wipes she always kept in her handbag sorted the sleeve out, for the time being. Then she was off to the school, all gratitude to the staff, delaying any explanations to the children until she'd got them home. She came to the point once they were back; no putting it off any longer. She herded them into the kitchen as they looked at each other, exchanging enquiring glances at this unusual turn of events.

How to tell them? No point in messing about, so she gave it to them straight; her own version, of course.

'Right. The thing is, there was no traffic delay. Your mother's had an accident. No, no, it's okay, she's alright. I found her when I got here and called an ambulance. They've admitted her and she's going to be fine. They're keeping her in, and your father's with her.'

'What happened?'

They spoke in unison, stock still, eyes wide.

'She meant to take some headache pills, but got hold of the wrong bottle; they're very similar, you know. I found her in the bathroom, it couldn't have been long afterwards. She was very groggy, but managed to bring most of them back up. But we got her to hospital in time and she'll be fine.'

They looked relieved, to some extent, if not entirely convinced.

'The really bad news is that you're stuck with me looking after you for the foreseeable future.'

Her attempt at levity lifted the mood a little, but not a lot.

'Your father's going to keep us informed, so the best thing we can do is carry on as close to normal as possible. So how about you go get changed and I'll make dinner?'

They were full of questions, in need of reassurance, so she did what she could. Ordering takeaway pizza seemed like a good way to lift their spirits, so after some deliberation as to the merits of a meat feast with extra pepperoni over a four-cheese with extra gorgonzola and a plain margarita for Penny, the order was placed and they rushed upstairs to get washed and changed. Homework had been done at school, in detention, which gained them both "street cred," apparently, so there wasn't much to do but eat, drink and watch some favourite films, interspersed with occasional worried enquires as to the welfare of their mother.

A phone call from Matt calmed their fears, with him talking on loudspeaker before short personal conversations with each of them. Finally they'd been despatched to bed, there to stay awake and play on their phones, if so desired. Penny wasn't going to check up on them, she was more tired than usual, which wasn't a surprise given the day she'd had. Now she sipped her coffee and wondered at what had happened.

Why had Jennifer taken an overdose? Because despite what she'd told Matt about the mix-up of tablets, Penny was convinced this hadn't been the case. The headache pills were in the cabinet, but on the shelf above the sleeping pills, so it wasn't a case of picking up the bottle next to the one required. It was still a possibility, of course, but Penny didn't think so. Jennifer hadn't been herself at all lately, hence her own increased presence in the house and general life of the family; but Penny was sure there was more going on that just being too busy and not getting enough sleep. She wasn't one to go on intuition that often—it not having served her well in the past—but in this case she had a gut feeling, and it wasn't down to being an interfering mother-in-law.

What could be so bad that Jennifer would want to kill herself? Penny'd had some bad times in the past, in her distant youth and more recent years, but nothing had ever made her want to end it all. Whatever it was that'd made Jennifer attempt suicide, or a cry for help, at the very least, what was Penny going to do about it?

'Mum?'

'Matthew.'

She hadn't heard his key in the lock, hadn't heard him come in, she'd been so tired and engrossed in her own thoughts. She rose and went to him.

'How is she?'

'Sleeping now, and they're keeping her overnight, at least. They intubated her, and put her on a ventilator, but she's responding well. It wasn't too bad, as these things go. Good job you found her so soon, and did all the right things.'

He slumped onto the sofa, closed his eyes and breathed out, hard. She sat beside him, put her arm around his shoulders. He relaxed against her for a long moment, then pulled away.

'I've got to get back. I just wanted to check on you and the kids.'

'You look exhausted. Have you eaten? I'll make you something.'

'No, I should go back. What if she wakes and I'm not there?'

'I'm sure they'll call you. Call them now, to check. You need to keep your strength up.'

He didn't speak but got out his phone, finding and hitting the number. A short exchange ascertained that Jennifer was sleeping peacefully, and without assistance now too. The nurse would be straight on to him if there was any change. He disconnected the call, his shoulders dropping.

'Okay. Just something fast.'

'Cheese on toast?'

'Good.'

He followed her into the kitchen, despite her entreaties that he stay comfortable on the sofa, sitting at the table absently stroking the heads of Duke and Prince while she rustled up a fast supper along with a mug of strong tea. He'd almost finished his meal when first Toby, then Bella, appeared at the door, hesitating uncertainly before running to him as he put down his knife and fork and wiped his mouth.

While Matt gave an update and reassurances to the children, Penny busied herself clearing away his dishes.

'Will you—?'

'No, I have to get back. I'll spend the night beside her. Are you okay to stay?'

'Of course. As long as you need me.'

He walked the children upstairs and saw them back to bed.

'I'm sorry to put this on you, Mum.'

'Don't be ridiculous. What are mothers for?'

'You haven't been home or anything. Will your place be alright? You didn't know you wouldn't be going back today.'

'It's fine. I never leave the dishwasher going, or the oven on, or anything like that, when I go out. No sense in asking for trouble.'

'I don't know how long it'll be, but I should have an idea by the morning.'

'Whatever. I'll be here, give them breakfast, take them to school, maybe then pop home for a change of clothes. You focus on Jennifer and getting her back where she should be.'

He reached out and hugged her, hard, as he hadn't done in many years.

Then he was gone.

26: MADGE

She leaned back and relaxed against the leather seat, which still had that reassuring new smell lingering on it. She caught the cabbie's eye in the mirror, then looked away. He's not looking at you, he's checking the traffic behind us. She closed her eyes, satisfied with her day so far.

The lunch had been delicious, the Sole Véronique exquisite, and she'd allowed herself more white wine than she usually would. Nothing wrong in over-indulging on occasion, and today she'd been in the mood. Good food, wine and conversation, girls' talk, without the need to play to a male audience, although there had been a few men congregating in the bar when she'd finished her coffee while waiting for her cab. She'd run into that chap again, the one she could swear she knew from elsewhere, and they'd exchanged smiles as they passed in the hallway. She'd spoken to him about it in the past:

"Excuse me for asking, but I'm sure I know you from somewhere."

"From here, I suppose."

His tone was laconic, and Madge wasn't accustomed to that. She'd persisted.

"Yes, but I'm convinced we've met somewhere else, other than here. You look familiar."

This time he'd smiled.

"Well, I've been told I look like Cary Grant, if that helps."

"'That must be it then.''

But she'd known it wasn't.

Since then they'd traded brief greetings whenever they met, but Madge still couldn't place him. Maybe it was the Cary Grant thing after all. She'd shrugged it off and forgotten about it. If there was another connection it'd come to her in time, she was sure.

'Just here alright, love?'

The taxi driver was slowing as he approached her house.

'Yes, that's fine. Just over here, yes, thank you,'

She paid him and descended onto the driveway. Frank must still be out, as his car wasn't there. She walked up to the front door, rummaging inside her handbag for her keys.

Humming gently to herself she unlocked the door and pushed it open, to step inside.

27: PENNY

It wasn't long after Matt returned to the hospital that Penny took herself off to sleep in one of the spares. She treated herself to a shower—she hadn't seen hot water or soap for what seemed like an eternity—and borrowed a dressing gown of Matt's from where it hung behind the door to the master room. She didn't like to take Jennifer's, although she'd be obliged to take a pair of her panties in the morning. They'd be a little tight, Penny was sure, but at least they'd be fresh.

In the event she borrowed a blouse and jacket too, her own in need of serious cleaning after she'd managed to get puke over the sleeve yesterday. They were all up early, the children unsettled by the situation, and Penny couldn't blame them. Washed, dressed, breakfast eaten, books and bags found, she got them into her car and safely into school. A fast trip to her own apartment—well, Simon and Dan's—for a check that all was in order, as well as a change of clothes, then she returned to Matt's place to clean up the en-suite bathroom after yesterday's scene in there. She hadn't felt it right to leave the children alone during the evening, so she'd just locked it to stop Toby and Bella wandering in and seeing the state it was in.

Mrs Jenkins was due today, she realised, so rang and stopped her, explaining about Jennifer's accident and it probably not being a good idea for the cleaner to come in until the situation was sorted. The house wouldn't die from a bit of dust, and she was sure Mrs J could find plenty else to do; and of course she'd be paid. The dogs could go into the garden until Penny had time to walk them later.

Bathroom sorted, and the medicine cabinet emptied of incriminating evidence, Penny was just putting the breakfast things into the dishwasher when Matt called.

'They're letting me bring her home, so that's something. I hate to ask, Mum, but could you come and get us? I've been up most of the night and I'm not safe to drive.'

'On my way.'

She hadn't been so useful in such a long time, Penny mused as she navigated the traffic on the ring road. It was a good feeling; and then she reproached herself, given what it'd cost her family for her to have that feeling. Still, she'd be there for as long as she was needed, which was for a few days more at least, given the paleness of Jennifer and the dark circles under Matt's eyes when she found them waiting in the reception area. They could've gone to Matt's office to wait in private, but he didn't want to advertise what'd happened to the colleagues he had to work with every day, Penny realised.

They sat together in the back while Penny drove. Conversation was rather strained, although Matt did his best and Jennifer joined in, in a somewhat wan and faint way. Comments were firmly centred on the children, were they eating, doing their homework, not watching unsuitable TV, that sort of thing. Penny answered in a positive tone, but then lapsed into silence to concentrate on the road, with an answering silence from the back seat. Jennifer had closed her eyes, she noticed in the rear-view mirror, while Matt had his arm around her as she leaned against his shoulder.

He took her straight to bed when they got back, refusing Penny's offer of tea. She made herself busy in the kitchen until he returned downstairs.

'She's sleeping, and I think I'll grab a few hours myself.

That way I'll be there if she needs anything.'

'Only a few hours? You look like you could use the whole day, especially given that you hardly slept last night.'

'No, I need to go back in later, check that things are going okay. Bradley's doing a good job covering for me, but it's not fair to put too much on him. And, of course, I need to collect my car.

'Sorry, Mum, I hate to ask again, but would you mind being here for the day? If you want to get home I can manage. This whole thing isn't fair on you either.'

'Don't be silly. Of course I'll stay. There's plenty I can get done here, the laundry for starters, and I need to take the dogs out.'

'You're a star. Could you wake me in about two hours? I'll need a lift back to the hospital, and the kids will need collecting from school.'

'Could you take a taxi? And send one for the children. I don't like to leave Jennifer on her own so soon.'

She didn't say "in case she tries it again."

'Sorry, Mum, I wasn't thinking straight. I'll call Bob in the village; we always use him if we need a cab. If I time it right he can drop me off and get Toby and Bella on the way back.'

He yawned, covering his mouth too late for good manners.

'Better get off to bed then. Are you sure—?'

'Don't worry about me. I'll set an alarm to wake you. Go, go.'

He didn't need telling twice, but disappeared up the stairs without looking back.

Penny made a coffee. She needed the break before she did anything else, not being used to such activity, satisfying as it might be. She lingered over it, indulging in some biscuits for good measure, then set to and put on a load of laundry before tidying up around the kitchen and lounge and checking the cupboards to make some sort of shopping list. Duke and Prince had to make do with a good run in the meadow at the end of the lane, because the two-hour period flew by; then the alarm was going as she was finishing off some sandwiches for Matt. She'd have liked to make him something more substantial, but she knew her son and realised he'd probably want these boxed-up to take with him.

She crept up the stairs and into the room, not wishing to wake Jennifer as well as Matt, then shook him gently by the shoulder.

'What? Oh hell, is it that time already?'

She put a finger to her lips, indicating the sleeping Jennifer at his side. He put a hand to his mouth and climbed out of bed with care, following Penny from the room and pointing towards the main bathroom down the corridor. There's be less chance of him waking his wife in there.

Penny had a mug of tea ready beside the sandwiches when he came down, dressed in more casual fashion than he'd adopt for work on a normal day; but this wasn't a normal day. To her surprise he sat and drank the tea, wolfing down the sandwiches with one eye on the window, watching for the taxi. Then Bob was stopping at the end of the drive, and Matt was dropping a brief kiss on Penny's cheek before rushing out to climb into the back. A quick wave and he was gone, the sound of the engine disappearing up the road as she made her way back into the house.

The trip to the hospital the cabbie had to take, with the detour to the school and return from there, meant Penny had an hour or so to pass before Toby and Bella were home. How to spend it? Putting the mug and plate into the dishwasher took seconds before she turned, surveying the kitchen to find something to do; but she didn't need to.

Jennifer appeared in the doorway, clad in dressing gown and slippers, hair mussed from sleep. For a long moment they looked at each other, then Penny sped to the younger woman's side.

'You shouldn't be up. Let's sit you down.'

She made as though to steer her towards the lounge, but instead Jennifer took one of the stools at the kitchen island.

'I'll be fine. I need to start getting back into it all.'

'Will you have some tea? And biscuits, or something more? You must be hungry,'

'Tea will be fine, thanks, although I should be making it for you.'

'Nonsense. You've been—unwell. I'm happy to help until you've got your strength back.'

She turned and busied herself making two mugs of tea, adding a plate of biscuits despite Jennifer's refusal. They sat in silence. Penny didn't know what to say, but then Jennifer spoke.

'You told Matt I took the wrong pills. By mistake.'

'Yes.'

All at once Penny became very interested in the contents of her mug.

'I have to thank you.'

Their eyes met.

'You know that wasn't what happened, don't you?'

'I didn't—I mean—It's none of my business, but I didn't want—'

'It's okay, Penny.'

She'd never called her by name before. She didn't usually call Penny anything, except "Gran" when talking about her to the children.

Silence.

'It'd have been embarrassing for Matt to have the whole hospital, the entire community, know that the female half of the perfect couple had attempted suicide. You limited the damage, and I'm grateful.'

'That wasn't my intention. I mean, yes. It's private, nobody's business outside this family. I care about you, Jennifer; I mean, I know we've had our differences. But you're my son's wife, and a good one, and the mother of his children. I don't want you to come to harm; any of you.'

She tried not to sound judgemental, but couldn't help the thought that Jennifer succeeding in her attempt would have left the children without a mother.

Jennifer looked away, inclining her head for a moment.

'I don't want to pry; it's not my place. But if there's something wrong between you and Matt—'

'There isn't. Not yet, anyway.'

'Whatever it is, Jennifer, I'm not asking. It's none of my business. But you ought to tell Matt, he deserves to know. You need to talk to him. He loves you, surely you can share it with him. Let him help you, get outside assistance if necessary. I can't bear to think there's something so bad that you—that you did this—the only way out. You know what I mean.'

'I do. But oh, Penny. How can I tell him?'

'You tried to kill yourself, Jennifer, and that suggests there's something seriously wrong somewhere. Whether it's about him or not, Matt deserves to know. God knows I've made a mess of my marriage, all my relationships with men. I wouldn't want to see you end up like me.'

She'd said it. Admitted more than she'd ever wanted to, even to herself; what did that mean? This wasn't the time, however; there was Jennifer to be helped. She was looking at Penny, her eyes vacant, as though not seeing her at all.

She slumped forward, head in hands, and then Penny was by her side, standing while the woman on the high stool leaned over against her, crying on her shoulder in the most literal manner.

The storm of weeping lasted a few moments, then

subsided. Penny put both arms about her, pulled her in again her chest and stood, stroking her hair.

'Whatever happens, I'll be here for you, I promise. You won't get rid of me that easily.'

A sniffle and a small smile rewarded her efforts.

'You can't be comfortable there. Come.'

Jennifer allowed herself to be led like a small child, taken into the lounge and seated on the sofa. Penny made as though to return to the kitchen, but the hands of the other wouldn't let her go.

'Stay. Please.'

Seating herself, Penny put out her arms and drew the younger woman in towards her, keeping them around her as Jennifer relaxed into her embrace. She leaned against Penny, who held her, idly stroking her hair in a rhythmic and soothing manner. She lost track of time as they sat like that, until the silence was broken by the sound of a car drawing up outside, then the sound of running over the gravel, a key in the lock. Jennifer sat bolt upright.

'The children. Oh heavens, I look a mess. I wanted to be dressed and tidy for them.'

'They don't care about that. They just want their mum back.'

Bella and Toby burst into the room, and into their mother's arms. Over their heads her eyes met Penny's, and the latter saw promise in them.

Let's hope she and Matt could sort this out. Whatever it was.

28: FRANK

Everything was ready. He'd been over a couple of days ago, while Madge was away, and made sure. Today was D-Day, and he wasn't looking forward to it, even though Madge ought to be in a good mood when he broached the subject at last. He hadn't dared, when she'd returned from her book-club away-day and stopover the morning after. She'd been a bit grumpy, not like her usual self, hadn't said a lot but declared her intention to go to bed for a couple of hours. "I'm just tired," she'd said, managing a weak smile and a peck on his cheek before disappearing upstairs. Hungover, he'd deduced, a drop too much the previous night, and whereas most people slept the sounder for that, for Madge it had the opposite effect.

He'd left it for today, therefore. Madge had a lunch to attend, an all-ladies affair at the golf club, and she always enjoyed those. Frank had dropped her off earlier, before playing a round he'd had arranged. Usually he'd pick her up, or collect her, but today he was finished before she was, so she'd get a taxi home later. He'd take the bull by the horns and confront her when she got back, while she was mellow from wine, although it was likely she wouldn't stay that way for long, given what he had to tell her. If things turned nasty he could decamp to the apartment without further delay. The rest could be sorted out later.

To give himself courage for the inevitable confrontation

he'd come around to check the place over again, to remember how it'd been living here before and think about how it'd be to live here again. Alone, with no-one to please but himself; and he knew how to find company if he wanted it.

He could see as he came up the final flight of stairs from the entrance hall that the apartment door wasn't properly aligned. He knew how it ought to sit, he'd lived here for long enough. He speeded up, took the last few stairs two at a time, was over the landing and pushing the door. It swung inwards and he entered at speed, only to stop abruptly at the sight which met him.

His gasp was audible at the scene of utter devastation before him. The hallway mirror smashed, the console table beneath it broken, as though an axe had been taken to it. The coat-stand by the door had been treated in a similar manner. The bare bulb swung from the ceiling by its cable, the lampshade which had hung there in tatters on the floor.

He moved along the hallway and gazed into the bathroom. Another smashed mirror, the toilet seat and upper body in pieces as though a lump-hammer had been used on it. The new bath and basin featured deep scratches criss-crossing the porcelain glaze; the work of a sharp knife, Frank presumed. He surveyed the broken picture frames on the floor of both hallway and bathroom, then froze. Was whoever'd done this still here? He moved on, peered into the bedroom on the left, the living-room and kitchen area on the right. He'd been a soldier, had served in the Falklands war and in Iraq; a vandal or two held no fear for him. Whether his physical fitness at his advanced years would have matched his bravery wasn't put to the test, fortunately, as there was no one in the place but him.

He heard a noise and jumped, not with fear but shock at the unexpected sound. He re-entered the hallway and approached the front door, from whence the hesitant knocking had come.

'Frank?'

It was Emma, his neighbour of many years, who still kept an eye on the place for him. She entered, tentative, looking around with disbelief. He took her arm and steered her into the living room, where together they surveyed the mess of slashed curtains and sofa, smashed TV screen, china and glass, dented fridge-freezer and kitchen cabinets, splintered table, chairs and picture frames, with what looked like burns all over the carpet. A strong smell of bleach hung over the whole.

'Oh Frank, what on earth happened here?'

Emma was aghast, as was he; angry too. All that work, all that money, and for what? He controlled himself.

'Did you hear anything?'

'I've not been here for a few days, I've been staying with my sister. She's not been well, needed a bit of looking after. I've only just got back. I didn't hear anything before I went.'

She was apologetic, as though personally responsible.

'Not your fault.'

His mind raced over what he needed to do. Call the police, was top of the list, so he did that, then went with Emma, at her suggestion, to wait in her place.

'You can't do anything here right now. You shouldn't even sit down. It's a crime scene, there'll be fingerprints, footprints, forensic evidence to be collected.'

His smile was faint. It was clear she watched detective dramas, with their current trend for forensic detail. He followed her as she led the way next door, to make him a consolatory coffee, as if that would do the job. He paused on the way, bending down to look at the broken picture frames. The photographs themselves seem to have only minimal damage. He returned to the bedroom, checking the frames there, fallen amongst the scattered duck-down from the shredded duvet and pillows. His erotic art prints. Like the photographs, those souvenirs of his seventy-plus years of life, they had survived. He was glad. A present from a long-ago lover, they meant much to him.

Frank supposed he'd better leave them where they were, although he desperately wanted to salvage them. That could be classed as interfering with a crime-scene, and possibly erasing evidence which could lead the police to whoever did this. Reluctant to leave, he went next door, where Emma provided hot drinks and awkward conversation to pass the time until the police arrived. He was conscious of being in her way. His problem wasn't hers, and she needed to get on with whatever she had to do, especially if she'd just arrived back from a trip away.

'You don't need me here. I'll go back next door and wait.'

She wouldn't hear of it. It was her problem too, she insisted. They were neighbours, and if his flat had been burgled hers could very well be next. She made him sit down and provided more coffee, and although he'd had more than the two cups per day he allowed himself, this was nothing like a normal day and he felt he deserved it.

While Emma went through to the bedroom to unpack, and whatever else she needed to do, his racing mind arrived at the ramifications of what this meant in terms of his moving back into the flat and instigating divorce proceedings from Madge. It was obvious that would have to be put on hold for now, and he wasn't proud of the feeling that he'd be using her; but what other choice did he have? His life was here, he couldn't very well go and land on Matt and Jennifer for an indefinite period; not that they wouldn't be glad to have him, but they had their own lives without an extra body creating work, even if his daughter-in-law was the perfect housekeeper, alongside her many other talents.

His phone rang. He looked at it, hoping for the police but

getting Madge; strange, as he'd just been thinking about her. He answered, ready to give her the news of the break-in, but he never got that far. Instead, he listened to his hysterical wife crying down the phone to him.

29: MATT/JENNIFER

The hotel was the last word in luxury, on top of a hill with its own beautifully-laid-out grounds, numerous varieties of trees, plants and flowers, with exotic species which could thrive in this sunny and south-westerly corner of England. The views over the Channel were stunning, and it'd be quite possible to spend the entire time up there, with the Michelin-starred hotel restaurant boasting the best cuisine to be had. The hotel had its own courtesy cars, however, to whisk guests down to the quaint seaside town which lay at the bottom of the cliffs, there to enjoy something more rustic and local.

They'd done the latter this evening, strolling along beside the sea before eating langoustine and crabs at a small harbourside bistro, washing it all down with white wine and finishing with Cornish ice-cream.

'Coffee here? Or back up top? I could use a good brandy.'

'Here, I think. The hotel's lovely, don't get me wrong, but down here there's more atmosphere; local colour in abundance.'

Matt pushed back his chair and relaxed into it, raising his hands behind his head in a fluid motion which managed to summon a waiter on the way there. Order given, he threw back his head to gaze up at the stars.

'Such a clear night, see those stars! The weather gods have been kind to us.'

Jennifer looked up. Such a mass of stars, planets, meteors,

satellites too, with one moving past right then. Stretching out into infinity and beyond, as Toby always said, the influence of the *Toy Story* films having stayed with him since his childhood. What did the affairs of the people down here matter, when set in the context of the universe? We're nothing, she thought, small as atoms, less than atoms, so why do we worry so much about our little lives?

She was worried, despite the break she was enjoying with Matt. He'd been marvellous, booking this at a moment's notice, arranging leave from the hospital, putting aside his concerns over the burnt-down clinic and focussing on her alone. I'm so lucky to have him, there are women who'd give their right arm for such a man; and I feel like a total fraud, because he doesn't know the truth. He'd accepted without question the version which Penny had given him; and there was another surprise, her mother-in-law coming on-side with Jennifer, so non-judgemental but so right at the same time.

Matt deserved the truth, although she got that strange trembling feeling inside whenever she contemplated telling him. She'd steeled herself twice already, when the moment seemed good, but she'd funked it both times. They'd be going home tomorrow, so she needed to get it done and over with, face the music and clear the air, take whatever consequences were forthcoming, negative thought they might be.

It had to be tonight.

*****

The bill had been paid, the hotel car summoned and now they were in their suite, taking off their shoes, preparing for bed. Jennifer stood at the window, looking out at the grounds, the strategically-placed lights in green and red reflecting off the trees and flowers in their paths.

It had to be. Now or never. Before her courage deserted her.

She felt the light touch of his footsteps on the carpet, his arms going around her as he pressed himself against her back. She relaxed against him, almost giving in the impulse of the moment. Then she pushed herself away, turning to face him where he stood, his brow wrinkled, his eyes darkened.

'We need to talk. About what happened.'

He was silent for a moment, his eyes lowered.

'Do we really need to? I mean, it happened, it was awful, but it's past. It's been wonderful, here with you, you're so much better than you were. I'm here for you, Jen, we all are. We can put it behind us. It was an unfortunate accident, Jen, but it's in the past.'

'It wasn't.'

'Wasn't what?'

His voice was almost a whisper. She couldn't meet his eyes.

'An accident.'

It came out louder than she'd intended, and then her face crumbled and the tears came. He looked at her, eyes wide, mouth open, then took her in his arms and steered her to the sofa. She leaned against him, crying for all she was worth as he held her close, stroking her back, head leaned against hers until the storm of weeping subsided.

'Why, Jen?'

She didn't raise her head, nor did he attempt to.

'I've been getting hate messages. On my email.'

Then he did move from her, turning her head to look at him. She raised her eyes, then lowered them again.

'Why didn't you tell me? I could have helped.'

'I couldn't. You have so much on, I didn't want to trouble you. I thought if I ignored it, it would go away. But it didn't, and it kept on—'

She started sobbing again. He waited until she'd regained control.

'How long has it been going on? Is this what it's all been about? You being off-colour, losing sleep, all of it? Oh Jen, why didn't you tell me?'

'I couldn't. I was so ashamed.'

'Why? You'd done nothing—'

'But—'

She couldn't bear to look at him, her voice a whisper when she spoke.

'I had.'

He was silent, digesting that. She stumbled on.

'I never said I didn't have relationships before I met you, did I?'

'No. Neither did I. I guess we both assumed we'd been with others before. I never spoke about mine because, well, there didn't seem any need. I knew when I met you that you were the one. But—.'

Her lips quivered. She didn't look at him when she spoke again.

'He was a photographer. Professional. There were—photos.'

'Ah. You mean—'

'Intimate.'

'And he's been sending them to you.'

'No. Not him. But someone has.'

'Why not him?'

'I searched for him. He's been dead a few years.'

'How old was he?'

'About five years older than me.'

'So how did he die?'

He had to lean in much closer to hear her reply.

'Substance abuse. He was a regular user. Class A drugs.

Accidental overdose.'

They were both silent, digesting the irony of that.

'So who—'

'I don't know.'

She broke again, everything flooding out.

'It's been horrible. Oh Matt, I got one and ignored it, and then another, and then they went quiet, and then another one, then another break. Every time I thought they'd gone away they'd be back, playing with me.'

'Did they ask for money?'

'No. Even if they had, I couldn't have paid them without you knowing, could I? Our accounts are joint. It's like they were trolling me, having fun torturing me.'

'And the pictures. You say they were—'

'Explicit. Yes.'

'And they could pop up anywhere, any time.'

'Yes.'

He'd stopped stroking her hair, and went silent. It lasted for so long that she pulled away from him, frightened to see his eyes, gazing before him, looking but not seeing, blank. She squeezed his hands, wanting some reaction, but still he sat, with unfocussed stare.

'Matt.'

She stood, the movement catching his attention. He turned in her direction, shook his head, focussed on her.

'We can get through this, can't we?'

The light had gone out of her face, her mouth turned downwards, forehead wrinkled, dark damp circles beneath her eyes. He wanted to go to her, but he wasn't ready just yet.

'I don't know. I'm sorry, Jen I—look, I just need some time. You go to bed. It's been a long day. No, honestly, get some sleep. I just need to sit awhile. I'll be in soon.'

She didn't look happy, but she went anyway. She must be exhausted with it all.

Matt sat for a moment, then stood and fetched himself a whisky. He didn't resume his seat, but wandered to the window, staring out into the darkness but not seeing.

It was a lot to get his head around, and he couldn't help remembering the disgusting contents of the package his mother had received, along with the trolling of Pippa and Graham. If somebody was attacking Simon and Dan through them, causing distress to their parents, it was beginning to look as though Jen might be included. And what about the fire at the clinic? He'd been appraised by the police that arson was suspected, which put a very different colour on the thing.

Is somebody attacking us? And if so, who? Matt had no idea, and was too weary with everything to think straight. He needed another mind on it, and he hadn't bothered Jen with any of it, given the recent state of her health. As to his mother, she'd got over the incident at her apartment, or at least there'd been no repeat performance. He didn't want to worry her again.

His father. Frank hadn't been involved in any incidents. Matt would call him in the morning, let him in on it all and get his opinion. A problem shared is a problem halved, and even if Frank couldn't come up with any useful ideas at least he'd be supportive.

One thing at a time. First Matt needed to sort out his feelings about Jen. He'd always seen her as perfect, the wife, the mother, the upstanding member of the community with a finger in every pie for the enrichment of their collective lives. He ought to have known, he'd been to university, hadn't he? There's no such thing as perfect; he'd been told that often enough; but off he'd gone, out into the world looking for something that didn't exist, and when he thought he'd found it he'd married it. And here they were.

You're a fine one to talk.

The little voice in his head, the one he'd pushed to the

back and drowned out with something else whenever it raised its head, spoke now; and perhaps it was the darkness and the silence around him, but he had no resources to quiet it. Instead he listened to the shame of the past he kept buried under the minutiae of the present.

He'd had a girlfriend, Chloe, when he was in his final year at medical school, and they'd started a full-on relationship very soon after meeting; they were students, after all. While Matt was pretty much living with her he'd met Jennifer, and been attracted to her instantly. She'd turned him down the first time he'd asked her on a date, claiming a prior engagement, but her manner had suggested that a positive answer would be forthcoming were he to ask again. He'd played the game and she'd agreed to go out with him; but when she did she wouldn't go all the way. She'd allowed him to hold her and kiss her, but anything more was strictly forbidden. She was a lady in the old-fashioned sense, her manner implied.

He'd been going crazy, not the least with guilt because he was still continuing in his relationship with Chloe, and neither girl was aware of the existence of the other. His mother, appraised of the situation by his brother Simon, who'd found out God-only-knew how, took Matt to task when he sought refuge from his complicated love life in the bosom of his family one weekend.

"If you're serious about this Jennifer you ought to be honest with Chloe and finish things with her, darling, because it's not fair on either of them. I thought we'd raised you to be better than that."

Duly chastised, he returned to the fray, but rather than doing what his mother had suggested he asked Jennifer to marry him, after he'd graduated and taken up the internship which was waiting for him. She'd accepted, and responded by giving in at last to his wishes. He was in seventh heaven after their first evening together in her bedsit, but to his consternation several weeks later she'd told him her period was late. So they'd married, a fast registry office affair, and too soon as far as Matt's plans to be established with an income to support a wife were concerned; but as Jennifer had miscarried not long afterwards he wasn't burdened with the support of a child too.

And Chloe? To his shame Matthew remembered how he'd been too afraid to tell her what was going on, until Jennifer was pregnant and their marriage pending. He'd been living with Chloe in a student house in the town, sharing a double while three others inhabited the singles, and at last he'd plucked up the courage and told her in the privacy of their room. She'd gone white when he told her, but remained silent and dignified. No shouting, or swearing, or name-calling, just a quiet statement when he fell silent.

"I think you need to leave now. You can collect your stuff in the morning."

He'd left the room, and she'd closed the door firmly behind him. He'd gone to Jennifer, where he was welcome now they were almost man and wife, and moved in with her. When he'd returned to his old house the following day he found his belongings packed in the suitcases in which he'd first bought them there, and waiting in the communal kitchen downstairs. Chloe was out, one of his now ex-housemates informed him, and the door to the room he'd shared with her had a new lock which'd been fitted the previous evening. It was clear that money was no object, even for a penurious student, when getting rid of a cheating ex. Feeling even guiltier, Matt had pushed some banknotes he could ill-afford under the door, so Chloe wouldn't have to bear the whole cost, financial and emotional, for his betrayal. Then he'd handed over his front-door key and got out of there fast.

He'd felt like a rat, but tried to put that out of his mind as he carried on and got married. Jennifer had continued working, when early motherhood eluded her, but nevertheless the first few years were a bit rough in the financial sense, and no way would Matt approach his parents asking for a handout, even though he'd pay it back when that became possible. They'd come through it, and were now very comfortable indeed, meaning Matt was able to put his plans for the clinic in motion; and now the results lay in ashes. Divine justice, perhaps.

It was his guilt over Chloe that had pushed him on to succeed, he thought. The need to prove to himself that he was a decent person, that his treatment of her had been a mere youthful indiscretion, over which he shouldn't still be beating himself up. She'd survived the experience, after all. He'd heard later, on the old friends' grapevine, that she'd graduated with a first, then gone on to a Masters and followed up with a PhD. She'd taught for some years at a top-ten red-brick university and had two children by a don she'd met there who'd recognised a good thing when he saw it, and snapped her up. They were living happily ever after, it seemed, and Matt was glad things had worked out so well for her.

He still couldn't get rid of the feelings of shame brought on by memories of that period of his life, however. It offended his sense of himself as a man of honour, an upright member of the community, a husband and a father.

And look at yourself now, starting an affair with a woman almost old enough to be your mother. A friend of your parents, for God's sake, years older than you. What the hell were you thinking?

No, he was far from perfect. Why then should he expect perfection from Jen?

*****

She felt his arms go around her where she lay, sleepless and miserable. She felt his lips on the back of her neck as he spooned her from behind.

'I love you. Nothing else matters.'

She felt happiness flood back through her as she relaxed into his embrace. She decided she'd see a therapist, get over her fear of surgery, get her body sorted out.

She loved Matt. The damage to their relationship could be sorted too.

30: FRANK

She didn't wait for him to speak, but launched straight in, her distress obvious.

'We've had a break-in! I just got back and I heard noises! I thought it was you but your car wasn't there and—'

She paused and gulped, trying to get her breath and some control.

'I heard them as I came into the hall. I thought—but you weren't there—I went into the lounge—. It's awful, the patio doors are open, and I think I saw someone—'

She was weeping and gasping, and Frank had to work hard to make out what she was saying. When he understood, his first thought was for her.

'Get out of there now. They could still be in there. Go next door, Madge, calm down, get out, go to Nick and Imogen, go now, okay? Get them to call the police, tell them what's happened. Go now. Are you going?'

He cajoled her into leaving the house, walked her through the journey to their next-door neighbours, then made sure she was there.

'Is that Nick? Give him the phone, let me speak to him'.

Nick came on the line.

'Frank, is that you? What's going on? Madge is in a right state. Yes, it's okay, Imo's looking after her.'

So Frank told Nick what Madge had told him, asked him to call the police, said that he, Frank, would be back as soon as possible.

He couldn't take it in. Both his flat and Madge's house, vandalised within a day or two of each other. What were the chances of that? Emma was there, she'd heard his side of the urgent conversation and was looking at him, aghast.

'I'm afraid I'll have to impose on you some more.'

His explanation was apologetic. Emma was sound, a good friend as well as a neighbour. She took his key, when he'd secured the flat, and promised to deal with the police when they arrived. She'd got his mobile number, so would call him and he could talk to them, tell them of the double break-in too.

It took all his self-control to drive home without breaking the speed limit. He was torn. He needed to get home and make sure Madge was alright. She'd been almost hysterical on the phone, and no wonder; but in his head and heart he wanted to be back at his trashed property, speaking to the police, securing the place. He was angry. All that work, and the flat in a worse state than when he'd started. It was lucky he couldn't get his hands on whoever'd done this. Questions were racing through his mind. How had they got in? There was a communal front door with security, and a hall with post boxes for each flat. They'd have had to get through that even before they got to his own door.

Why had nobody seen them? There were two flats below on the ground floor, and two above on the second floor, with Emma next door on the first. Even though she'd been away, he'd have thought another of his upstairs or downstairs neighbours would've seen or heard something. He got on well with them, they'd all been living there for some years and had good relationships. Everybody looked out for each other and each other's property; no way could it have been an inside job. And Madge's home had been broken into as well. He couldn't think it a coincidence, but neither could he think that someone was deliberately targeting them out of malice.

Nick came straight out when Frank pulled up on the drive. It was clear he'd been looking out for his neighbour.

'Is Madge—?'

'Yes, she's okay, shaken, but Imo's with her. I've been inside; it looks as though she may have disturbed them. Thank God they ran away when they heard her, or it could have been nasty. I've alerted the police; they should be here soon.'

They entered Madge's house, and Frank saw what Nick meant. The lounge was in a similar condition to his flat. Slashed armchairs and curtains, smashed pictures, sideboard drawers emptied onto the floor and the contents ransacked and destroyed, shattered glasses and ripped tablecloths. But there the damage ended. The patio doors which led out to the back garden and thence onto the woods were wide open, the remnants of the curtains flapping in the breeze. It looked as though the intruders had entered and made their escape through these, as the metal frame of one door was buckled around the lock area, from the blunt force of a crowbar, Frank guessed.

A quick check of the rest of the place showed that no other rooms had been touched. It looked as though Madge had interrupted whoever had done this. It'd be possible to live here and repair the lounge in a relatively short time, once the police had done their work.

It was too much, coming right on the heels of the destruction of his place, and all of a sudden Frank felt tired, exhausted. He couldn't give in to it, however; there were things he had to do. He went next door with Nick, to find Madge being consoled by the resourceful Imogen. She was shaken, as Nick had said, but seemed to be making a brave effort to overcome her feelings. The police arrived soon after Frank and, with the usual effect of everything happening at once, his phone rang with a call from Emma, who now also had the police on site.

Another drive, more being torn over which crime scene he ought to be at. As he'd discovered the break-in at his flat and Madge had disturbed that at her house, it seemed logical that he'd return to his place. Nick and Imogen were only too willing to be there for Madge, and it wasn't fair to expect Emma to deal with the police on his behalf. To top it all off, the stomach issues which had been plaguing him recently returned, brought on by stress, he was sure. If he ever got hold of whoever did this—

*****

In the event, the results of the police investigations were inconclusive. They found no credible forensic evidence at either site; the perpetrator or perpetrators seemed to have been very careful to leave no traces. The downstairs neighbours at the flat had heard what sounded like the TV, or the radio, and a few banging noises; but as they were used to Frank being there renovating the place quite late on occasions, they'd just assumed it was him.

It was fortunate the house had been spared the liberal application of bleach which the flat had received, Madge apparently having disturbed the intruders before they could complete their activities. It was a more recent innovation in burglaries, the police told them, to destroy fingerprints—although they'd probably been wearing gloves—and any other tell-tale signs left behind; they were seeing more and more of it. Emma didn't hear about that on her TV programmes, Frank thought, inconsequentially, but then returned to the serious matter in hand.

Locks were duly changed, security cameras installed, although intruders would probably just spray those with paint to obscure any footage recorded. Any other security measure available was taken, but before that the mess at the house was cleaned up, there not being too much damage. Curtains and sofas needed to be replaced, true, but Madge enjoyed shopping and the insurance would pay for it all.

The flat would take far more time and energy, and Frank wasn't sure he had enough of the latter. There was also the cost, which would put a strain on his finances until the insurance payment came through. Madge wouldn't protest over him not paying his way in terms of everyday household costs, he knew, but he was determined to take no more from her than he had to. Instead he had a talk with Matt, embarrassing but necessary, especially as he and Jennifer had problems of their own at present, concerns over her health as well as the fire at the building site. He didn't quibble about a loan, and Frank was grateful for the tact and support of his son.

It cut both ways, because the morning after the vandalism of his and Madge's properties, Frank had received a call from Matt, fresh back from his trip away with Jennifer and now aware of the online harassment she'd suffered. He'd already told Frank about the fire at the building site, but now mentioned the suspicion of arson too, as well as what'd been going on with Jennifer, and the incidents involving Penny, Pippa and Graham; but not before his father had told of the attacks suffered by himself and Madge on their properties.

"It looks as though somebody's targeting us as a family," both were thinking, if not saying. But who? And why?

When they'd ended the call, Frank couldn't stop thinking about it. The damage was bad enough, but the idea that they'd all been deliberately singled out didn't bear thinking about. Who'd want to do this to them? To my family, he corrected himself, because the letter Pippa and Graham had received concerned Frank's son as well as their own. Prior to Matt's call he'd been concerned solely about himself and Madge, because both homes within hours of each other suggested some kind of vendetta, rather than random vandalism. But who? The thought went around and around in his head. Not everybody Frank had known over the years had liked him, and vice-versa, but he couldn't think he had any enemies who'd go to such lengths to demonstrate their dislike. Somebody who had it in for Madge? She couldn't think of anybody, when they discussed it. There were other men at the golf club who'd wanted a serious relationship with her, whose hopes had been dashed when Frank had stolen her out from under their noses; but it was hardly a reason to go on this sort of rampage.

Further, although they could understand somebody coming through the woods to access the house via the back garden, it was far more difficult to understand how they'd got into the flat. There was no CCTV, regrettably, but there was the security system, plus the lock to the flat itself; you'd think one or the other would have registered something, or prevented entry.

And now there was the information Matt had passed on, bringing the entire family into the affair. It wasn't a good feeling, knowing there was somebody out there who wished them ill. They had little immediate option, however, other than to take comfort from their increased security and get on with life as best as they could.

Yet Frank couldn't stop trying to work it out.

His family was in danger, and it was his responsibility to protect them.

31: MATT/ABBY

He couldn't leave it at that, of course. Couldn't just leave Abby dangling. Some men would, and he'd known too many who had, but that wasn't Matt's way. He was out of order, well out of line, and he knew it; he needed to tell Abby to her face that it was over. But how?

The university came to his rescue. Back at home, domestic harmony restored, he sat in his study and went through the backlog of emails which he'd left while getting Jen away to help her back to her old self. More than that, and unexpectedly, their relationship was better than it'd ever been, Jen even agreeing to work on getting her bodily problem fixed. If this blackmailer, or troll, or whatever the hell they were ever showed up again Jen wouldn't have to deal with them alone. They were a couple, and whatever transpired they'd face it together.

For now, fortunately, that piece of human garbage had gone quiet, and in the light of the clinic burning down Matt had put increased security in place at the family home. There was also the issue of the vandalism of his father and stepmother's properties, and the troll letter and package Pippa, Graham and his mother had received; but Matt could only cope with so much. His father and Graham were ex-Forces, not exactly helpless even if they were getting up there age-wise. Matt put it all from his mind, therefore, and concentrated on catching up with work.

Among his neglected email correspondence he found one from Philip Grove, the university professor who'd engaged Matt for the lectures. The message was good news. The professor once more apologised for the inconvenience Matt had suffered recently through the last-minute cancellation. In order that this situation not be repeated, therefore, he'd reshuffled the schedule and swapped Matt's 11 a.m. slot with one at 4 p.m. on the same day. That way, should any more wildcat strikes occur, he'd be able to let Matt know well before the latter set out on his journey to the university. Should he be obliged to stop in the area overnight because of this late slot, the department would be more than willing to cover the cost of accommodation.

Matt's shoulders relaxed as he leaned against the back of his chair. Manna from heaven. He'd had to leave at 7 a.m. for the 11am lecture, it being a 3-hour journey and Matt being a firm believer in leaving extra time to allow for untoward traffic occurrences. He'd got the call at 09.45 a.m., more than halfway there. Ultimately it'd given him the day with Abby, leading to the night; and then he'd had to rush away on receiving the call about the clinic fire. He'd called her later, and she'd been fine with leaving things in abeyance until Matt had his life under control again.

She was due a call then, meaning he could inform her of the later lecture slot, embellishing this with the news that he was due in surgery early the following morning, so couldn't stay the night. A lie, but a white one, and there was a good chance he might in fact need to be in theatre on the following day. He'd tell her he wouldn't think of anything rushed at her house—a euphemism he'd never used for sex before, he reflected—but how about he meet her in the village for a drink on his way? He'd like to see her, even if for a brief time.

Pleased with his plan, he put it into operation as soon as possible. The professor had supplied the date for the next lecture, some weeks hence, so first Matt replied to him, apologising in his turn for the delay at his end and accepting, if the offer was still open. When he received an answer in the affirmative he made the call to Abby from the hospital car park, as he was about to set off home. She understood his reasoning and accepted the invitation, so they'd arranged to meet at the village pub in the market square.

He'd tell her then, and hoped they could be amicable about it. Matt regretted it, but Abby was a grown woman of the world and he thought she'd understand. He knew what was what now, what his priorities were. He'd had a wake-up call from the business with Jen, and was committed to improving his work-life balance. Less work, more family would be his watchword from here on in, and there'd be no dalliances on the side. What he had was too valuable to throw away for a whim.

Something else almost sorted out.

*****

Clicking off the call at her end, Abby heaved a sigh of relief. There'd been no time to think, the morning after her night with Matt, what with helping him get ready to rush away to deal with the fire at his building site; but once he'd gone she'd considered the matter in some depth.

It'd been good, made her feel young again, and that was enough. A swansong, a signing-off from that section of her life. She'd never planned for things to go that far, however, for him to stop over and—well, what happened had happened, and couldn't be changed. They hadn't been supposed to spend the day and the night together. It was down to his university messing up that it'd worked out that way, and so much had gone wrong for him since. He'd been very open about it all, issues at home, his wife ill, his mother helping out, the need to find her a new place as his younger brother was coming home soon and needed the apartment where Penny was living at present. It didn't bother Abby to hear them mentioned. She'd been under no illusions, and on balance she thought it better if they didn't take it any further. Leave it as it'd been, in a good place, remain friendly. Meeting him for a drink would be a good way to wind things up, so she'd suggested the pub where they'd had lunch and he hadn't protested, hadn't acted surprised that she hadn't invited him to the house as a matter of course. Maybe he was seeing sense too.

Abby wasn't complaining. That family owed her something, and she'd collected, even if not quite in a way she could ever have imagined. But Matt was married, had a wife and children, and she wasn't looking to take him away from them. Not that she wanted to; she was quite content being on her own, for most of the time anyway, and she was pretty sure Matt wasn't looking for anything more permanent.

The idea was ridiculous, and she'd made up her mind it mustn't happen again. They were both grown adults, she more than he, there was no reason they couldn't put a stop to this amicably, accept what'd happened as just one of those things and move on. She'd been planning to tell him, most likely over a drink, the next time he suggested a meeting. Now he'd handed her the ideal opportunity, and Abby intended to grasp it with both hands.

Then she'd be quits with the family. Chapter closed.

32: THE PAST (4)

It'd been a party, so long ago, at somebody's house, somewhere. She'd had far too much to drink, they all had, but she didn't tend to overdo it to this extent. They were all young however, having fun, making the most of life in the heady days of youth. It'd been a summer night, warm, balmy, even though it was late and dark by now.

The fun had shown no sign of abating, and things were getting more raucous and rowdy. Dancing, singing-along, laughing, telling jokes, splinter groups forming in the kitchen and hallway. At some point she'd gone into the garden, wanting some fresh air; not because she felt ill, on the contrary, she felt fine. It was just for the feeling of freedom, to get away from the crowded house, to see the sky and the stars above her. She looked up, threw out her arms and twirled in delight at the coolness. She could see the house every time she turned in that direction, every window lit up, people moving, the sound of music playing, and then she'd see the darkness and isolation of the garden in the other direction.

She felt dizzy, staggering and sitting down clumsily on the grass, panting to get her breath and laughing quietly at the same time. She put her head down, between her legs, to counteract the slight giddiness she still felt and to get her balance back. She heard a noise, footsteps, none too steady, and then someone flung themself down beside her.

"Good idea. Get right away from it all. Get a breather."

His voice was slurred, from the booze he'd drunk and still continued to consume, from the wine bottle he had with him. He took a long pull at the neck, offering it to her when he'd finished. She took it eagerly, did the same, threw back her head to try to clear it.

"What's that?"

"What's what?"

They both collapsed with laughter, as though the exchange had been the height of sophisticated humour.

"That. Those. Over there."

He indicated a spot by the side wall of the house, something standing there, more than one but difficult to make out in the dark. Squinting, they tried to identify the objects which had suddenly become so important to them. She got it first.

"I think it's scooters."

"What?"

"Scooters. Scooters, you know, you stand on it, one foot, hold the handlebars and—something—oh yes, push along with one foot. Or something like that."

"Oh yes."

They sat for a moment and contemplated the intricacies of scooter-riding.

"Race you."

"What?"

He'd lumbered to his feet somehow, holding out a hand to help her up.

"Oh no, not now. Can't be riding now."

"Yes you can. Come on!"

He waggled his fingers, extending his arm even further.

"Come on!"

The mischief in his voice was infectious, and she threw out her hand to grasp his, pushing awkwardly with both feet to help him pull her up. Laughing, they staggered over to the scooters, fumbling with the handlebars, pushing them towards the long path which led to the end of the garden.

"Last one to the bottom's a—"

She lost his last words as he sailed away, then clambered aboard her own machine and set off in pursuit. The path was wide, but not wide enough for two of them abreast, and it looked like she'd lost before she even started. Desperate now to win she pushed hard, coming up to the back wheel of his scooter, which wobbled precariously before falling over sideways, depositing itself and its erstwhile rider into a flower bed. She might have worried about him being hurt, but she could hear his drunken laughter as he lay among the flowers, not attempting to get back into it.

Triumphant, she wobbled on her way, speeding along and flying with a flourish onto the grassed patch onto which the path led.

"I've won!"

She jumped off, the scooter going one way and she the other, stumbling as she fell, unsteady on her feet and falling forwards, winding herself and grazing her knees. She rolled onto her back and then sat up, slowly, gasping, wheezing, to get her breath.

"You okay?"

Scooter forgotten, he'd come down the path at a part-run, part-stagger.

"I—just—need—to get—my—breath."

He fell down beside her and waited while the sounds of her laboured breathing slowed and quieted.

"I won!"

Stability restored as much as it was likely to be, she looked towards him where he lay in the grass.

"So I get a prize."

"What do you want?"

"I don't know."

She lay back beside him, looking skywards as she vaguely considered the matter.

"I could pick you some flowers."

He made as if to rise, but abandoned the attempt. They lolled around, oblivious to the faint sounds of the party still in full swing up at the top of the garden.

The Devil—or the alcohol—took her.

"Kiss me."

"What?"

"I mean it. Kiss me. That's my prize."

"But—"

"Don't think about it. Do it."

He did. Rolled over, hung above her for a split second, then lowered himself to brush her forehead with lips which hardly made contact.

"Properly. On the mouth."

He hesitated, then obliged. It was surprisingly soft, and gentle, and she responded, more than she should have, but she was in the moment and it felt so good, so right—

Abruptly he parted from her, moved away, sat up. She lay bewildered, then felt his hand on her shoulder, reassuring.

"We're both drunk. It's nothing, nothing to worry about, okay? I think we'd better get back inside."

Sobered, they stood, each careful to manage alone, to not make physical contact with the other. He found her scooter, wheeled it up the path until they reached that which he'd used.

"Can you—?"

She took charge of the first, while he extricated the second from the flower bed. Together they replaced them by the wall, then returned back inside to the crowd and the noise and the party, determined to continue into the early hours.

"Get you a drink?"

"No, that's okay. I'm all in. Probably time to find—"

As if on cue, her husband appeared at her side.

"Are you okay? I couldn't find you."

"I'm fine, just needed some fresh air. I'm feeling a bit tired."

Her garden companion disappeared in the direction of the kitchen, to her relief.

"D'you want to call it a night? We can stay if you want, but I'm happy to go. You can only have so much fun."

"No, I think we should probably be getting back. I've had enough to drink to last me a week."

They found their hosts, said their goodnights to them and other friends, and resisted all attempts to get them to stay 'just a bit longer.' He was among them, the other one, with his own wife in tow, she making similar 'time to go' noises. He acted as though nothing had happened, and the incident was never referred to again by either of them.

*****

"I do love you."

"I love you too."

As she snuggled down beside her husband she knew it was true. It'd been nothing, a bit of alcohol-fuelled silliness between two friends who ought to know better. She had a husband, he had a wife, both wonderful people to whom they were devoted, in their own ways. It'd meant nothing.

So why did she continue to feel guilty for years afterwards?

33: MADGE

Returning to the car park, Madge felt more relaxed that she had in some time. She'd been on edge since the day the house had been vandalised, and even though she'd been to the golf club multiple times, and shopping with friends on a few occasions, she hadn't felt loosened-up enough to enjoy herself as much as she'd like.

Today, however, something seemed to have clicked into place, leaving the bad memories behind. The police hadn't come up with any answers as to who'd trashed not just Frank's flat but the lounge at her own house; still—

She put those thoughts from her. It was all in the past, extra measures had been put in place, and Madge felt secure once more. She'd passed a wonderful morning with Gillian, discovered a suit in just the right shade of lavender to compliment her fair complexion and found shoes which matched it without even having to try. She'd lunched on chicken salad washed down with a small glass of chilled chardonnay, and thought she'd have a gin and tonic when she got home to keep the upbeat mood going. Humming a little tune to herself she entered the multi-storey and ascended the stairs to the second level. As she approached the bay where she'd parked she rummaged around in her handbag for her keys, then brought her head up. She stopped abruptly, her eyes bulging and her mouth falling open.

Long black gouges decorated the nearside of her car, from

nose to tail, most likely made by dragging a sharp metal object along the paintwork. The roof had been similarly treated, while the wing mirrors hung loose, smashed from their armature with a hammer, perhaps, or an iron bar, or another heavy object. Headlights and tail lights had received identical treatment, while tyres front and back hung to the ground in loose folds, from where they'd been slashed with a blade. Fragments of windows and windscreen were held together by dint of the lamination, but only just, and the scratched bonnet bore the legend "SLAG."

When Madge managed to collect herself enough she moved to the other side of the car, dragging her feet; it matched the first side in every respect. She stood, stupid, in shock, hardly able to take it all in, never mind take action. Fortunately she was saved the trouble.

'Are you alright? Oh, my God!'

She jumped at the unexpected exclamation, but turned to see the young man, in his thirties, she guessed, standing as aghast as she was.

'What? Oh, God.'

The woman, his wife, was walking behind him, her attention inside her handbag where she scrabbled around for something. Colliding with his back she looked up, to see just what he'd seen.

Both were very good, the wife getting straight on her phone to call 999, but wasn't impressed by what the operator told her. Take photos, the woman said, there's so much vandalism the police don't come out to it as a matter of course. Scandalised, Madge's new best friend took the operator to task. There was an elderly woman here—Madge winced, but clamped her lips shut—with her car in a multi-storey with a barrier, so it should have been safe. It wasn't just an isolated act of tyre slashing, or keying the paintwork; the entire car had been trashed in a thorough manner which must have taken some time.

The operator knew she was beaten, putting the irate caller on hold and returned within a minute to inform her there was a police car in the area, which would be with them as soon as possible.

'So it bloody ought to be.'

Scandalised, she clicked off her phone, then turned her attention to Madge at the same time as her husband spoke.

'You can wait in our car.'

'No.'

He was trying to be helpful, but his wife shot him a look, with do-you-honestly-think-she'd-sit-in-some-stranger's-car written all over it.

'Over here, look, you can sit on the wall. D'you want a tea, or a coffee?'

'Tea, thank you. You're very kind. If it's not too much trouble.'

'Not at all. There's a coffee shop opposite the entrance.'

The husband was despatched to get it, while the wife waited with Madge, who perched precariously on the edge of the external wall, the metal bars fixed into it preventing a more comfortable seat. It'd have to do however, as her legs had almost collapsed under her. Her companion made sympathetic noises, then became practical.

'Do you have someone you can call?'

'Yes, my husband, I suppose. I'm sorry. You need to be getting off.'

'It's not a problem. But you'll need to get home somehow. The police might drop you off, but I'm not sure. In any case, you shouldn't be alone.'

True. With shaking hands she located her phone in her handbag and called Frank. She let it ring, but no response. In unsteady tones she left a voicemail, and then they waited.

He called within five minutes, appalled. He was on the

golf course, at the sixth hole, but the game would go on without him. He'd be there, and soon.

The husband returned and Madge drank the hot tea, which did make her feel stronger. The police arrived not long afterwards, with Frank not far behind. Photos were taken, details given, arrangements made for the car to be collected by a tow truck and taken for repairs. Thanks were given to the helpful passing couple, with money offered and refused for the tea, after which they departed, leaving Madge and Frank alone. He put his arms around her and squeezed hard.

'I'd better wait for the truck, make sure everything's done right. Would you feel okay going home in a cab? It might be a while.'

'No, I'd rather stay with you. I'll be fine in your car while you organise things.'

So they sat and waited, with comfort offered and received. Both were thinking the same thing, which continued to go through Madge's head when the truck arrived and Frank went to direct operations.

Who did this?

*****

There was the matter of the insurance claim, and a form of multiple pages to be completed. Was the car locked? Yes, she was always very careful, plus the advanced security system would've sounded an alarm, had she forgotten to lock the car; but she hadn't. So many more questions that the police had already asked her. Was anything of value left in a visible position inside the car? No, Madge was always careful not to leave anything where it could be seen.

But the box wasn't big enough for the whole answer. She

threw down the pen and put her head in her hands, fighting back tears.

'Why can't they let us fill in the bloody thing online, instead of having all this hassle with pen and paper? I've had to squeeze the writing up, and now I've made a mistake. I'll have to print off another copy.'

'There, there, why not let—'

'Don't "there, there" me. I'm not a child!'

She stormed off to the kitchen.

Frank heard the bang of the fridge door, the squeak of a lid, the glug of liquid pouring and the click of a lighter. He hesitated, then lit his pipe and approached the kitchen door, standing in the frame rather than going inside. She looked across from the island where she sat, their eyes meeting and locking. She looked away first.

'I'm sorry. I know it's not your fault. But—.'

She took a large gulp from her wineglass, then drew on her cigarette and slowly exhaled the smoke.

'Can I get you one?'

'No, I'll do it.'

He returned to the lounge, poured a generous measure of scotch into a tumbler, returning to the kitchen to add the required amount of cold water. He sat, drank, reached out to touch her hand.

'It's been rough, I know, and you didn't need this nonsense on top of it all. Let me do it for you.'

She gave a thin smile as he stood, putting his pipe in his mouth and extending his free arm, which he wrapped around her shoulders as she followed his lead. They moved back to the lounge, where he deposited her on the sofa before sitting down beside her. For a while they sat, drinking and smoking, silent, each locked in their own thoughts.

It was bad enough before, went through Frank's mind, and now this. He'd just about got Madge calmed down over the break-in at the house, and he'd got the other worry of what'd been done to the flat on his mind. She'd been jumpy enough over all that, heaven knew, and with this car business she was way beyond what she'd been then. It was too much for both of them, but life had to go on, and he'd got strong shoulders, even if a bit less so than when he'd been younger. He drained his glass and squeezed her hand.

'Let me do it for you, eh? It's been a nasty shock for you; there's no shame in being upset. Sit here and just give me the answers. I'll make sure they fit the blasted form.'

She closed her eyes, inclined her head and leaned it back against the sofa. Leaving his empty glass on the coffee table and now-extinguished pipe in the ashtray he went to the study, returning with a new insurance form printed out and seating himself at the dining table, copying the answers for the first few questions from the spoiled form and then addressing Madge, faithfully recording her answers.

'Will they pay out, d'you think?'

'They ought to. We pay enough for the bloody policy.'

'Yes, but—'

'It's fully-comprehensive, and not with any old insurance company. They're a motor-focussed provider, the biggest roadside assistance company in the country. Reputable.'

'I know.'

Her smile was wan as she turned to face him.

'It's just that I remember trying to keep costs down when we bought the car.'

'I didn't listen to you, which is fortunate as things turned out. It's an expensive car, costly if it needs major repairs, and the excess—well, I went behind your back, I'm afraid. Got vandalism cover, all the bells and whistles, so to speak. So yes, they should pay out.'

'You mean—'

'Don't worry, my dear. I paid the extra from my own

pocket. My wife deserves the best, after all.'

She stood and went to him, leaning down to drop a kiss on his forehead as her arm went around his shoulders.

'I don't deserve you.'

He squeezed her hand as she stood, awkward for once at her own unaccustomed display of affection.

'Let me make you a nice dinner.'

She turned towards the kitchen.

'No, you should take it easy. What say we go out? Or—'

Maybe leaving his car in a car park, or even the courtesy car provided by the insurance company while Madge's was being repaired, wouldn't be the smartest move at this particular time.

'We can get a takeaway delivered, what d'you say? Chinese, Indian, Italian, whatever.'

'I'd like that. If you're sure.'

'Wouldn't say it if I wasn't.'

She moved to the kitchen, to find the menus for their perusal, while Frank considered the fact that her extra-clingy and nervous state was going to make it even more difficult to break it to her that he was leaving her.

At least he didn't have to do so just yet.

34: PENNY

It was only about ten days later that Jennifer and Matt gave Penny to understand that they'd got their household under control again. She'd known it was coming, could feel it in the air. Whatever had been troubling Jennifer, and Matt too, she could tell it was fixed. She was his mother, after all. They'd been very grateful, thanking her endlessly for all the time she'd given while things were up in the air, but now they'd worked things out and wouldn't allow them to get into such a muddle again.

She needed a rest, they both insisted, she'd been working far harder for them than she'd been used to, and she wasn't getting any younger. Thanks for that, Penny'd thought in the acerbic manner she'd abandoned while holding up the household. I'm not exactly dead and buried yet. She'd smiled, however, if somewhat thinly, and with an effort pressed her lips together. They'd be asking for her help again soon, they'd promised. When the insurance paid out—and they'd confirmed a few days ago that a payment was in the pipeline—Matt wouldn't be starting again with the new clinic, but having the site cleared and putting it up for sale. His workload at the hospital was more than enough, and he needed to spend time with his family.

To the same end Jennifer was cutting back on her activities in the community. There were others keen to have a shot at running things, so although she'd still take a part in fund-raising for the church steeple, or fun-running for various charitable institutions, she too would be making more time for the family.

Penny was pleased for them, but she couldn't help the empty feeling inside as she drove home. She'd got used to it all, stopping over, helping get the children up and off in the mornings, going to the shops until Jennifer got the supermarket deliveries going again; she'd even taken over dog-walking duties from Mrs J, and enjoyed chatting to the locals as she did so. She'd felt useful, and now she didn't, not to mention the fact that it'd kept her away from the apartment and that slight tension she couldn't help feeling whenever going to check the mail. She'd kept an eye on the place, popping in now and again to make sure that all was well, and that there were no more unwelcome items lurking in the mailbox, which there hadn't been. In terms of housework, however, she'd done nothing. The place wasn't a tip, *per se;* Penny was too organised to keep an untidy house, but it had a rather fusty odour about it. The windows all needed to be opened, to let some fresh air through, then a good dust and vacuum. She'd got rid of the food she'd had in the fridge, taken it over to Matt's, or thrown it out if it couldn't be avoided, although Penny abhorred waste; but now it could do with a good clean before she did the shopping and restocked it.

It all felt rather cold, sterile and lonely. She'd got used to having children around again, her own and the grandchildren, along with the noise they inevitably made, of phones ringing and the conversations which ensued both on those and otherwise, the TV, Toby playing games on his X-box. And now, all gone. She dashed away the tears which came unbidden to her eyes.

She turned on the TV, flicking through the channels and finding a wildlife programme, the best on offer. She wandered into the kitchen, opening the fridge and pulling out one of the non-perishable items which she'd neither taken to Matt's nor needed to throw away.

She opened the bottle of white wine and poured a generous glass.

*****

Moving with care across the room with the full glass in her hand—her second—she caught a glimpse of herself in the mirror above the console table. On an impulse she went closer, too close for comfort, and started away from the image that stared back at her. The eyes, bloodshot from weeping and drinking, the crows-feet wrinkles that splayed out from the sides of them, the over-creased forehead and the lines of bitterness which dragged down the corners of her mouth.

She sought refuge back on the sofa, gulping her wine and grimacing at the memory of what she'd just seen. Not a hint of the girl she'd been, but that was so long ago. She thought back, remembering how her future life had been determined when the older girls at her school were invited to attend a social function with the cadets from the military academy for officers which was located in the neighbourhood. These events had been going on for years, social evenings at Sandhurst when they'd bring in just the right type of young ladies to teach the cadets how to socialise and, more important, who to socialise with; and it was at this gathering that Penny had met Frank. Met him again, that was, because they'd known each other as children, as they discovered in conversation. Frank had lived in the same village as Penny for a few years, and their families had interacted with each other when the two were young. Memories of childhood were raised between them, of times before Frank, a few years older than Penny, had departed at the age of eight, and moved thereafter into a military career of his own.

He made it obvious that he was more than keen on the pretty blonde young woman, now grown from the little girl with a tomboy streak and pigtails that he used to pull. Her fellow students teased her about it on the journey back to school, and Penny had lain awake half the night thinking about the encounter.

What was she to do with the rest of her life? It was the second half of the twentieth century, with so many new opportunities now available for women. Penny could have done whatever she wanted, but she didn't know what that was. Frozen inside after the too-fast events of the year before she'd come to school, all she wanted was to hide away, from her old home town and its memories, from her mother, from her past life, in whatever safe haven she could find. Could Frank provide that? Penny decided he could.

He was handsome, upright, well-spoken and well-mannered, a sportsman from a long line of military men; everything that could be expected from one of his privileged social class. He was smitten with Penny, that was clear, and of course he'd offer marriage. No gypsy he, to do a midnight flit after a roll or two in the hay, and being in the Forces, he'd be living overseas for much of his career, taking his wife with him; away from her mother and the perpetual air of derision which Penny felt aimed in her direction.

A month or so of dating later, all with school and parental approval, of course, he popped the question, and Penny was pleased to accept. The marriage was set for after Frank had passed-out from Sandhurst as a Second Lieutenant, at which time Penny would be leaving school. She'd accompany him on his first posting, overseas, to Germany, meaning she could leave behind the emotional baggage which had been weighing her down for all this time. She felt no passion for her husband-to-be, but wasn't averse to the well-controlled kisses he bestowed on her. He made no attempt at much more, respecting his bride-to-be too much to try anything irregular. Their union would be consummated at the correct time, on their wedding night after a traditional military ceremony at which Frank looked very dashing in his number-one blue dress uniform, while Penny was radiant in virginal white.

As they stood for photos under the arch of swords held aloft by Frank's identically-clad fellow officers, she caught the unmistakeable—to her—shadow of a sneer on her mother's face, and blushed despite herself. The effect was captured on camera, and any joy Penny might have taken from looking at that picture in the future was spoiled by the knowledge of her mother's undoubted thoughts that Frank had been duped by the unmarried mother of a bastard child who was passing herself off as a virgin.

This unwelcome reminder had more unfortunate and further-reaching effects than a few uncomfortable moments outside the church. Penny had given little if any thought to the wedding night, preferring to let matters take their course when the time came. She didn't hold back in drinking the free-flowing champagne at the reception, and felt pleasantly prepared for what was to come; it wasn't like it was anything new to her, after all. Come the crucial moment, however, she was horrified to find her body freezing-up against Frank's amorous advances. Try as she might, she couldn't muster the correct response, as thoughts she'd buried deep at the back of her mind asserted themselves in the physical sphere.

It was fortunate that the overall impression confirmed Penny as the blushing, virginal bride she was supposed to be, and Frank didn't try to force the issue. Patience, understanding and sensitivity would be his watchword over the next few weeks. It'd all happen with time, and to some extent it did, although the best Penny could ever muster had been a rather mechanical response. Frank was very good about it. She was a well-brought-up young lady of an aristocratic family, after all, and he could hardly expect from her the free-and-easy goings-on of certain young women whose acquaintance he'd made on evenings out with his friends.

Those days were behind him now, and together they embarked on married life as the perfect couple. The young officer and his lady, always the ideal companion at mess functions, the capable hostess at the dinner parties they gave, a credit and an asset to her up-and-coming husband, for whom promotions had arrived with more speed than was the norm. Children had come too, although it had taken six years before Matthew was born, followed by a three-year gap before Simon made an appearance. Penny settled into her new life, once more the obliging and sweet-tempered person of her early youth, now the flawless wife and mother.

Having the boys had been a blessing, her pregnancies giving her the perfect excuse for refusing her husband's physical attentions. When her babies were born she immersed herself in motherhood, and if Frank thought her wifely role suffered thereby he never reproached her for it. He'd long ago acknowledged that Penny wasn't "like that," and accepted the minimal conjugal relations she allowed him. She was queen of the coffee mornings and other functions of the Wives' Club, leading the other women of all ranks by example as her husband did his men. They were the best of their class, and appeared content with their lot.

The trouble set in thirty-something years into their marriage. Posted to a small unit, Frank by now of a senior rank, they were expected to lead by example as they'd been doing all along. The problem now was that there was a riding club on the station, and although Frank had never been a rider, Penny had. She'd never gone back to it after the unfortunate affair of Jed, but her husband was aware of her knowledge of "horsey things" and asked her to get involved.

She was reluctant, pleading the passing of too many years, but he was insistent.

"Riding a horse must be a bit like riding a bicycle, if you know what I mean. It'll come back, once you're in the saddle. Take it slow, don't risk anything. Just get involved in grooming, if you don't want to ride. But I could do with your input on this, please Pen. You've got the time, now the boys have flown the nest."

It was true. She missed Matthew and Simon, grown to manhood and living their own lives by now, only visiting on occasion; yet still time hung heavy without them. How then could she refuse what Frank asked?

It did indeed all come back, including the bits she'd rather forget; stolen kisses in the tack room, snatched moments of passion in the hay, the feel of that hard male body. She'd ride out across the open terrain—the unit being in an isolated area—hat deliberately left behind, hair flying out behind her in reality this time, trying through the physical activity of galloping on the horse beneath her to forget that other passionate activity beneath her former lover.

It did no good, and Penny was forced to live with the torment. Returning to the UK for their next posting, and preparing for Frank's retirement, they bought a house in their location of choice which happened to be not far from a riding club; and Penny by now being addicted to reliving those passionate memories, she became a member. It was never going to end well, and it didn't. History seemed doomed to repeat itself when she met Jeremy, a few years older than she and in excellent shape for his age, doubtless kept that way by regular riding out into the countryside, in which she was soon accompanying him.

It started in all innocence, but a meaningful eye-meet as he tried to help her into the saddle on their first meeting, and which she'd refused, had led to an apology and much joking banter on his part thereafter. When he suggested one day that she ride out with him she knew she should refuse; but there she was, accepting, mounting and trotting out, to take up the challenge of a gallop across the meadow. It had been exhilarating, with dismounting at speed at the edge of the woods on the other side the most natural thing. There was barely time to tie up the horses before they were in each other's arms, hands everywhere, tearing at each other's clothes; history repeating itself, in essence.

There was a difference, however. For Jeremy, a divorced man, this was no meaningless affair, a few tumbles on the grass and a passion which would wear itself out in a few months. He wanted her to be with him, not just for now but for the future, till death us do part, in fact. He raised the subject one afternoon as they lay in post-coital bliss in bed at his house, whence they'd moved their physical activities when it became clear this was a serious relationship.

"Come away with me," he urged, when she pleaded her long and functional yet passionless marriage to Frank. "You've raised your children, they're grown men, long gone. They don't need you anymore."

"And what about Frank? He's been a good husband. I can't leave him alone after all this time."

"Yes you can. You already have, and he doesn't need you. He's away most of the time."

It was true. As Frank's seniority had grown, so had the responsibilities that went with his rank. He was away a great deal, which was why Penny had decided to live in the house they'd purchased, rather than accompany him to his current posting and live in yet another shabby married quarter, frequently left on her own. It also enabled her to spend a great deal of time with Jeremy without having to lie, which would have troubled her more than she was already troubled.

She loved Jeremy, of that she was sure, and he loved her too. The passion between them had taken her by surprise as much as her first affair with Jed, about which she'd been open with Jeremy. There was no need to lie to him as there had been with Frank. The floodgates of her pent-up passion had opened again after all this time, and she was making the most of every illicit moment snatched with her lover. She was seriously tempted by his offer, and felt he was right. The boys had flown the nest, and Frank was hardly ever home with her, so what was the problem? Why did she feel so ashamed about the idea of leaving her husband?

Guilt. She'd lived with it ever since that teenage fling and the physical results, the child which'd been torn from her before she'd even seen it. Her mother's barely-concealed sneering reproach at the daughter who'd let the side down and brought shame to the family; it was there and acknowledged, even if hidden from public view. She'd always felt bad about deceiving Frank concerning her past, and she'd tried to compensate for that and her semi-frigid state by being the perfect wife and mother in all else. But now—

Why shouldn't she take the chance to live for herself? She wasn't getting any younger. Well-preserved she might be, but Penny was aware that from here on in it was downhill all the way. This shared passion with Jeremy could very well be her swan-song. What else did life have to offer this more-than-middle-aged woman? Apart from the daughter-in-law already acquired, and on whom she wasn't keen, plus the grandchildren, and being used as a free-of-charge babysitter, expected to drop everything when the need arose. It wasn't that Penny didn't care, but she'd had her share of nappies and sleepless nights with the boys. She didn't need any more of it.

And Frank? He could live comfortably in the mess, which he was already doing anyway. He wasn't too old to find somebody else, as Penny had done, so he could have a partner with whom to set up his own household. In any case, she'd suspected him of having at least one affair over the years. She'd never said anything, as it kept him from making unwelcome demands on her, besides which she still felt a sense of guilt for her own lack of response to his sexual needs.

She could still remember, although she tried hard not to, her own awakening to passion, her awareness of Jed, his crooked smile, his wide dark eyes, the way she'd jumped as though electrified the first time his hand brushed against her bare arm as they'd engaged in some stable task together. Virgin though she'd been, that first time in his stable lodging she hadn't needed any showing what to do. All had come naturally, her instincts and desire working together to ensure her first experience wasn't the awkward and painful mess which friends were later to confide in Penny as having been theirs.

If Frank had been looking for the same passionate response from his wife he'd been sorely disappointed, so maybe he'd found it elsewhere, over the years. He'd been loyal to Penny, never tried to leave her for someone else, although there'd been *that* time. She'd been jealous, worried, panicked even, at the prospect. There was something different about *that* woman which might cause him to go. Penny'd known, she could tell, they'd been having an affair, she could feel it. She'd been resentful at first, then desperate, sure he was working up to telling her their marriage was over. She'd thrown herself into doing everything she could to keep him, talking about the boys, what they'd do when they came to visit, pulling every string possible to remind him that he belonged here, with Penny, fulfilling the role she'd allotted him of husband and protector.

Then that final, desperate attempt, throwing herself from her horse at full gallop. She hadn't meant to cause quite so much damage, hadn't intended to be a touch-and-go case, to spend all that time in hospital with a broken back even when she'd got through the initial damage and surgery. It'd worked, however, and Penny had survived to be pleased at having done whatever it took to keep Frank by her side. The affair was finished, she knew. She could imagine him telling the woman how he couldn't leave his wife when she'd suffered so much. She'd felt his sense of loss, even while realising his total withdrawal from that other one, and when they'd been posted away he'd thrown himself into his work with all the discipline to be expected from a military man. If the passion he'd felt for that one was anything like what Penny'd felt for Jed, back in the day, he'd never given any indication, and if he'd found consolation for his loss in the succeeding years his wife had never noticed. She was sure he had, because ageing or not he was still attractive and charming in an older-man way. No, Frank would have no trouble finding somebody to keep him company, in the event.

Little by little Penny'd made the case for leaving it all and following Jeremy who, sensing her weakening, urged and encouraged her. On her own account she could never have left Frank; it was a comfortable setup, no worse than the marriages of countless others. With a lover pleading his case on the sidelines, however, it wasn't difficult.

She'd gone for it, and what had she got for it? A big fat nothing, that's what. It turned out that the everlasting love which dear Jeremy had sworn was a relative thing, only lasting until he met another woman, to whom he'd no doubt sworn a similar affection; and she'd been let down in her turn, from what Penny'd heard. A serial everlasting-lover, it would seem, and she'd fallen head over heels for his superficial charms, leaving everything for his version of happy-ever-after.

The ever-after was the problem, because Penny had been obliged to leave the house where she'd lived in what she'd thought was eternal bliss with her new—husband, she would have said, but the proposed marriage had been put off for one reason or another, by accident or design she couldn't say. There'd been the need to wait for her divorce from Frank to be final, and although he'd been a gentleman about it—when wasn't he?—it still took time. He'd been shocked when Penny had summoned up the courage to tell him, but he'd remained calm and not reproached her, which had been a relief. Once he'd got over the shock he'd been civilised, even over the immense settlement which Jeremy had encouraged her to claim.

When her decree absolute had come, Jeremy'd got cold feet.

"Living with your divorce has brought my own back to me, and it wasn't a clean-cut thing as yours was. Hazel took me to the cleaners, and I'm lucky to have this place, albeit with a mortgage around my neck for years to come. I know it's irrational, darling, but what if anything were to happen between us? I know we're very happy now, and there's no one with whom I'd want to spend the rest of my life, but I couldn't go through anything like that again. I just couldn't."

Penny had been at pains to reassure him, but the upshot was still that he wanted to wait for a while, until his irrational fears had subsided, before their wedding could take place; and of course, it'd never happened. Worse, as they'd only been together for about ten years, and as Penny had neither a financial stake in the house, nor a long-term marriage to plead, she'd been out in the cold in every sense. She had children, thank God, and Matt had taken her into his house while seeking an apartment for her in the area, so she could maintain her independence, he'd said. Penny didn't see why she couldn't have stayed there, but Matt had been insistent. The layout of their house didn't make it easy for him, Jen and children Toby and Bella to co-exist with Penny thrown into the mix.

Fortunately it hadn't been an issue, as Penny'd met Ross, and a relationship had blossomed. She hadn't believed her luck when he'd asked her to move in with him, although with hindsight she ought to have given it more thought. The need to move out of Matthew's house had been preying on her mind however, so she'd chosen the easiest way out and taken up Ross on his offer; and then history had repeated itself as he finished it and asked her to move out.

So here she was, in this well-appointed but cold and clinical apartment owned by her youngest son; all alone, and lonely. No man, woman or child to sit with her, or sleep with her, instead just the memories of what a mess she'd made of things. Was it any wonder she drank, in a futile effort to forget about it all?

She took a gulp from her glass, and her eyes narrowed.

Frank. He should be here. She'd been a good wife, hadn't she, for all those years? Kept whichever house they'd lived in—and there'd been more than a few—immaculate, made a home from impersonal married quarters countless times. She'd been the perfect hostess, a credit to him in every sense, without a doubt playing no small part in gaining him the promotions he'd received. She'd put up with his physical requirements without complaint, so what then if she'd given in to a fit of passion for another in her middle years? He'd been unfaithful on occasions, Penny knew, and she'd never mentioned it, just maintained a dignified silence. Surely that counted for something. Where then was he in her hour of need?

She drank deep from the glass, almost draining it.

With that other woman, that's where. The one he'd married within not that many years of his split with Penny. Why couldn't he have waited? Then he'd still have been free when Penny needed him back. But no, he must marry that woman, move in with her, live in her old house rather than be a man and buy one of his own so he'd have a home to offer Penny.

She drained her glass and set off in search of another.

It's not right. After what I've been through, to be alone like this.

I deserve better.

*****

She felt different when she awoke the next morning, without her customary hangover. Amazing, especially as she hadn't drunk much for some weeks now. Perhaps that was a sign? She couldn't explain it, but just accepted that she felt better, lighter, as though a weight had been lifted from her. Every grievance she'd been nursing for some time, not gone, but accepted. Telling Jennifer that she, Penny, had made mistakes, had messed up her own life; perhaps that'd been the catalyst for her facing up to her past. Yes, she hadn't made what she might have of her life, but there was no going back, no changing anything. The best she could do was to move on, try to do better in the future.

Just because she wasn't running Matt and Jennifer's household on a daily basis anymore didn't mean she'd been cut out of their lives entirely. When they got things sorted out—and the positive air around them now suggested they were on the right road—she'd be back visiting, helping out when necessary. Jennifer had already asked her to come for lunch on Sunday, and she wouldn't feel like cooking if she wasn't getting better, would she?

The future could hold a role for her in the lives of her children, and grandchildren. That'd be her focus from now on in. Simon and Dan were due back from their summer lives soon, and they'd be needing their apartment back. She'd better begin looking for a place in the area, somewhere between both her sons, their partners and Matt's children. Time to put a positive slant on things.

The past contained one nagging thought that wouldn't leave her. Maybe she wasn't finished with it after all. Perhaps Simon would help her. He might be shocked, as would Matt, when the time came, but he'd get over it. After all, he'd been the victim of discrimination in his life, he and Dan, on account of their sexual orientation. He if anybody could understand.

They might not want to know, but that was a risk Penny was prepared to take. But she owed it to them all to see if she could find the child she'd been forced to give up.

35: FRANK

The vandalism to his wife's car caused Frank to spend even more time trying to work out who was to blame for that and everything else which'd happened. He thought he'd got it figured out, although he didn't like the conclusion he'd arrived at. The party. Graham's birthday party, the reunion of people who'd kept in touch, of others who hadn't seen each other for years. The revival of friendships; and possible enmities.

In the following weeks and months his family had been the victims of various attacks. His own flat vandalised, along with Madge's house, and now her car. Matt's clinic burned down, his wife Jennifer subjected to trolling via emails, his mother Penny the recipient of a vile package; although whether that had been aimed at her or their younger son Simon and his partner Dan was uncertain. As Dan's parents, Pippa and Graham had received hate mail about the couple, Frank thought it had to be about the boys; but their parents had been caught in the crossfire.

The culprit? Somebody with a grudge against him, Frank, and it seemed clear who that was. Seeing them all together, under one roof, that of Pippa and Graham, his oldest and best friends and parents of Dan, partner of Frank's son Simon; that had to have given rise to the idea of getting at him through them all.

Her. It had to be her. Frank hated the idea, but he couldn't leave it. He had to confront her, and soon. It was still early in the day but Madge was already well into a round of golf, and it was about an hour-and-a-half to where she-who-must-be-confronted lived. He could get there and back in the space of a day, and now he'd had the idea Frank wanted to get things done, get it out in the open and stopped. He'd have liked to ring ahead, check that she was there, but forewarned is forearmed, as they say, and he preferred to take her by surprise.

He was feeling tired too, had been that way a lot lately. He hadn't been sleeping well, which wasn't surprising given that his mind was always working, trying to find the culprit. When he did fall asleep he often awoke of a sudden, bathed in sweat. It couldn't be helped, however. He had to do this, so fortified himself with plenty of coffee before he set out and took a flask too, to help keep him sharp.

A final freshen-up and he was ready to go.

*****

He didn't have any issues of sleepiness on the way there, no need to pull into a layby and take a nap. He put this down to the sense of purpose now that he'd decided on action, the almost-automatic sharpness learned through years in the military, needing to postpone basic bodily needs like sleep when in the field. He made good time, the mid-week traffic being lighter than he'd been expecting, but the satnav wouldn't play for the last half-mile of his journey so he'd been obliged to stop and ask directions at the supermarket.

The last house in the lane, on the right, old style rendered with modern execution, copper-coloured Lexus on the drive.

Found it, and the car was there, so she was at home. He hesitated, then left the car, locked it and strode up the path at speed, ringing the bell before he could talk himself out of it. He stood a moment, hearing nothing but silence from within. He looked around, caught the twitch of a curtain from the window to the left. Footsteps inside, the click of the lock, the rasp of a bolt being withdrawn, the door pulled back, and then she stood before him, unsmiling and unwelcoming.

'Frank.'

'Abby.'

*****

They observed each other in silence.

'May I come in?'

She moved aside, her face hostile, her posture stiff, then gestured him inside and closed the door behind him. In silence she stood, looking at him.

'How did you find me, Frank?'

'I—Graham—.'

He hadn't liked having to ask, but there was no other way. Graham was his oldest friend, trustworthy, but doubtful.

"Is this a good idea, Frank?"

"Not what you think. I need information, and she's the only one who might have it."

Graham hadn't asked any more, but provided the address and other contact details. It was none of his business, but he'd keep it to himself and not tell Pippa. Frank knew he didn't have to check on that.

"Just be careful," was all he'd said, and that was that.

'I see. And to what do I owe the pleasure, Frank?'

Abby was waiting. There was no easy way to do this, so he plunged straight in.

'Since Graham's party someone's been targeting me and my family. Pippa and Graham received an anonymous homophobic letter referencing Simon and Dan. Penny's received hate mail which looks to be the same, while Jennifer's had a string of offensive emails which look as though they're leading up to blackmail. Matt's new clinic burned down—the police suspect arson—and I found my flat trashed on the same day as my wife's house was vandalised, along with her car not long afterwards. I have to protect my family, and I'm sure the police will take a dim view if I give them the name of the perpetrator. I have a suspect in mind.'

He'd kept his eyes focussed somewhere to the left of her as he spoke, but now they moved to meet hers full-on. Her gaze never wavered; he was first to look away.

'And you—you think this is *me,* Frank? *Me?*'

He was silent as he looked at her again.

'Jesus Christ, Frank, it's been years and years. Do you honestly have such a bad opinion of me that you think I'd do anything at all, let alone wait all this time? Bloody hell!'

'Why now? I mean, it started soon after the party, and it's my family and friends—'

'And I'm not one of those, of course. It figures. You and your bloody family get targeted and it has to be me, because of course nothing bad's happening to me, is it? Never mind that I've got a stalker.'

'What?'

'You heard me. I keep on feeling it, around the village, like I'm being watched, but when I look there's never anyone there. It's freaking me out, but there's nothing I can do, so obviously I've got time to harass you and your effing family.'

'But—'

'Don't "but" me.'

Her hands bunched into fists at her sides, her mouth tightened, a vein stood out in her neck. For two pins she'd have hit him, driven a fist into that smug mouth that dared to come and accuse her in her own home, and pushed it right down his lying throat. It wasn't to be borne, and she was tired of it all.

'Go on then, Frank. Go ask your precious eldest son how I managed to burn down his clinic while he was in bed beside me.'

His eyes widened, his gulp was audible.

'Oh yes, it seems I hold a special attraction for the males of your family.'

He noted she didn't say "men."

'How about your youngest? Is he just gay, or bi? Doubtless if it's the latter I'll be getting a call from him soon.'

Their eyes locked again, and once more he was first to drop his.

'Look, Abby, I'm sorry. It just seemed—'

'Oh yes, it just seemed like you could put two and two together and come up with me. You know what, Frank? I don't want to hear it. You can get out of my house and get fucked—but not by me.'

She strode to the front door and threw it open, glaring at him.

He gathered such dignity as he could muster and walked through it, moving down the path without looking back. He heard the crash behind him, the splintering of glass, but resisted the urge to turn and go back. He reached the car, got in, turned on the ignition and put distance between them, as fast as possible.

36: ABBY

She stood stock still inside, listening until she heard the sound of the engine, starting and then disappearing into the distance. She'd thought he might return at one point, but it was fortunate he didn't as she might well have grasped one of the larger shards of glass and slashed his lying throat. Instead she went for a brush and dustpan and cleared up the mess before googling a local glazier. For an exorbitant price he came out within the hour, boarding up the panel in secure fashion and promising to return the following day to reglaze it.

An expensive episode. Something else for which Frank owed her.

She threw herself onto the sofa, stretching her neck and massaging the area before lying back, eyes closed, until the tears squeezed themselves out from under the lids. She didn't know how long she lay like that before sleep overtook her, and when she awoke it was dark. She was hungry, and thirsty, but she couldn't find the energy to go to the kitchen.

Instead she just sat there, thinking.

She remembered it, the beginning, how it'd come to be. That night, just one night when everything had happened, all at once. The Christmas Ball, the special night of the year, when the wives all went out and bought new dresses, ballgowns, to give them back that special feeling they'd had on their wedding days. She'd bought one, black and gold, tissue and net, a beauty, and had her hair put up for the occasion. It was meant to be wonderful, and it was for about an hour; and then came the message from work, the situation room, something developing, and Mr Workaholic just had to go in, didn't he? Anybody else would've delegated, got the most senior person present to deal with it and send him updates if necessary. Not Gerry though. He couldn't resist it, so off he went, apologising, but still leaving her on her own.

Not that she couldn't cope with being alone at a party. God knows she'd done it in the past, when he'd been away, and there were enough singletons around doing it that way as a matter of course. But that hadn't been how it was supposed to be for them, had it? They were a couple, meant to be there together, and he'd welched on the deal. She remembered there'd been a photographer. They always had one, on occasions such as these, with a flowery-bower sort-of set up, so everybody could have a picture as a memento; men in mess kit, women looking like princesses, something to hang in the downstairs loo for visitors to admire whilst "freshening up." Abby'd gone and had hers taken anyway. Might as well keep a record of the dress, which went to the charity shop not long afterwards. Standing there on her lonesome, looking soulful, Diana at the Taj Mahal before there was a Diana at the fucking Taj Mahal.

She'd drunk, and picked at the buffet, chatted with friends, danced with some of them; and then *he'd* asked her to dance. A surprise, but a pleasant and flattering one, given that he was so much more senior and she barely knew him; and that's when it'd happened. Maybe it wouldn't have, if she hadn't been alone; but she was, and it did, and there was no changing the outcome.

Heaven, remembering how much he'd desired her in the beginning. Hell, knowing what he'd just accused her of. Why did you have such a low opinion of me? Why didn't you have more faith in me? I was there for you for so many years, and I didn't see you for ages at a time, but whenever you came back I was always happy to see you, and you always went away wanting more, coming back again and again. You loved me, I know you did, even though you never said it, always avoided admitting it; because you thought, maybe, that if you said so it would be out there, in the open, you wouldn't be able hide it away again and I might just want you to do something about it. I'd never have asked you to do anything you couldn't. I know you'd never have left your children; but you risked so much, everything, to be with me when you could, in the beginning. You must have loved me.

Or else you were a fool, she thought, bitter at the idea. Did I love a fool? He could've lost his wife and children, his career, everything; because if we'd been found out they'd have had him out of there before his feet could touch the ground, on the next plane and out, his career over, his pension gone. It's bad for morale, not to mention a security risk, to make oneself vulnerable to blackmail by foreign agencies, as well as those with whom you're involved; myself, in this case, and Gerry, for that matter. A high-ranking and important officer seducing the wives of his subordinates: not to be thought of, and he'd have been made an example of, if caught. His whole life up in smoke for love, which is at least admirable; or was it just for the sake of a bit on the side, which is cheap and detestable and the action of a fool?

She sighed. What was the point? Why did he have to come here, dredging up the past, spoiling the good memories with ridiculous accusations?

Screw it. She pushed herself to her feet, went to the kitchen and made sandwiches, took a glass and a bottle from the fridge, carried the lot back to the lounge and sat, flicking through the catch-up channels on the TV to find a good film or series to watch. It reminded her of when she'd sat here with Matt, watching *Turandot* and discussing it, before things had taken a more intimate turn. He wasn't much older now than his father had been back in the day, and in the dark—.

Surreal. It was in the past, best to leave it there. She'd meet Matt, as agreed, but let him go as gently as she could.

No more dealings with either father or son.

37: FRANK

He didn't feel good at all when he left her, shame setting in before he'd even reached the end of the lane. He pulled over, wanting to go back, to apologise, but there was no point. It was more than his life was worth while she was in a fury; he needed to wait until she'd calmed down, but see her he must. The gentleman in him had to put things right.

What she'd said about Matt, however; was it true, or was she just trying to rattle him, bait him because he'd insulted her. It was offensive, to think that of her, when he remembered all she'd been to him, and he to her, in the past.

His mind wandered back to when he'd first met her, a beautiful, sweet, caring individual. She'd come through a door one day, and into his heart at the self-same moment. It was some function, a school prize-giving day, and he there to award the prizes. He'd controlled himself, as he'd been trained to do by his own steel will and Sandhurst, but managed to speak to her in the natural course of things when people were milling about talking after the ceremony. No, she didn't work at the school but was there to help out a friend, one of the teachers. She was a "wife-of," but had no children of her own.

After that he'd seen her about on a regular basis; it was a small community, after all. Then there'd been that night, the function at which they'd both been guests. He'd joined the group of which she was a part, managed to get her talking, then music started and a dance seemed only natural. What more to say? He'd spoken, she too, and from there came stolen meetings, infrequent, risky but heavenly, with talk as well as love before the unwelcome departure back into their own everyday lives. The difference was that she'd opened up to him, in those talks, and he was ashamed of his own inability to reciprocate. He couldn't even tell her he loved her, being unable to share his life, what had happened to him in the past.

He remembered his childhood, his father, cold and unsmiling when he was around, which wasn't often as his military duties frequently kept him away. Frank was sent to boarding school, and he understood why. It was the tradition, character-building for the sons of officers and leaders, who'd be expected to lead in their turn. He'd wanted his mother but instead had found bullies, other boys handy with their fists and members of staff with darker motives. He'd had to defend himself, and survived the experience, but he'd seen others not so fortunate.

He'd got through, and succeeded in life, following his father into the military. He was a survivor, albeit with the secret of the horrors he'd witnessed locked inside, never opening up to anyone, male friends, girlfriends, even his wife. He'd realised later that, without conscious thought, he'd chosen a wife who was likewise closed-off, not sharing herself, and he'd felt secure with that. Penny never invited him into the sanctum of her inner self, and vice-versa; they'd talked only of the peripherals of their life, her interests and his, their friends, the parties they'd attended, those they'd given in reciprocation. It occurred to him that she too could be hiding something which had damaged her inner core.

When the boys came along they'd become the perfect excuse for their parents to talk about them too, how they were growing, teething, night-time feeds, which schools to sign them up for, because the children would follow the tradition of boarding schools, too strongly ingrained in Frank to be resisted, despite his own negative experience. His sons had come through okay, it seemed, but how would he know, unless they'd opened up to him?

He should have done something about it all, yet he'd always maintained the *status quo* and let sleeping dogs lie; lying being the operative word, or more correctly economy of the truth, to use a modern expression. But then there'd been Abby, with her wonderful openness and her love which wore out because he couldn't talk to her as she did to him.

No use thinking about it now. He'd concentrate on getting home, when he'd managed to put behind him the almighty mess he'd made. First he'd better find a service station, use the restroom, drink some tea. He was perspiring slightly, his breathing laboured; signs of stress brought on by the confrontation which he ought never to have provoked.

Signs of a life which could have been lived better.

38: PIPPA

'It's lovely to see you, darling, but a shame Simon couldn't come with you.'

'He'll be here, in a day or two. He felt it best to go see Penny first, given that we're about to make her homeless once more.'

He reached out and squeezed her hand, and Pippa squeezed back, harder, if that was possible. It was always a good time when Dan and Simon returned from their differing summer pursuits. As she made coffee, while Dan carried the plate of biscuits through to the lounge, Pippa thought briefly of the toxic email she'd received from some anonymous troll, slandering their relationship. So what if they were gay? They were happy, and had a much better relationship than many hetero people she'd known down the years, she was sure. How many couples, respecting their differences and need for "self-time," agreed to spend the summer apart, in order to enjoy those things they didn't have in common? No way would it work if Dan tried to paint onboard the yacht Simon had been crewing for the past few months. He needed a quiet place, a tiny old house on the hillside above a Greek village this year, where he could paint around the area to his heart's content and sit drinking ouzo by the harbour while Simon was having a beer onboard as he coasted above the blue depths of the Med.

The arrangement worked well, giving them plenty to

discuss when they got back together in the autumn. Most often they'd return and meet first at the apartment they owned, then visit their families once settled back in. This year however Penny was living there, after the untimely demise of her relationship with Ross, and they weren't about to put her out on the street. It'd been arranged that she'd go and stay in the granny annex which adjoined Matt and Jennifer's place. They'd tried this once before, and it hadn't worked out, but Penny seemed to be getting on better with her eldest son and his wife these days, from what Pippa had gleaned from the phone call she'd had with her old friend just last week. Jennifer had been ill, and Penny had been drafted in to help keep the home running. It'd been good for her, Pippa thought, because Penny had seemed far more positive in attitude. It sounded like she was over the Ross debacle and taking more interest in her grandchildren.

She was glad for her old friend. You never knew what went on within a marriage or any partnership, or where the fault lay when things went wrong, as they had on a disastrous scale for Penny. If she was coming through it, wonderful, and with luck she'd continue on this upward trend; and it was no hardship for Pippa and Graham to have Dan staying with them for a few days while Simon helped his mother decamp to Matt and Jennifer's place. They had all the summer to catch up on, and love Simon as she did Pippa was enjoying having her younger son to herself for a while, Graham having gone to the chiropractor because his knee was playing up, an old rugby injury aggravated by a bit of arthritis.

'So, what did I miss at the party? I'm dying to know. I hope you didn't get up to any of the shenanigans of your misspent youth.'

'Misspent? Darling, what do you mean?'

'Dad told me once about some party years ago, where things got totally out of control. Not exactly wife-swapping, he said, but it got a bit heated.'

'Ah yes. The "Burco Bash".'

Graham had arrived back and caught Dan's comment as he entered the room. Helping himself to a handful of biscuits and taking a seat he proceeded to elaborate.

'Someone, Ted and Lynne it was, I think, gave a party. They had this "Burco," a machine for boiling water. You got all sorts of things in married quarters back in those days, and they'd got this, although they didn't use it. They decided it'd be ideal for a party, it had a little tap on the bottom, you know? So they threw in a few bottles of wine, with some soda to add a bit of fizz and a few orange and lemon slices, and that was the punch. Anyone arriving with a bottle—and we all did, "bring a bottle" was the order of the day back then—they were told to put it in the Burco.

'It worked fine, until someone who hadn't got the "wine-only" message arrived with a large demijohn of brandy, cheap local stuff; it was Cyprus, after all. Well, they threw it in and things got really uncorked. Out of our skulls doesn't do it justice, but I think we managed to stay on the right side of decency; just. I have a memory of sitting on the sofa beside some bosomy beauty, leering into her cleavage before I passed out into it, they told me when they woke me up. I don't remember much of it, except they were nice and soft, but firm too, you know?'

He wiggled his eyebrows at his audience, and Pippa laughed despite herself. Dan tried, but he had to look away.

'Dad.'

'Why is it that children, even when they're grown adults, get embarrassed at the idea of their parents having a sex life? You did ask, Dan. You can lower your eyebrows.'

Dan, abashed, managed to laugh at his own reaction.

'No harm was done, Dan. The lady was very good about it, when I'd sobered up and apologised to her later. Hell, nobody behaved very well that night. I even saw Uncle Frank kissing your mother in the garden, before they both staggered back inside.'

Pippa went very still.

'I repeat, no harm done, not by us, at any rate. I can't answer for anybody else present though. Maybe an affair or two started that night, who knows?

'Anyhow, I'm hungry. What say we send out for a Chinese? Save your mother cooking?'

He pushed off from his perch on the arm of the sofa and moved into the kitchen, to rifle around in a drawer for takeaway menus.

*****

Later, when they'd all retired for the night, Pippa looked at the ceiling and spoke with care.

'I didn't know you saw me and Frank kissing that night.'

'Well, I wasn't exactly blameless, taking a nap on some other woman's breasts, now was I? We were all smashed, Pips, more under the influence than usual. You don't drink spirits, not back then and never since, so it probably affected you worse than most. Moments of silliness, that's all they were.

'And I far prefer your boobs,' he added by way of an afterthought.

'Oh?'

She turned to him.

'Hers were too big.'

'I thought bosoms could never be too big.'

'Yes, they can. If you can't get your hand around the whole thing it's a waste. Now these—'

He stretched out and demonstrated with Pippa's own assets, and she didn't stop him.

'You're a far better kisser than Frank, too.'

'Really?'

'Yes. He was a bit too—wet. Plus I know he's always smoked aromatic tobacco, but it's still there, the taste. Not like you.'

She kissed him, lingering over the action.

'You always taste clean, like soap and shampoo.'

'Like this?'

He kissed her, the lightest touch against her lips.

'Yes—a bit harder though.'

'Like this?'

He obliged.

'Yes, much better.'

He went in for the clinch, and they subsided onto the mattress together.

As his body moved across hers, Pippa nevertheless felt a great weight lifting from her.

39: FRANK

He hadn't been himself at all lately, feeling ill in a way he couldn't put his finger on, but lacking in energy and motivation, apathetic, disheartened. He put it down to the attacks on the flat, not to mention Madge's house and car, and who wouldn't feel down after that? All the work he'd put in, all the money he'd spent, and now having to do it again; after cleaning up the mess, of course, and he just couldn't stir himself to do that, beyond the retrieval of some personal bits and pieces.

He hadn't told Matt, who had his hands full with sorting out the burned-down clinic, and Jennifer's recuperation, not to mention Penny in need of new accommodation, all having to be coped with along with his workload. How he managed his father didn't know, and didn't want to add to his worries; so thank God for Simon and Dan, who'd returned from their summer meanderings around the Med and pitched in without question when Simon had rung Frank soon after their return. They had some pretty good practical skills between them, and they'd spent a week with a skip, bucketloads of cleaning materials plus paint and brushes. They'd got the place into a liveable condition, with the addition of some cheap, off-the-shelf curtains and the like, and Frank had put it on the market. He couldn't face living there after this; better to unload it, even at less than he might have hoped to get for it.

His family being attacked, via the flat and Madge's house,

her car, Matt's clinic plus the postal and online trolling, had been and still was stressful in the extreme. Add to that his disastrous and erroneous confrontation and accusation of Abby, which had left him feeling ashamed, and it was no wonder Frank felt ill. The resulting negativity had manifested itself in increased and irrational irritation with Madge, because it was going to be even more difficult to leave her now; but it had to be, in order to facilitate his new plan.

Despite everything, he intended to approach Abby once more, ask her to forgive him and let them start again. He'd have liked to have a place to offer her, to demonstrate seriousness on his part; but now he'd be a man asking to move into her place, which put him at a disadvantage. He hoped to God she'd understand, and forgive him; it wasn't too late. Frank was determined to make it happen; if only he didn't feel quite so strange.

What was the matter with him? He'd been getting himself back in shape, the last few months, taking exercise with his golf along with walks in the woods behind the house, the push-ups and other general fitness exercises he did at home. He'd begun watching his weight too, in a sensible way. No fad diets for Frank but healthy eating, a balanced plan with plenty of fruit and veg, wholewheat, low-fat and low-sugar products where possible, sweetener in his coffee and tea and on his cereal; and now, for his age, he wasn't in bad shape at all, better than a lot of the younger people he saw around, in fact. Whatever was wrong with him, it was a wake-up call.

He'd considered himself awake already, but now he focussed on the fact that he was up there in his seventies, the majority of his life behind him, and in front of him, who knew? The chances got more rather than less the older you got, and he'd known enough people who'd passed away well before they reached his age. People who'd kept fit and healthy too; one man he'd known had suffered a heart attack at the gym, when only in his late fifties. Who knew for certain, when they went to bed for the night, whether or not they were going to wake up the next morning? Frank didn't, and the way he was feeling—

It was time. No more sitting around waiting for the ideal time, like those people who wouldn't exercise whilst on a diet, because they'd didn't want to look bad, jogging in shorts. The apartment could take a while to sell, as it wasn't the ideal time of year, and he might have to wait six months or even a year. No more tenants though; he wanted a lump sum to buy a new place, but he couldn't wait any longer.

Throwing off his lassitude he went upstairs and put some things into a bag. Madge was out, so he couldn't speak to her now, but to hell with it, he wasn't waiting. He'd call her later. In the en-suite he freshened up, throwing cold water on his face. Back downstairs he took bottled water from the fridge to keep hydrated; he had a long drive ahead of him. He could find coffee when he topped-up the tank, and take breaks in service-station car parks.

He was ready. Standing at the front door he took one last look around before turning his back, stepping out, resolute, locking the door behind him. He wanted to post the keys through the letter box, but that would worry Madge before he could speak to her, and he wasn't that much of a heatless bastard; plus, in the event of another break-in it would be giving unlimited future access to the criminals, and oblige her to get the lock changed. He pocketed the keys. He could post them back to his soon-to-be-ex-wife.

Frank was going to reclaim the woman he loved.

He didn't look back as he pulled off the driveway, indicated left and headed down the road.

And the watcher in the car parked not far away pulled out and followed.

Time to talk.

40: MATT/ABBY

'I'm glad we could meet like this. Do things in a civilised manner.'

'Me too. I just wish—'

She reached out and put a finger across his lips.

'No more. We've been through it all, and it makes sense, Matt. What happened, happened. We can't change it, and perhaps we wouldn't want to.'

'Would you?'

'Would you? Don't answer, neither of us is telling and we should leave it like that. We don't take it any further and I hope we both have some good memories. You've got far too much on your plate, you don't need this added complication. So, we have a drink, an affectionate kiss on the cheek, and then we walk away.'

'You're right, I know it. Will you be alright?'

'Of course. I was alright before.'

You were just an optional extra, she didn't say, a windfall, an unexpected bonus. I'd have been fine if you'd never come along. And, given what your father just accused me of, it's better like this. I don't want to see you or any of your benighted family again.

They drank in silence for a moment.

'D'you want another?'

He indicated his empty glass, alcohol-free as usual when

he wasn't overnighting. She drained hers.

'No. Probably better to go. The evening's getting on and you've got a long drive.'

'Can I drop you home?'

'No, it's not far. The walk'll do me good.'

She'd have liked a lift, as that strange sense of being watched was still with her. But better in this instance to part with Matt as soon as possible.

He went inside and paid the bill. She stood as he returned, waited as he donned his jacket, then accompanied him across the square to the car park situated behind the mini-market.

41: FRANK

It was a strange feeling, heading back to her, and not just because he'd committed at last. The odd feeling he'd had before he set out wouldn't go, a bit of heartburn, perspiration, some shortness of breath. Stress. He couldn't let it get the better of him, he needed to get there, get to Abby. She'd forgive him, she'd help him at least to get some medical attention, if these strange symptoms didn't leave him. Ignore them, think of something else.

He couldn't make it happen. He looked out for a layby, but it was several miles more before he found one and pulled in, killing the engine and closing his eyes, reclining in his seat. He reached out and found the water bottle in its holder close by, drank half the bottle—so thirsty—then poured some of the remainder into one palm and applied it to his face.

Time to get on. Not far to go now. He felt like hell and wanted nothing so much as to curl up and go to sleep, but he wasn't going to let this stop him. Just a few more miles.

He pulled up outside her house, struggling out of the car, wincing with the effort, but forced himself up the path and leaned on the bell.

No answer.

He moved back down the path, looked up at the building. All windows closed, no lights on. He listened, to nothing but that particular silence which indicates that nobody's home.

Damn.

He got back to the car, sat, rested. What to do? He should have checked, but if he'd called she'd have hung up on him, he was sure. He could wait, he supposed, but what if she was away, not just for this evening but for a few days, a week or more?

He needed help, he accepted that at last. He managed to drive back into the village square, taking it slow, saw the "P" sign with the arrows pointing down a side road. He found a space, because it wasn't busy at this time of the evening, and parked up. Waves of dizziness went through him, and he almost passed out; but he bent forward, over the steering wheel and waited for it to pass, then climbed out of the car.

And his follower, who'd been with him unnoticed ever since he'd left Madge's house, pulled in nearby.

42: MATT/ABBY

'What's going on?'

There was unusual activity, people rushing from different directions towards the same place. Others stood and looked across, pulling out phones. One man could be heard shouting into his.

It was clear, now that they were closer, that a man lay unconscious on the ground, the man on the phone crouched beside him while others stood around gawping, or filming the scene.

'Bloody ghouls. For God's sake, why don't they help, instead of taking their fucking footage to put on social media?'

Matt heard Abby's outrage behind him as he went into action, running over and getting to his knees beside the supine body, positioned on its side.

'What happened?'

This to the man on his phone.

'I've called 999, they're sending an ambulance. She's telling me what to do.'

'I'm a doctor. Let me speak.'

He took the phone, a brief exchange ensued and then Matt gave back the phone, shaking the prone body by the shoulder, asking if he was okay, hoping for a response, his attention divided between the man on the ground and the man on the phone.

'What happened?'

'He got out of his car and keeled over. I saw it, I'd just pulled in beside him. He got out, closed the door, then bent over, clutching his stomach. He held onto the car, trying to keep upright, and then he just went down.'

'Okay. Stick around.'

He'd been raising the knees, loosening the belt while speaking, not looking up. He'd received no response and now loosened the tie before carefully turning the casualty onto his back to check his breathing. It was then that he recognised the too-pale face.

His father.

*****

He heard the gasp as recognition also hit Abby, standing somewhere behind him. The doctor pushed aside the son, commencing CPR when he found the breathing to be irregular and laboured.

'Is there a defibrillator around here? One of those phone boxes with one?'

'The other side of the square. I'll go.'

Abby took off, angry with herself that in her shock she hadn't already thought of it. What the fuck was Frank doing back here? Come to have a go at her all over again? Whatever, it was clear he was ill, and she wasn't the sort of person to gloat at a time like this.

Matt continued, relieved when Frank began to show signs of life. The sound of a siren, getting louder as it got closer, told him help was at hand. By the time Abby returned, defibrillator in hand, the paramedics were attending to Frank, preparing to put him into the ambulance. She stood behind

Matt, who continued to speak to the driver, turning to her as the man returned to his cab.

'I'm going with him, in the ambulance. I'll get my car later.'

'But what was he doing here? Was he meeting you?'

'No. He didn't know I'd be here. Coming to see you, maybe?'

'Not as far as I know. I've never given him my address, and I haven't seen him since Pip and Graham's party.'

A lie, but Matt didn't need to know that. Anyway, she hadn't sought Frank's unwelcome company.

'That's not important now. They're ready, you need to get going.'

He squeezed her hand. Her lips brushed his cheek.

'I'll call you.'

Then he was gone, into the ambulance, the back doors closed behind him, with a swirl of blue lights and the shriek of the siren.

And the man with the phone climbed into his car and followed.

43: ABBY

Her walk back home was slow, her body heavy, her mind numbed from what had just transpired in the village. It was too much to take in, she couldn't believe it, everything happening all at once like that. Why the hell had Frank returned, and what was wrong with him? He'd been so ill, almost—

No point in going there, torturing herself. She crossed the square, becoming aware of the now-redundant defibrillator in her hand and returning it to the old-fashioned phone box now used to house it. She forced herself onward, across the High Street, along the lane, aware that there were more people around than was usual, more noise, more chatter. A man collapsing in the centre of town, a desperate attempt to save his life, ambulance bells clanging, blue lights flashing; that'll get people talking every time. She just wished she hadn't been connected to it all so closely.

She reached her gate, closed it behind her as she moved up the path, locking the front door behind her with her usual care, even if she was on autopilot. It was getting dark now, that time of evening when she went around closing curtains, after checking the windows and doors covered by them were locked and bolted, but tonight she didn't have the energy. With an effort she kicked off her shoes, then went to the kitchen, finding the chilled bottle in the fridge and pouring a large glass. She'd had a couple with Matt, but she needed more now.

She took both glass and bottle and returned to the lounge, sitting without lights in the gathering gloom, gazing blankly before her as she gulped her wine, trying to make sense of the events which had just unfolded.

Frank. How awful he'd looked, unconscious on the ground, white-faced and shrunken-looking. She remembered the last time she'd seen him, before Graham's party, before their recent disastrous encounter. He'd been getting red-faced and podgy back then; it must have been about sixteen or seventeen years ago, and he hadn't improved in the interim. He'd looked terrible at the party, in her eyes. He'd grown even stouter and his walk, once so confident and with what she could only describe as a military swagger about it, had become slow, ponderous and hesitant; a prematurely-aged man's walk. His face had become flabby, sagging around the jowls, the skin coarsened in texture and reddened in an unbecoming fashion. His lips, thick and sensual as they had been, seemed smaller in ratio to the now-inflated face, framed by hair which was thinning and a light grey for the most part.

What'd bothered her most was his eyes. They'd been blue, to match his almost-fairness, which Abby had found attractive when she'd first met him, despite the fact that she'd always been drawn to dark colouring. He wasn't her type at all, but those eyes were mesmerising. She could feel them following her around even when she wasn't looking at him, and when she did look they bored into her, burning with desire, holding her within their blue fire. She'd always been powerless to escape from them.

At the party they'd appeared as if clouded over, the fire extinguished and his passion for life with them. Their focus wasn't here, in this world; they'd been looking elsewhere, towards a place to which nobody could go with him. Surely he wasn't thinking about death, she thought, with an involuntary shiver. He's only in his seventies, and if it's not exactly teenage it's not necessarily the end of the road either. He could have another twenty-five years in him. I know people go much younger—look at Gerry—but that isn't always the case.

She remembered after the party when, safely ensconced in her hotel room, she'd grown exasperated at the thought of what he'd been, and what he'd become. For Christ's sake, she'd addressed him in her mind. You're a soldier, or you were; why the hell don't you *fight?* Stop shuffling around like a living corpse and *do something,* sort yourself out and start to *live* again! She'd burst into tears of frustration over this man, who she'd loved so much, and what he might have been, and what he'd become instead. She'd cried until she couldn't cry any more, restraining herself as best she could in case anybody else heard; which was silly, she was in a hotel. What did she care if the next room heard her sobbing?

She'd let it all out as best she could, and when she'd finished a cold anger took hold of her. Why doesn't he look after himself better, she'd thought with fury. Why isn't that fair, fat and fifty-something—yeah, right—bitch taking better care of him? Her rage knew no bounds. He could have had *me,* but no. Was I so bad, that he preferred *her,* that great pudding? I loved him, I'd have looked after him. My houses have always been spotless, I can clean and launder and iron with the best of them, and if I'm not MasterChef I'm not a bad cook. Gerry always ate everything I made, and came back for more, and he was a notoriously fussy eater.

Bloody Frank. I'd have got the weight off him, and kept it off, because I know diets, who better? I've spent half my fucking life on them. I'd have put him on one so subtle he wouldn't have known he was on it. I'd have got him fit again, taken him for country walks with me, as well as encouraging him to play more golf. If he'd gone drinking in the clubhouse afterwards it would've just have meant the diet would take a bit longer, but at least he'd have been getting some exercise. And of course I'd have made love to him, whenever and wherever and however he wanted. He'd never have ended up in this state if I'd been looking after him.

Her rage had found another focus then, and she'd cursed that skinny blonde bitch Penny for what she'd done to him. To leave him when he was still relatively young and handsome, when he was surrounded by people, in the middle of his career, when he could have found someone else, was one thing. But to leave him when he was on the verge of retirement, expecting to settle down with her after a life of travelling wherever they were sent, was cruel. Abby couldn't have done it, and it'd hurt her to think of him, ageing, alone and unloved. Everyone needs someone to hold and be held by, and he was a very physical man, as she well knew. Even his children couldn't do much to fill his need to be held, because he only had sons; and although the man-hug existed, daughters were more prone to hugs, and cuddles, but he had none. She'd thought of the little girl they might've had, if things had been different, but they hadn't; so with his need for physical contact unfulfilled, it was no wonder he'd married the pudding.

She'd tried to be fair. Perhaps Penny'd been struggling with her own mid-life crisis, with a bit of empty-nest syndrome thrown in when her sons left home. Nevertheless, Abby found it difficult to excuse the woman. Her bruised and battered feelings went around and around her head, and she ended up back where she'd started. He must have been so hurt when Penny left him, but he'd have coped, and then he could have found *me,* and said, Now I can marry you, my darling. But no, he went to *her,* married *her,* that great lump! How insecure must he have been.

How the hell had she allowed him into her life anyway? She'd been married, ought to have been happy, all things considered. It wasn't a bad thing, a lifestyle unlike that I'd lived before. Gerry was ambitious, each successive promotion meant moving elsewhere, so for those years we lived in rented accommodation; a bit ragged around the edges, but streets ahead of where I'd lived before. It was fun, shopping to find the personal bits and pieces which would turn them into homes, and I didn't have to work, although he made it clear I was welcome to if I wanted. I didn't. He was earning enough to support us both, and it sounds crazy to say it, but I enjoyed being a housewife. It was poles apart from how I'd kept house before. No limited budget and no unhealthy diet of cheap foods; instead fresh fruit, vegetables, meat, and Gerry loved his meat. I had fun learning to cook, rather than reheat, and I bought recipe books for the first time.

I had my own washing machine and tumble dryer, bought and paid for, rather than sitting in the grubby launderette with drug dealers coming and going, having whispered conversations while goods and money changed hands. I had a dishwasher and a vacuum cleaner and my husband, a generous and civilised man who came with me to buy sheets and towels and all sorts of things and didn't watch every penny as I'd had to do in the past.

We'd had a registry office wedding, just a few friends present. I had no dreams about spending a small fortune entertaining hundreds of people. We bought new clothes, a suit for him, a smart dress for me, outfits we could use again. I didn't want a white dress; it would've been impractical and probably would've got stained at the gastropub where we went for a meal afterwards. We went to a country house hotel for a long weekend by way of a honeymoon, country walks and meals from the hotel's award-winning restaurant. And sex, when it arrived at last, wasn't bad. He was considerate and patient, and it was satisfactory. I couldn't see what all the fuss was about, but it was a part of my big new life and I was satisfied, overall.

It didn't last. A few years into marriage the novelty of it all was wearing off, a workaholic husband leaving me lonely. I could cope with that, but I'd been alone for most of my life before marriage and I'd hoped for more companionship. Gerry was a good man, but like everyone he had faults, and I suppose he was what would be called obsessive-compulsive these days. He drove me mad, wiping the sink, or the shower, into a state of perfect cleanness and dryness after every use; lots of little everyday things like that, and if we had a function to attend which didn't require mess kit he'd obsess over the dress code, and whether or not he should wear a tie.

He carried this fixation into his work, in which he demanded no less than perfection. To this end, he frequently went in early, came home late and skipped lunch most days of the week. He'd work at weekends if necessary, and it was often necessary. I began to feel resentful, that I came second to the almighty workplace, which didn't have an improving effect on the romantic side of our life.

Starved of the trappings of romantic love. No wonder when it came knocking I fell right in. Could I help—

The shrill insistent sound of the doorbell jolted her out of her thoughts, causing her to jump. Who, at this late hour? She knew so few people, nobody came calling on her even during daylight hours.

Matt. It had to be. Why was he here, why not in the ambulance with his father, or already at the hospital and the urgent treatment which Frank needed. Unless—

No, please no. She raced to the door, all caution to the winds, threw it open without checking through the spyhole—and then fell back before the stranger who stood before her. They looked at each other.

'Hello, Mother.'

44: ABBY

Her heart skipped a beat at the sight of the man before her. Hard, cold eyes, no smile. Not Matt, but an unwelcome visitor from the past.

'Bryn.'

Her voice was barely a whisper. That bastard, come back to haunt her.

She noticed the look of confusion that passed over his face and re-adjusted. Not that bastard. Too young, she realised.

'Robert.'

He responded to her correct recognition, his tone less certain than it had been.

'We need to talk. May I?'

She stood aside, too shocked to refuse. He moved past her, into her home, her safe space. When she didn't follow he came back and closed the door, then stood, staring at her.

'You do know me then.'

His bitterness wasn't lost on her. She said nothing, just stared. He tried another tack.

'Who's Bryn?'

She'd got herself together now. She could do this.

'Your father. But I'm not your mother. I'm your half-sister.'

His turn to be shocked.

'You're lying.'

Something snapped. How dare he, the son of such a father, accuse her of lying.

'No. Ask Kathleen, if you don't believe me. Kathleen and Pat. They raised you, didn't they? I don't know what they told you about who you were before they adopted you, but they knew. Maybe it's them you should be questioning, instead of turning up on my doorstep like a thief in the night.'

She reached out and pulled the door wide open, inviting him to walk out through it. He stayed stock still, his face working, confusion replacing the bitterness.

'No, please. I've come too far. I mean, I need to know. They didn't tell me. That I was adopted, yes, but no more, nothing. I've been checking for myself, since she died.'

'Kathleen's dead? And Pat?'

'A few years ago. Her, about ten months back.'

He staggered a little, putting out a hand to steady himself.

'Look, I'm sorry. Could we—.'

She could see his turmoil, so took pity on him; he was the baby she'd cared for, after all. She led him to the kitchen, indicating a chair at the table whilst taking water from the fridge and pouring a glass, which she handed to him without a word. He drank it, in similar silence, then looked up at her as he put down the glass.

'Wait.'

She left him there, going through to the lounge to open a cupboard in the sideboard. Kneeling down she sorted through mounds of paperwork, at last bringing out a folder from near the bottom. Returning to the kitchen she sat opposite her unwelcome guest, sorting through the contents and extracting one document, then another.

'Look.'

She showed him the birth certificates. One for her, one for him. Same mother, different fathers.

'Your mother was mine, Irene Lewis, an ordinary working-class woman who slaved to raise me alone when my father went. Left her one day, didn't even say he was going. Just went off to work as usual, she told me, and didn't come home. She later found he'd gone off with another woman, had a job all lined-up in the Gulf, with good money; but nevertheless he cleared out the bank account before he went, leaving Mum penniless.

'She had to do it all herself, cleaning, child-minding, taking in laundry, whatever she could fit around caring for her child; me.'

His was not the only bitterness in the room now.

'She had no life, it was all work, for others or for me. Then *he* came along and seduced her with his smarmy charm and fake promises. Took her out, dinner, drinks, dancing, cinema, you name it, and she fell, hook, line and sinker, fell in love with him, that phoney, and I was happy for her, at first, and then—

'She didn't know she was pregnant with you until he was long gone, the scummy bastard, and good riddance to him. Oh yes, and between seducing her and vanishing he tried to rape me, that piece of shit. It got him nothing but badly-bruised balls, prick that he was.'

Her eyes gleamed, then darkened as she saw his wince.

'I'm sorry. I know he was your father. But if you'd seen him, met him—'

She choked, then continued.

'It was hard for her, the prospect of another child to raise alone, and she much older than the first time around. I was seventeen by then, able to work and contribute some cash to keep us going.'

She looked away, as he was unable to do.

'There were complications in your birth. Even the caesarean they tried couldn't do it. It saved you, but not her.'

She raised her burning eyes, and he couldn't look away.

'I tried to raise you. You were my mother's son, why wouldn't I? But it was difficult, because I couldn't help but see him in you. I managed for a bit, gave up my shop job and started cleaning work, so I could take you with me, in your little Moses basket, and you could be there with me while I worked. That's how I met Kathleen. She used to come home early, before I'd finished. She liked playing with you, she'd do that while I finished up, then she'd put the kettle on and we'd have a cuppa, you on her lap, and have a natter.

'That's how come she asked me if she and Pat could adopt you. They couldn't have their own kids, same old story, but it was clear she loved you; she was besotted with you. She saw how I was placed and offered to babysit, kept you overnight sometimes, so I could get out and have some of the life a young woman ought to have.

'Then they suggested adopting you, and it was like manna from Heaven.'

He interrupted.

'There was no birth certificate in Kathleen's papers, although I didn't expect one. I'd checked it, and found that adoptive parents get a certificate of adoption instead. But I couldn't even find one of those. There were just some papers with your name on them, a sort of informal, home-made document agreeing to pay you eighty thousand pounds.'

His eyes were hard again. She lowered hers from that fierce gaze.

'It wasn't a regular adoption. Kathleen worked as a teaching assistant. She didn't need to, they were well-off, with Pat owning a building company. She loved children, you see, and this way she could be with them. Some kid had made an allegation against her. It was untrue, and proved so; you only had to see her with children to know she could never hurt one. The brat blamed Kathleen for bad exam results, rather than her own lack of work, and thought she'd get revenge. The little bitch fell apart under questioning, and Kathleen was exonerated, but mud sticks, and she was worried it'd be held against her, so she wouldn't apply again. They'd done it before, you see, but the social worker assigned to profile them wasn't convinced they weren't still hoping for their own biological child.

'When I brought you into her life Kathleen fell in love with you. She loved playing with you, babysitting you, having you stop over. When she realised that looking after you was depriving me of my own life she came up with the idea of taking you on herself.'

'What about Pat?'

'He cared for you too—but more for Kathleen. He saw how having you around affected her, and wanted to make her happy. If keeping you did that then he'd do it. Whatever she desired, he wanted to give it to her. He loved her, even to the extent of breaking the law by buying a child for her.'

'So you sold me to them.'

'What did I have to look forward to? A life like my mother's, minimum-wage work, raising a child not even my own, no education, no social life, no boyfriends. They were offering me the chance to get all that, as well as an enormous sum of money. Of course I sold you. What would you have done?'

She challenged him, although her eyes were softer now, a wry smile on her face, while his mouth had loosened around the edges.

'I need coffee. You?'

'I guess.'

She began the process, surprised to find him beside her searching for the jar in the cabinet while she found the mugs. They worked together, sitting at the table to drink the reviving brew. Draining his, he leaned back in his chair.

'I'm sorry for ambushing you as I did. I've been so unsure about confronting you. I've kept meaning to, almost done it, and then funked it. Tonight I—'

'Do you mean you've been here before? Have you been watching me?'

'Yes. I couldn't quite bring myself—'

'I knew it. I kept having this feeling, but whenever I looked around there was nobody. It's been freaking me out.'

He had the grace to look ashamed.

'I don't know what else to say. I wasn't sure if you were the right person. I mean, everything I found out suggested it was you, and when I saw you I thought—. Well, I don't know what I thought, to be honest. It's not easy, approaching a total stranger. Then tonight I got angry with myself, and sort of turned it against you for abandoning me—I mean—I didn't know—'

He trailed off, and their eyes met. He looked away first.

'I don't know whether to be angry or relieved. Certainly the last. At least now I know what's been going on. Okay. How did you find me?'

'It wasn't easy. There was no adoption certificate, like I told you, and no birth certificate. Mum, Kathleen, that is, she told me just before she died. It was a lot to take in, I'm sure you can imagine. She told me about you, how you'd worked for her, the area where you'd lived, but apart from that, there was nothing. I had to do a lot of digging around, hire specialists, but at last I tracked you down.'

'I stopped working for Kathleen after she took you, although we kept in touch for a while. It made it possible for her to tell people that she'd adopted you through regular channels. Not long afterwards I met a man. He was in the Forces, and when we got married I went overseas with him; so if any of Kathleen's friends asked about the young cleaner who'd had a baby she could tell them the truth, and they'd just assume the baby had gone with me. At a certain point we lost touch; it seemed better to break the connection. I know it doesn't sound great, but I hope you understand.'

'I suppose.'

His smile was shaky, but brightened as he raised his eyes to hers. She gasped.

'What?'

'Your smile. You look just like her. Mum. Our mother, I mean.'

She watched, entranced. It'd been so long since she'd seen that expression. At last she broke the spell.

'So, tell me about yourself. What do you do?'

'A builder. Pat left the company to me, so I run it now. I started working for him in my teens, from the bottom up. The best way to get to know the business, he said, and I agreed. I loved it. They'd have sent me to university if I'd wished it, but building was all I ever wanted to do.'

'I see. Any family?'

'A wife, Moira, and two kids, Ben and Jessie. Jessie's married with a girl of her own. You should meet them.'

'I'd love to.'

She meant it. She'd been alone for too long. Abby was good at being by herself, but wasn't averse to company, and this was family, something she'd been lacking for most of her life.

She made more coffee, and they sat through the night, catching-up.

*****

She hadn't forgotten about Frank, and Matt, but managed to put them out of mind. Robert had gone by the time Matt called, which was just as well, given what he had to tell her.

She sat up, unable to sleep, trying to take in the momentous events of the evening, and the potential fallout.

45: MATT

He emerged from the ward where Frank was on life support, being monitored and tested, the cause of his collapse as yet undetermined, to be accosted by a flustered-looking man who looked vaguely familiar

'Please, I need to speak to you. It's urgent, but I can't get the staff to take notice as he's not a relative. He's your father, I gather. Please, this could save his life.'

Recognition dawned on Matt, although he didn't take in everything that was being said to him.

'The car park. You called the ambulance, right?'

'Yes, and—'

'Thanks for being there for him. You didn't have to come, I mean—'

'The thing is, I wasn't there by accident.'

Matt turned to him, head on one side.

'Look, can we talk? Please. You want him to live, don't you?'

Matt didn't know what to think. Too much had happened in the space of the evening, coming on top of a mind already exhausted by the misfortunes of months past. He looked the guy up and down; he seemed serious, earnest. Maybe he was genuine, but then again there were so many nut-jobs around these days—

He looked up and down the corridor. Plenty of people, members of the public and staff. He noted a security guard stationed not far away. If he stayed in public and on his guard it couldn't hurt to listen.

'You say you weren't there by accident? In the car park?'

'No. I'd been following him since he left home. He stopped a few times and I just thought he was taking a break, so I did too. Then he collapsed when he got out of the car.'

Matt turned away, looking around for the security guy, spotting him and raising his hand.

'No, please, listen.'

He reached out and grasped the extended arm, Matt pulling away from him. The security man, sensing trouble, began moving towards them.

'Look, I'm Richard Sadler. Madge is my stepmother.'

He had Matt's attention.

'Everything alright here, sir?'

The security guard had arrived, ready to break up anything before it got started.

'No, thanks very much. We're all good here.'

The man gave them the once-over, then nodded and moved off, back in the direction from which he'd come.

'Let's sit.'

Matt indicated the line of fold-down seats for those who waited.

'In a bit, but first, it's important. Tell them to check him for arsenic, or another poison. Please, I'm telling you. You're a doctor, aren't you? You know it needs to be done right away.'

Matt gave him a long look, then whirled to re-enter the ward, where he imparted the information he'd received. They took notice, knowing him for a doctor; but what if I hadn't been, he wondered. Would they listen to anybody who wasn't a part of the medical profession? Maybe not, or maybe they'd arrest him as a suspect.

As it was, Matt returned and sat with Richard, listening to

his incredible tale while waiting to see if his information was correct. Richard Sadler, son of David Sadler, Chief Pharmacist and experimental pharmacologist at a prestigious teaching hospital. Richard had broken off contact with him when David divorced his first wife, Richard's mother, to marry Madge, who Richard never liked. Smug, self-satisfied, sly and superficial, only out for herself and what she could screw out of his father. Besotted as he was with his "blonde bombshell" David couldn't see it; but Richard could.

He'd made it his business to find out everything he could about Madge, which had turned up the information that her first husband had died in unsavoury circumstances; an instance of "erotic asphyxiation," it'd seemed, the man having been found with a ligature around his neck while suspended from a coat hook in a cupboard. Madge hadn't exactly advertised the circumstances which had resulted in her first widowhood, it being somewhat seedy to say the least, but she'd confided in David, her new target, who'd fallen hook, line and sinker for her weeping-widow act.

It wasn't long before his own death that David had contacted his son, desperate it seemed to speak to him again, and although he didn't know why, Richard had agreed to meet him. He'd been shocked at how different his father had looked, thinner, greyer, frail even, although David had dismissed his concerns and announced himself "in the pink of health," although certain contradictory statements he'd made in their ensuing conversation suggested he was anything but. He was feeling his age, not always able to keep up with his much-younger wife, and Richard had received the distinct impression that his father was no longer as enamoured of her as he'd once been.

He felt there was something David wanted to tell him, but wasn't doing so, and when the son asked outright his father had denied any such thing. His aim in meeting seemed almost to be to say goodbye to his son, as though he had a premonition of death. Richard had dismissed the idea out of hand, as his father feeling a bit down and giving in to morbid thoughts. Nevertheless, it was only six months later that David passed-away, with a verdict of accidental death given when it appeared he'd become careless in the lab and managed to ingest a poisonous compound.

'The thing is, he was never sloppy in his work. He couldn't afford to be, given the hazardous materials he worked with. He drummed it into me, from a young age, the need to be careful and precise in whatever I did, and he set a good example. I remember him telling me how once, when he was in his teens and working in a lab, he'd experienced a burning sensation across the front of his thighs. A switched-on member of staff, who'd been there for years, rushed him outside, shouted at him to take off his jeans and hosed him down. It turned out that a very disorganised member of staff, the stereotypical mad-scientist type, had been working with sulphuric acid at one of the sinks outside the fume cupboard; an absolute no-no, as you're aware. He was given a warning, and fortunately my dad didn't get any permanent scars from the incident. What puzzled him more than anything was why there was a connected hosepipe in the yard outside the building; but he took the lesson to heart and made sure he always did things by the book.

'I couldn't accept that his death had been an accident, and I couldn't help feeling that Madge had been involved somehow. You might say I'd watched too much TV, real-life crime stories of "black widow" women, serial husband-killers, that sort of thing; but she'd already been widowed once. I tried to be fair, to feel it was my dislike of her twisting things, but however hard I tried I could never lose this gut feeling that it was her behind it. I couldn't prove it, however; I had absolutely no evidence, and I tried to put it behind me.

But then I joined a golf club—my old one had to shut down, some dispute over land ownership—and as it turned out it was the one where Madge was a member.

'I hadn't known. My father never played. Too busy with his work, and he wasn't an outdoor person, happiest at home with his head in a book. But there she was, at the bar surrounded by men like moths hovering around a flame, and there was I. She didn't recognise me because we'd never met. I'd always refused to have anything to do with her, even before I cut the old man off, and her with him; but I'd seen her from afar. I'd followed him when my mother confided that she thought he was having an affair, so I'd tailed him a few times, and got lucky and seen him with Madge. And here she was, still playing the flirt with the men of her own age, and I didn't join them because I'm a lot younger than her.

'It became a thing to keep an eye on her. Not follow her, as such, but see her around the club, laughing and drinking with her circle; so I heard about it when she married your father, and I couldn't help being worried for him. That's all I did, honestly, watched them both; and then he started to lose weight and look a bit drawn, so I followed him a few times, although I never approached him. What could I say, without looking like a fool? But I saw him the other day and he looked terrible, so I took my courage and went round to the house to have a word.

'I knew Madge was at a lunch at the club. I'd seen her there, so there was no danger of her coming back any time soon. But when I parked up outside the house there was Frank, coming out the door looking thin and pale, and I knew something was up and determined to follow him. I didn't know he'd be taking such a long journey, but I had nothing else to do and it seemed important to speak to him, now I'd made up my mind. You might think I'm crazy, but I followed him into the car park, and saw him collapse, so went to him and called the ambulance. Then you turned up, and here we are.'

'And if it is what you think it is—'

'Arsenic.'

'Then we might have your proof.'

They looked at each other, silent, then Matt bent over and put his head in his hands while Richard leaned back and looked at the ceiling. After a long moment he stood, going to the water cooler along the corridor and returning with two full cups. They drank, and waited, and waited—

'Doctor Fairfield, please.'

Matt opened his eyes to see the doctor who'd been attending to Frank standing outside the ward door, beckoning him. He stood, turned back to Richard.

'You'll wait?'

'I'm not going anywhere.'

46: MADGE

The police have been in touch. A gang has been apprehended. Vandals, one of the car park employees in league with them, switching off the CCTV cameras and looking the other way while they went to work. They were looking for cars to steal, and mine being such a superior vehicle I'm sure they were attracted to it. The security system being so sophisticated they couldn't break in, however, so it appears they vandalised it out of frustration and spite.

Mindless morons. Disgraceful. But at least now I know, and that's one thing less to concern me. I have other, larger, matters on my mind.

I wait, and I watch, because I'm sure the police will soon be turning up on the doorstep to inform me. Such bad luck, people will say, and I'll play the grieving widow to perfection; I've had enough practice. I shall be dignified in my mourning, and admired for my fortitude. I shan't marry again, although I'm sure I'll have offers enough. Three is plenty, however. I've had enough of this nonsense, and it's so exhausting. I'll be social, of course, accept invitations to dinner, the theatre, everything I enjoy and that's available to me; but I'll come home alone, in a taxi. No need for those soulful looks after accepting a lift, all that "Aren't you going to ask me in for a coffee?" rubbish. We all know what that means, and I'll be having none of it.

I see them coming now, and I know. They park on the driveway. Why can't they leave it on the street? This is private property. Even if their business is with me, they ought to know how to behave. I'll have to let it go, however; there are more important things to be done here.

They're coming up the drive, two of them, one male, the other female; appropriate for attending to a distressed woman. I calm myself, compose my features. I know how to comport myself in this situation. I've been in it before. The worried wife, soon to be the grieving widow.

They're knocking at the door. A real door-knocker, antique brass, no common electric bells in this house, so vulgar, so modern-day. I like whoever comes to know that here at least may be found some class, some style.

I don't make them wait too long. I open, my calm smile turning to anxious when I see the uniforms. It's the recommended reaction when the law comes calling and, although it grieves me to behave like the common herd, I must adopt the behaviour most expected and accepted for such a situation.

I gasp. There's no need for words. My fallen face, my open mouth, the question in my eyes, these things say it all. They ask my name. Mrs Fairfield? I incline my head, just so, and speak the prescribed words. What is it, what's happened?

They speak again, but their words—I don't believe them. This is not what they should be saying. The script is wrong, my anxiety real now. I'm in shock, not feigned, I'm paralysed with terror. The female speaks; I incline my head. I gather up my dignity, what's left of it. I take my coat from off the peg, handbag from beneath it. Such automatic gestures. I'm in a bad dream, a nightmare. This can't be happening.

She guides me to the car, helps me into the back. My legs are jelly, won't support me. She sits beside me, while he drives. I sense the people watching us, watching me, as he backs us down the drive, along the street. The neighbours' curtains twitching, the eyes that peep between Venetian blinds, the man at number forty-two out with the shears, the mower, the woman further on, bucket and hose in hand, to wash her car.

I see it all, and then I'm back where I should be, inside my own head. At last, rage takes me.

How dare they do these things to me! Not just these functionaries, wearers of ill-fitting uniforms, but all of them. You, Carl, you who started it, when you married me and swore to be the world to me. How you failed me. You seemed the real thing, the genuine article. A man of business, well-set-up, handsome in a rugged sort of way, divorced. I ought to have considered that more deeply, but you were so attentive, too much so, I fear. Business trips everywhere, first-class flights, the best hotels, the finest foods and wines. Bringing me presents, flowers, chocolates, jewellery—oh such jewellery—and then the lingerie—and the rest. Wanting me to wear certain garments—or not—to sit with you, watch those vile videos, look through those disgusting magazines, then join with you in some of the revolting acts we'd seen in them were doing. And you wouldn't take no for an answer.

No more. You had to go, degenerate that you were. It wasn't difficult, although distasteful, to lure you into a trap of your own making. Erotic asphyxiation, it's called, and you were fascinated with the idea, with a little encouragement from me. How easy, once you were on the hook—in every sense—to push you forward, beyond the perverted pleasure you sought, into the abyss. I played my part to perfection, afterwards, weeping and wailing and conscious of the disgrace of the manner of your passing from this world. I inherited everything, of course, and I kept this house. People thought I stayed to be reminded of you, to be close to the ghost of my beloved husband. Nothing could be further from the truth. I wanted to forget you, sick bastard that you were, but this was my house now and it pleased me to stay, to move my new husband in and laugh at you, Carl, because I had the last laugh, didn't I?

I wasn't looking for another husband. Or so I thought, because one day there was David, a fellow guest at some gathering or other, and clearly smitten with me. How could I resist? She wasn't right for him, that first wife of his; it became clear after several conversations. Such an intelligent man, thoughtful, an academic, unlike the self-made wide-boy who'd blinded me with bling. David had that way with him. A mere bunch of flowers, given with the right words; why would I want more? He'd have given expensive gifts, I'm sure, but I fell in love with his delicacy of manner. He was sensitive to my every need, and I loved him for that.

He didn't attempt to anticipate our marriage, but waited while his divorce went through, and then, joy of joys, he was a sensitive lover, undemanding, which suited me just fine. I'd had enough of sex, with Carl and his warped ways. If David wanted to put me on a pedestal I was more than happy to be up there, looking down and favouring him with the sunshine of my smile; and we were happy, for a while.

It didn't last. You couldn't help yourself, could you, David? You neglected me in favour of the health of the nation. Married already to your work, you let me slip into the background, into the role of little woman. You gave me what little time you had left over at the end of each long working day, but you didn't give me children, by way of compensation. You could at least have made me a mother, justified my existence in that way. But what did I become to you? A housekeeper, cooking, cleaning, shopping, washing, gardening. Keeping a comfortable home to which you could return, your important mission of the day accomplished.

My position was untenable, yet your purpose nourished mine. The stories you told me, each evening, the events of your day. Chief Pharmacist, overseeing everything drug-related at the hospital, relaying to me the characteristics and uses of a variety of drugs. Who would think to look to me, the little wife, when your own death occurred? You never brought any drugs home, which would be illegal, but the necessary substances aren't hard to come by, if you know where to look; and I made it my business to find out. Your death was assumed to be through accidental ingestion of toxic substances used in pharmacology, at your place of work. Poor David. Hoist with your own petard. Tragic.

As to your widow, I became the toast of the golf club, my pastime, my relaxation, my escape from the domestic drudgery to which you'd abandoned me. I wasn't exactly in love with the game, but it made for an outing, a social balance to my drab and housewife life. I preferred to hold court at the bar, to talk to others, and when you died I had my pick of the men, even the married ones. I wouldn't have taken one of those, I'm not the marriage-breaking-other-woman type—not since you, that is.

I had to take more care, this time around. To lose one husband looks like misfortune, as Oscar Wilde said, two like carelessness; or criminality. Widowed twice, through unnatural causes, the police might look more closely. Who would I choose, from all those ready to console me for my latest loss? They all faded into insignificance when you joined the club, Frank. I knew as soon as I met you that I favoured you over the others, with your husky voice and winning ways. I wanted you, and I got you. I cared for you, fed you the right foods, encouraged you to exercise. I succeeded, but you failed me too. I knew you'd fallen out of love with me, if you were ever in it. Was I a mere convenience, a provider of home comforts to you, as I was to Carl, to David?

I knew you were planning to leave me. I checked the estate agents' websites for rental properties, perused their windows when in town, I even went inside and enquired, but yours wasn't there. You weren't hard to see through, Frank. Don't think I didn't find out what you were up to. I know when you're lying, I've watched you over time and I can see the signs. I knew you were renovating your flat for yourself, so it had to be "vandalised" when you were about to move in, and my house had to be "burgled" around the same time; but not so badly that we couldn't continue living there together.

You fool, Frank. You couldn't even work out that your flat was trashed when I was away on an overnight with my book-club friends; or so I told you. Not difficult to let myself in during the evening, after dark, with the key I'd had cut from the impression I'd taken of your own. It took a bit of time, wrecking the place quietly, but I managed it, with some music playing. The neighbours were used to you being there, knocking things about as you renovated it, so probably didn't even register any sounds I made. I had to leave quietly, drive a distance and sleep in the car; not wonderful, but necessary, and no wonder you thought me grumpy on account of a hangover when I came home in the morning. The fact that your next-door-neighbour was away for a few days, so that you discovered the damage yourself, with no warning to soften the blow, was the icing on the cake.

It wasn't difficult then to do a bit of damage to my own lounge, a few days later, with a hammer and crowbar from my own garden shed. Easy to pretend that intruders came through the woods and used my own tools to break into my house, too easy for me to come home and "interrupt" them, running next door to raise the alarm. A lucky break for me that my car got vandalised. Even though I hated it, it made the case for me being targeted as well as you. The gods of chaos were with me.

No one divorces me, Frank. I'm a desirable woman. I had my pick, and I chose you, but see how you repaid me. Preparing to leave me, me, the toast of the golf club, who could have had anybody but chose you, you, washed-up petty little soldier-boy. You were nothing compared to my previous husbands, professional men both, with letters after their names, and not a few of those either. Did you really think a pathetic little military rank could come up to either of them? I think not. Professional or not, they had their own nasty little habits, and they paid for those as you should now be paying for yours.

There's no such thing as a "black widow," which is what they'll call me. So unfair. I was widowed twice, although it should have been thrice, and it wasn't my fault; I was forced to it by Carl, by David, by you, and you all had to go, I merely did what needed doing. It wasn't difficult to feed you poison in the sugar substitute I gave you on your breakfast cereal every day, and in your coffee and tea. It's such a sweet substance, artificially so, ideal to cover anything extra you might detect, although that was unlikely. Arsenic famously has no smell or taste, and it isn't used too much in rodenticides these days; but I know that rusty old tin in the shed contains one which David bought years ago. I don't know where he obtained it, but I do know that you'd been using it in recent months, Frank, when we saw rats in the garden that had presumably come from the woods behind the house. That's what I was going to tell the authorities, at any rate, when you were dead of arsenic poisoning.

You, Frank, you should have been my salvation. You should be dead, not somewhere in a hospital bed, recovering. That's what I assume, from what they said. Not "murder" but "attempted murder." I'm no murderer; I merely give certain people what they deserve, and if that happens to be death, well, so be it.

As for that boring party, all your old crowd, your family and friends.

They all think Madge, stupid Madge, lumpy, dumpy, Madge; let's walk all over her. What did I ever do to them, to deserve their contempt? I'm better than all of them. Your drunken ex-wife, your goody-good friends Pippa and Graham, your disgusting homosexual son together with theirs. Dog-dirt for her, a few home truths about the sexual-deviants for them, and then there's your other son. The doctor, oh so superior with his private clinic to supplement his already-obscene salary from the NHS. I burned down his pretentions, reduced them to ashes, and destroyed his happy home. His ageing whore, that disgusting bitch who was yours before. I saw you looking at her, and I know that look. Can she console him? I doubt it.

And of course his domestic goddess wife, the ex-porn model parading as a model of virtue. Thinks she's fucking Kate Middleton, so wonderful, so distributing of largess to all and sundry. I saw her in all her sordid glory, in those magazines my pervert first husband used to buy. The gods wouldn't let me stop buying them in secret, perusing them in fear lest Carl had submitted the pictures he took of me for others to leer at in those repulsive pages. It was never about blackmail, just to tear down her façade of respectability in her own eyes. Just sending the pictures was enough to let that so-perfect self-satisfied little bitch suffer.

Thought you were so superior, didn't you, Jennifer, looking down your haughty long nose at me, along with your husband and the rest. Me, Madge Palmer, neé Fox, neé Sadler, now Fairfield, beautiful, accomplished, the toast of the golf club, respectable widow of not one but two professional gentlemen; although I use the term advisedly. And what were you? The cover and centrefold of dirty magazines, for a bunch of filthy perverts to slobber and do we all know what else over. Revolting creature; and you dared to patronise me! I wonder how you felt as you were gulping down those pills. Not so wonderful then, I'm sure.

I despise you all. I'm a beautiful woman. I could have had my pick but I chose you, Frank, who let me down every bit as badly as Carl and David. Use me as some sort of inferior creature, just about good enough to perform domestic duties for you in your declining years? Oh no. I deserved better.

EPILOGUE

It'd been a long few months, Matt thought, but so much had been resolved in that time, and now at last they could move forward. He thought back to that terrible night, waiting at the hospital while the staff fought for his father's life, which in the event was saved by one unknown to them all, who'd watched from the sidelines, waiting for any piece of evidence, however small, which could right a wrong from years ago.

So much else had been put right. Jen had seen a therapist, and been able to overcome her fears enough to undergo a procedure under general anaesthetic. A short and routine operation, performed by a colleague who Matt knew as one of the best. Run-of-the-mill for him perhaps, but an Everest to climb for Jennifer. Matt had been present, which his special status allowed, and seen that all was well, being there when Jen awoke in the recovery room. The surgery, along with a reduced workload for both husband and wife, meant matters between the couple were improved, with regular weekends away as the icing on the cake.

The home was looked after by Penny, happy to take charge and look after the children, the pets and the house while the parents were gone. She also helped care for Frank, who stayed in the main house upon his discharge from hospital and with whom she'd made her peace. In the same spirit of coming to terms with the past she'd had a heart-to-heart with both Matt and Simon, disclosing the information of the child she'd had prior to her marriage. Both sons were supportive, and Simon having a more flexible occupation was helping her seek the child, now a fully-grown woman; because the baby had been a girl, that much they'd ascertained so far. Whether or not she'd want to establish contact remained to be seen.

Simon and Dan made frequent visits, as did Pippa and Graham, whose relationship was better than ever. Frank was only to be there while he regained his strength, however, and Matt had made a plan for when his father was ready to return to some form of independent living. He'd dropped the idea of his own clinic. There were things more important to him, he'd realised. The health of the nation needed help, but that was up to somebody else for the time being. He'd wanted to spend the proceeds of the land sale, minus the cost of clearing the debris, on a property of her own for his mother; but after some thought she'd moved back into the granny annex at Matt and Jennifer's place, with the blessing of the entire family. Both sides of the connecting door respected the privacy of the other, with nobody from either side passing through without knocking, or even phoning ahead.

Instead, Matt had decided to invest the money in a place for Frank, who'd been well enough to be discharged after two months. While he regained his strength living with the family Matt searched for suitable accommodation, finding it in a Star and Garter military retirement home which had a good reputation. Frank would have his own en-suite rooms, with care staff around if needed and meals provided; there was even a bar, and a golf course not far away, if Frank ever felt up to the sport again. One step at a time, however; at present he was just grateful to be alive.

Once he moved into the home he called Abby, who'd visited the hospital, when it was touch-and-go regarding his survival. When Frank was able they'd talked, wiping clean the slate of their negative history, including an apology from Frank for his recent gaffe, and putting the past to rest. Abby'd agreed to visit him on a regular basis, although she'd stipulated that she not have to see any of the rest of the family whilst there.

As soon as it was evident that his father was going to make it, Matt recalled certain facts of the evening when Frank had collapsed, including the question of why he'd been in Abby's village. Another conversation had revealed the relationship she'd shared with Frank many years ago, and it was clear he'd been on his way to see her with a view to getting back together. Madge it seemed had somehow been aware of his plans to leave her, hence her murder attempt.

Whatever. Matt didn't want to get into the details. His own connection with Abby was discreetly forgotten by both parties, in the manner of grown and reasonable adults. Visits to Frank and to her half-brother and his family, with whom she was building a relationship, gave Abby some company and a link to other people which had been missing previously.

Then there was Madge. Over-confident and caught unawares, she hadn't disposed of the sugar substitute, which she'd cut with arsenic, by the time the police came calling. She'd tried to tough it out, but they'd got sufficient evidence of her attempt on Frank, which was enough for them to look once more into the deaths of her previous two husbands. She'd been remanded into custody, when nobody would stand bail for her, and was at present awaiting trial. Matt hoped she'd be put away for a long time.

Her life had changed drastically, he thought. No more sitting at the golf club bar holding forth to an audience.

The party was over for Madge.

The guilty party.

THE END

A REQUEST

If you've enjoyed this book, I'd be very grateful if you'd consider leaving a review on Amazon. It doesn't have to be much, one line or even just a star rating.

The amount of reviews authors receive determines the level of publicity which Amazon gives to the book, helping us to increase its visibility and get it in front of more eyes, potentially gaining more readers.

Please see my Amazon Author Page at:

https://www.amazon.co.uk/~/e/B088QFJJ3Q

Thank you.

Laura

SOURCES CONSULTED

https://www.healthdirect.gov.au/addiction-withdrawal-symptoms

https://metro.co.uk/2020/10/14/what-could-go-against-you-in-the-adoption-process-13334271/

https://www.tracingfamily.co.uk/blog/what-happens-to-original-birth-certificate-after-adoption

https://www.parentkind.org.uk/for-parents/home-and-school/involvement-in-school-life

https://my.clevelandclinic.org/health/diseases/24727-arsenic-poisoning

ACKNOWLEDGEMENT

The greatest possible thanks to Amanda Sheridan, friend, author and beta reader for *The Guilty Party*.

Special thanks go to Amanda for providing her unending kindness and patience in teaching me the skills needed to make promotional posters and videos, as well as those needed to make my own book covers. I'm by no means a professional, but if anybody had told me, when I began writing and publishing books, that I'd also be making the covers, I'd have laughed at them. I owe her a great deal.

ABOUT THE AUTHOR

Laura Lyndhurst was born and grew up in North London, England, before marrying and travelling with her husband in the course of his career.

When settled back in the UK she became a mature student and gained Bachelor's and Master's degrees in English and Literature before training and working as a teacher.

She started writing in the last few years in the peace and quiet of rural Lincolnshire, and published her debut novel, *Fairytales Don't Come True,* in May 2020. This book forms the first of a trilogy, *Criminal Conversation*, of which the second is *Degenerate, Regenerate* and *All That We Are Heir To* the third. *Innocent, Guilty*, the first of another trilogy, continues the story told in these three books and leads on to *The Future of Our House*, which is followed by *Uphill, Downhill, Over, Out* as the sixth and final book to end the series. *An Honourable Institution* was published as a stand-alone novel in January 2025.

Laura also developed a taste for psychological suspense, which led to the writing and publication of *You Know What You Did*, to which *What Else Did You Do?* is the sequel.

Laura has also published four small books of poems, *October Poems*, *Thanksgiving Poems and Prose Pieces, Poet-Pourri* and *Social Climbing and Other Poems.*

BOOKS BY THIS AUTHOR

An Honourable Institution

MARRIAGE IS AN HONOURABLE INSTITUTION—OR IS IT?

Cressida's a rock chick, living her life as she likes—and to hell with anyone who doesn't like it. It's about to be turned upside down, however, and there's little she can do about it.

Losing his parents as a child, Jay's had a difficult life—and despite his efforts he's had difficulty keeping on the right side of the law. Change is in the air—but for the better, or the worse?

Hugo's a privileged blue blood with a sense of entitlement. He's not ready for the sudden challenge to his place in the world, or for who's making it.

Justin's getting married soon—or thinks he is. He doesn't react well to an unplanned change.

There's a reason Janine's called 'crazy'—but unforeseen circumstances show an unknown side of her.

Five people, getting on with life, unsuspecting of events soon to affect them. Can they meet the trials which lie ahead, and emerge unscathed?

Fairytales Don't Come True: Volume One of the Criminal Conversation series.

LIFE IS ALL WE HAVE ... ONE CONVERSATION AT A TIME.

When middle-aged nurse Dora Stuart-Frazer is assigned to provide end-of-life care to ex-prostitute Magdalena, she suffers a failure of sympathy linked to the woman's career and her own marital issues. It's her job—her vocation to care. Trying to overcome her prejudices against her patient and the other members of the all-female household, Dora is drawn into their world. Mags has cancer and it won't be long now. She is an unwilling listener to the sordid life-story that her patient wants to recount in her last few weeks of life. It's her dying wish to get her story out and as such, it's Dora's job to listen. However, every night as her patient's story unfolds, Dora needs more. She is transfixed and a willing listener as she compares the life of the story teller to her own and forces herself to confront her mid-life crisis. In this race against time, Dora has to know it all—but fears Mags won't make it to the end.

Degenerate, Regenerate: Volume Two of the Criminal Conversation series.

LIFE IS ALL WE HAVE ... ONE CONVERSATION AT A TIME.

Police officer Stephanos Stephanidou is given a dead-end posting to a small Greek island. It has an ageing population and all the young people have left. In despair, he considers that his career is over, and possibly his life, too. With nothing to do and no crime to involve himself with, he reads some old files and a cold-case from many years ago sparks his interest. He's walking on the cliffs above the beautiful Mediterranean coast when he meets one of the case's main players. This could be the key to his solving the cold case mystery and reviving his career. As the story unfolds, and the clues have to be found, Stephanidou finds new hope. Time is all he has, but can he solve this old crime before time runs out?

All That We Are Heir To: Volume Three of the Criminal Conversation series.

LIFE IS ALL WE HAVE ... ONE CONVERSATION AT A TIME.

Her mother died when she was a little girl. She has never known her father. Katie is growing up with her adoptive family and is surrounded by a world full of love. However, she is older now and she has questions. You know that thing where you walk into a room and the conversation stops? Or when you ask a question and the subject is changed—Katie knows them all too well. To confront the past—she has to know it. One day a strange man comes to the house. He asks to speak to her. And he has a story to tell. Will he have the answers she needs?

"I recommend this novel for its daring to flow against the current. For its unique perspective on what makes somebody a criminal."
— Amazon Reviewer

Innocent, Guilty: Volume Four of the Criminal Conversation series.

THE CONVERSATION CONTINUES … YET NOBODY WANTS TO TALK

It's some years since the deadly events which decided Katie on her life course occurred, and matters seem settled for her and her extended family. Working, eating, sleeping, living and loving, they're content to live a quiet life out of the limelight.

Life has other plans for them all, however. Several quirks of fate, along with one desperately-sought answer to a niggling question, ensure that events, and their lives, soon spiral out of control.

Solutions are sought, but there are no easy answers, and relationships come under pressure in the quest to do the right thing.

The innocence of some is obvious, as is the guilt of others, while elsewhere it's not so clear-cut.

Difficult decisions have to be made, with results not always satisfactory, and repercussions which could echo down the generations.

The Future of Our House: Volume Five of the Criminal Conversation series.

THE CONVERSATION CONTINUES … YET NOBODY WANTS TO TALK

Time has moved on, and Katie has taken to spending most of her time on the Greek island of her ancestors. Miles—while passing every possible moment there with her—has branched out into the world of motor racing, his fledgling team poised for success, with Greg and Josh behind the wheels and negotiating the twists and turns of their high-speed lifestyle, both on the track and off.

In Miles's absence, his business interests continue to flourish in the capable hands of Alec, ice-cold in both her work and her attitude towards her would-be suitor, Siegfried Markham—heir to the family law firm Markham, Markham and Manners, which provides steadfast support to Alec.

Love and business vie for attention, in both fast and slow time—with unwelcome attention being paid to both families, without their knowledge. Crime and law make uneasy bedfellows, and tensions abound as all parties seek to come out on top—but there's only so much space up there.

Uphill, Downhill, Over, Out: Volume Six of the Criminal Conversation series.

THE CONVERSATION CONTINUES … YET NOBODY WANTS TO TALK

It's the end of an era. The passing of a patriarch signals changes in the lives of the Dukakis du Cain family members and friends. Time to move on, time to move out, as far as Alectrona's concerned, to leave behind a place that's finished and start over in a more congenial environment—yet there are a few accounts to be settled first.

For Greg too there's a goal achieved and another one to aim for, if only he can find the courage to try for it—because second-best isn't good enough, and failure is not an option.

Meanwhile, back in Broken Britain, Sig Markham faces further challenges within his dysfunctional family, as well as the consequences of a life not well-lived. There's music to be faced, but it's out of tune and the lyrics aren't encouraging.

The final chapter of the 'Criminal Conversation' series sees the characters looking towards a future shaped by the events of the past. How brave will their new world be?

You Know What You Did:

TWINKLE, TWINKLE, LITTLE STAR—WE ALL FALL DOWN.

Amanda Roberts has it all—a rich husband, perfect children, and a prosperous life.

But all that is about to change. As a successful author, she has established herself in the elite world of glitz and glamour. But her marriage comes under pressure when she suspects that things aren't as they should be. If only that was the end of her problems. When paranoia takes hold, Amanda spirals into a nightmare abyss of immense proportions. There's no way out, and the clock is ticking ...

There's somebody in the shadows and they're looking at YOU.

What Else Did You Do?

'When you reach the top, the only way is down.'

Amanda Roberts knows this only too well. It's been three years since her life imploded, with devastating consequences. But now she's determined to build a new life for herself, and put the past behind her.

Meanwhile, her nemesis has scaled the heights as a rising star, to enjoy the view from the top of the tree. Now though, it appears that somebody else is unhappy, and gunning for both of them. Or is it just meant to look that way?

Amanda's back. With attitude. But is she back for payback?

October Poems:

These poems were all written, one each day, in October 2020. They are about aspects of contemporary life, in both its humorous and serious aspects. They began about mid-September 2020, when I was invited, by Nancy Bonnington, to join a Facebook group for writers. Within a week or so, she announced "Writober", to begin on 1st October and go right through the month. She would post a picture every day, and the task was to write a short story, of one to three paragraphs, of whatever the picture inspired in us. So, on the first day, I sat down with the picture in front of me, and wrote—and what came out was not prose, but poetry, which I duly posted. Nancy pronounced it "Wonderful," and some others were kind enough to 'Like' it, and I was energised, and challenged. On the second day I produced poetry again, and that was it. I challenged myself to write a poem each day, to the prompt, and this book is the result. Some of them have been tweaked, while others, like 'Skin Deep', were not the original poem but another, equally valid, and which it seemed a shame not to publish alongside the other. So here they are, in the order in which they were written. Some are better than others, depending on what the picture-prompt of the day suggested to me. They may not be perfect, and I don't say they're the greatest poetry ever written, but they're mine and I'm proud of having written them. I hope you enjoy them.

Thanksgiving Poems & Prose Pieces:

I'd just about finished writing and publishing *October Poems* at the beginning of November 2020 when my friend and mentor, Nancy Bonnington, announced that during the month of November she would be putting up prompts – word prompts, rather than pictures, this time – to inspire short pieces of writing from the members of her Facebook group. In the event, the prompts all centred around the subject of Thanksgiving in the USA, which was to happen on the 26th November. I rose to the challenge, although as I was rather tired from the effort of writing the *October Poems* it took me a few days to rest up and get my poetic head back on: which is why the first few pieces I wrote were in prose, rather than poetry. I have included them, however, as they form an integral part of the whole—and are referred back to in at least one of the poems which I later wrote.

Poet-Pourri:

I wasn't sure if I'd continue to write poetry after I'd published *October Poems* and *Thanksgiving Poems and Prose Pieces* in quick succession. Writing my psychological suspense thriller *You Know What You Did* took over, the idea having come to me while I was writing the poems and needing attention therefore when I'd finished publishing the poetry. When that was also sent on its way into the public domain I had to get back to my *Criminal Conversation* trilogy, finishing and publishing *Degenerate, Regenerate* in January 2021 and moving on immediately to *All That We Are Heir To* in the face of wishes expressed by readers of the first two books to know what happened next.

I'd been writing a few poems in the background whilst writing those books, as well as beginning a couple of new psychological thrillers, but poem ideas were coming to me all the time, helped in no small measure by some prompts supplied once again by Nancy Bonnington for both poetry and prose. I therefore felt it expedient to finish and publish this new set of poems, interspersed with some pieces of prose, and *Poet-Pourri* is the result.

The poems and prose are, as usual, a mixture of humorous and serious, touching upon social issues on both the darker and the lighter side of life. There's little else to say, except thank you for reading and I hope that you'll enjoy them.

Social Climbing and Other Poems:

I had no plans, after publishing *Poet-Pourri*, to write any more poems, at least not in the near future. But while I was in the prepare-to-publish stage of that book, I made the acquaintance of photographer Clive Thompson and his large archive of photographs, put together over quite a lot of years. Scanning through these on the internet I found the picture of a discarded Father Christmas chocolate-bearing Advent calendar, which immediately said 'poem material' to me. I wrote the poem and presented it to Clive, who loved it, and there was born the idea of a collaboration, my poetry written to the prompts of some of his photographs.

The photographs I've used for the pandemic-themed poems were taken quite some time before that ominous word had become a part of all our daily lives, but they seemed to fit the subject and I therefore took the liberty of utilizing them in that way. The results of my poems joined to Clive's photographs I present here, as Social Climbing and other poems. It may not be the catchiest of titles but it works for me, and for Clive, and for you also, I hope. Enjoy.

Printed in Dunstable, United Kingdom

68142222R00181